Kit Parker has loved writing almost as long as she's loved reading, though that took a little encouragement, and a lot of Roald Dahl, in the beginning. Since attempting her own sequel to Matilda, aged eight, she has continued to write stories with a large dollop of the fantastical.

Also being a fan of stories on screen found Kit working at a cinema during her student years and taking a writing degree in Southampton with a media twist.

She currently lives in Sussex and can often be found listening to a rather bonkers selection of music.

Also by Kit Parker:

Coming soon:
Blood Bound
Angel Wings

Feels Like Home

KIT PARKER

First published in 2022 by Hellcat Publishing

Copyright © 2022 Kirsty Sian Small
Writing as Kit Parker

Kit Parker has asserted her right to be identified as the author
of this work in accordance with the Copyright, Designs and
Patents Act 1988

A CIP catalogue for this book is available from
the British Library

ISBN: 978-1-915462-00-8

Cover design by Hellcat Publishing

Discover more at www.hellcatpublishing.com

For my parents, sisters and brothers-in-law.
Thank you for never telling me this was a stupid dream.
Even though I suspect there were times you wanted to.

ONE

It had been raining since Jet stepped off the plane, and she was beginning to feel as though New York wasn't that pleased to see her. What kind of a welcome was that, when the city enticed her back so often?

Though this time, she didn't plan on a fleeting visit.

Arriving from London with little more than a lengthy hotel booking and a small amount of cash from her savings account would have been considered an indulgent holiday to most. A rookie move as a starter plan for a new life as a Manhattan novelist, perhaps.

As it was something she had set her heart on for many years and to make sure no one tried to talk her out of it, she hadn't told anyone.

That's what they did in the movies, after all.

Anyway, that's what social media was for, wasn't it? Bragging about your new life, taking gossip-hungry people on the journey with you.

She made a mental note to take a super-happy selfie from the top of the Empire State Building as soon as it

1

stopped raining.

Her parents knew of course, they'd probably seen it coming longer than Jet had. She'd let them know she'd made it through her first night alive, they were happy enough with that. After all, her father was a native New Yorker who had fallen for an English girl working in the city more than four decades ago, making London his home when the publishing company she worked for transferred her back. His only regret was selling his Upper West Side apartment when property prices boomed.

It was the city her parents had met and fallen in love in, the city was a part of her own DNA, but having only made it across the pond a handful of times, and mostly to visit elderly relatives, Jet was ashamed she didn't know it better.

Glancing again at the coffee house window, steamed up thanks to the sopping wet punters sat around her, she drank in the atmosphere. Many of the other patrons were huddled together in the hopes of drying off a little and warming through in the time it took to sip their extra-large lattes.

Nudging her rucksack with her foot as it sat under the table, she realised that even more water had dripped onto the floor whilst she'd been drinking her coffee and glanced around guiltily as she wondered how much of a puddle it had yet to impart on her local Starbucks.

It was still raining.

Reaching up to touch her long mahogany curls, knowing they would require the aid of a hairdryer if she was ever to feel warm again, Jet ran her fingers through a section at the front, plucking a loose strand from where it had stuck to her jaw, before wiping her wet fingers on her wet jeans.

Jet wanted nothing more than to head back to the hotel and change into some dry clothes or take a nap, perhaps even work on her latest novel, but she knew she couldn't hide in the hotel room and wait for the rain to ebb.

She had a job interview to go to, and instead of hailing a cab like any sensible interviewee, she'd decided to break up the walk with a coffee in the hopes she wouldn't get too wet.

A tech company two blocks over had responded to her resume. Knowing the city was too expensive for a small-time author like herself to even play at being a penniless artist for too long, applications had gone out before she'd left England.

Jet had forgotten how the rain could feel as though it was coming straight up as well as straight down in Manhattan, bouncing off the concrete as though thrown from the very rooftops of the buildings around her.

Wrapping her hands back around her cup, she lifted it to her lips.

As she savoured the hot, syrup-laced coffee and the additional warmth it offered, Jet watched the people around her. A middle-aged couple in the corner were playing with their mobile phones as their drinks steamed in the middle of the table. A muffin was placed between them, cut in two but otherwise untouched, while they checked in on Facebook, loaded their latest holiday snaps to Instagram, Tweeted, or whatever. Tourists, she'd already decided. Perhaps lost tourists, she pondered.

Manhattan may have been a giant tourist trap from Central Park to Battery Park, but having known that already, Jet had chosen a hotel in the financial district. A woman on the table nearest to her was hunched over a laptop looking stressed, a half-eaten sandwich and what was almost certainly a cold mocha sitting on top of a pile of red-penned paperwork.

Her eyes scanned the rest of the punters but landed on the front door which was closing behind a tall man as he shook the water droplets off his coat onto the entry mat. Clearly agitated by the rain's effect on his day, he shoved the hood off his head and ran his fingers through a messy mop of blond hair, which only sought to spread the rain from his face into the tresses.

Jet was a sucker for long hair and gave the guy more than a once over as he crossed the store to the counter.

He wasn't dressed like a wolf of Wall Street, far from it. Though neither, she decided, did he look as lost as a tourist in his heavy boots, flannel shirt and jeans. His generally aggressive demeaner and five o'clock shadow suggested he'd had a rough night. Maybe he'd pulled an all-nighter. An IT nerd for one of the bigger companies perhaps, stressed by all the suits asking him how a new system worked. Letting her eyes travel, Jet considered that he might even be a bit too buff under all those layers to be an IT geek.

Berating herself for making such assumptions, she barely realised she was staring.

Beneath his scowl, he was exactly the kind of handsome she'd write as a love interest, in fact he looked almost identical to one of her earliest heroes, a character she had first dreamed up in college, only a good fifteen to twenty years older.

As he reached the counter, as if feeling watched, he looked straight at her for a split second before the barista greeted him by a name Jet didn't catch and set about making his coffee. A regular then, she assumed.

People watching was one thing, but Jet didn't like to be caught gawping. Looking around for a fast distraction, she stared at and toyed with her cup of coffee, realising that it wasn't warming her fingers as well as it had been.

When she looked up again, he was watching her as he put sugar into his drink.

Staring at her was more like it.

Blushing, Jet lifted her cup to her lips to finish the last lukewarm mouthful, only to find the cup empty. While she tried to pretend it wasn't, he tugged his hood back up and left. Daring to glance up as he walked up the street, she made eye contact when he looked back, directly at her, a confused expression creasing his brow.

TWO

'Did you get the wrong door, Miss?' a voice called across the lobby after Jet had all but fallen through the revolving door in her haste to get out of the rain.

Taking a moment to compose herself and remove her hood, Jet spotted the security staff on reception smirking at her.

'I don't think so.' Jet glanced around and realised that he wasn't the only one to witness her entrance. An immaculately dressed pair of women were also giving her the once-over on their way to the elevators. 'I'm looking for Virgo. The technologies company.'

As she spoke Jet kept her chin up, there was no way she was going to let two fashionistas make her feel her choice of attire was inadequate. Tech companies were renowned for being more laid back than that and as an ex-manager had once told her, you could wear anything you wanted to almost any occasion, if you had the gumption to pull it off.

'Then you do indeed appear to be in the right place.'

He leant over the counter to look her up and down with a level of camp exaggeration. 'You just don't *appear* to be in the right place.'

'I'm here to see Leon, I have an appointment,' Jet said, using her overly pleasant professional voice to sound smarter than she looked, dripping onto the polished marble floor.

'Let me just call their front desk to confirm.'

Eyeballing her again, less friendly and more suspicious this time, he reached for the phone. As he lifted the handset to his ear, Jet managed to catch the name on his name tag, Leroy.

'Thanks, Leroy.' She smiled, trying not to appear as relieved as she felt.

'Hi Rachel, are you expecting a half-drowned visitor for an appointment with Leon this afternoon?'

'It's an interview,' Jet muttered as her head fell to review the state of her rain splattered clothes.

'Go on up,' Leroy was suddenly saying, having already hung up. 'Third floor.'

'OK, great.' Jet shrugged her bag further onto her shoulder.

'Rachel knows all about it, apparently.'

'Great . . . thank you.'

'I'm not sure you should, but you're welcome,' Leroy sassed as she began to walk away.

Wondering what he meant, she was thankful that the elevator arrived to spill existing employees into the foyer seconds after she had pressed the button. She let the doors close behind her before she turned to the mirrored walls and took a deep breath to compose and relax her face with a deep breath.

As the elevator reached the third floor, she met her own chestnut-coloured eyes in the reflection. Sure, she looked like a drowned rat, but she knew she had skills to offer this company.

The doors opened onto a black glass reception desk, the company name 'Virgo' etched on to the glass as though it was the constellation itself.

Rachel had clearly been watching the doors and on Jet's emergence, jumped up, smoothing her brunette bob and black shift dress.

'Welcome to Virgo, are you here about the content writing role?' Rachel extended a hand for Jet to shake, glancing towards some frosted glass doors to her right.

'That's right. I'm Jet.'

'Jet, Leon will be right out.' Rachel glanced again at the doors and Jet realised she was looking for someone. 'Can I take your coat for you? You don't look anywhere near as soaked as Leroy suggested,' Rachel said with a little wink.

'That would be great, thanks.' Jet held her shoulders where they were, to prevent the threatening shrug before slipping out of the soggy garment.

'If Leon keeps you long enough, it might have time to dry a little bit.' Rachel smiled, her eyes meeting Jet's again. 'Please have a seat.'

'Thank you,' Jet said again, handing the coat over.

Venturing towards a small snug of a seating area in the corner, she was in the process of taking a seat when the glass doors slid open, and a middle-aged hipster strode through from the open-planned offices beyond.

'Jet, is it?' He ignored Rachel completely as he thrust a hand in Jet's direction three long strides before he reached her. 'Sorry the weather hasn't been on your side today. Follow me.'

Turning on his heel, he headed back towards the main office.

'Batman is free,' Rachel called out.

'Perfect, thanks Rachel,' Leon called back over his shoulder as Jet scurried to keep up. 'We name all our meeting rooms after DC characters,' Leon explained as he showed her inside a room made entirely of glass panels, one of a nest of four in the middle of the generous office space. 'Batman, Superman, Wonder Woman and Aquaman are here in the middle, Harley Quinn, and Joker are in the far corner.'

Removing his suit jacket to reveal a silk waistcoat, Leon motioned for her to take a seat.

Holding his hand out a second time as soon as they were settled, Jet could only interpret the motion as being expectant of her resume. Swallowing down a scowl, she quickly retrieved one from the plastic folder in her rucksack.

While Leon read in silence, Jet studied him.

Quaffed hair, well-tended beard and moustache, both peppered with streaks of grey. Laughter lines appearing through the concentration as he read her extensive list of experience.

She was just estimating his age at around forty-five

when he dropped the document onto the table between them.

'It's good to see you've worked with online learning before. With technologies so in the forefront of everyone's minds these days, every graduate out there thinks that they're qualified to write for AR, VR and AI purely because they were born in a different century to you or I.' Leon folded his fingers across his waist as he sat back. 'Your experience is impressive.'

'Thank you.'

'The last tech company you worked for is a bit of a behemoth, we've lost good designers to them since they expanded across the pond. What have you been doing since you left . . .' he paused to review the document, 'five months ago?'

'I've been freelancing for the last eight years, between clients I write fiction,' Jet explained.

'This is a permanent role.' Leon lifted his eyes from the resume to meet hers.

'And New York is an expensive city,' Jet countered.

'We expect the right candidate to be able to upload their content too,' he challenged.

'That has been standard with some of my other clients. Just show me how your content management system functions and I'm sure I'll be able to work with it.' Jet resisted the urge to bite her lip, instantly regretting being so candid.

'Great, can you start Monday?'

'If you need me to,' Jet answered, though something in her gut churned at the urgency. 'Don't you have other candidates to see?'

'None that can start immediately. See you Monday at 9a.m.'

Five minutes later, Jet was stood back out in the rain staring across the street wondering what the hell she had just gotten herself into.

THREE

'No Mum, I'm fine, I've got the hotel room until the end of the month.' Jet smiled fondly but rolled her eyes as she paced the room. 'I start Monday, and I'll ask my new colleagues for accommodation advice.'

'Well, don't go bunking in with any dodgy roommates,' her mum fussed.

'They're the best kind!' her dad called from the conservatory.

She could see them in her mind. Her mum sat in front of some documentary on the History Channel while her dad read in the conservatory. It had been their evening ritual for as long as she could remember.

'I'll see how it goes,' Jet soothed, glancing at the television she'd automatically put on for company when she walked in the door. A news channel was wittering away to itself.

'Get to know them first,' her mother clucked.

'I will, I will. Rachel, the office manager, has already invited me out tonight as it happens.' Jet smirked. She wasn't much for hitting the town, never had been, and wondered if the Big Apple had the capacity to change that.

'Oh, and Gwendoline has been asking after you again.'

'Really?' Jet scowled and nudged her rucksack further into the bathroom with her toe to check that it wasn't causing any mild flooding.

'She wants to know when we'll see some material.'

'Who's we? You said my novels weren't suited to your mainstream lists, that they were better placed with a horror or fantasy press.' Jet ran her fingers through her hair and remembered that it was still sopping wet. The rain hadn't eased at all during her interview, and she'd been less inclined to care how wet she got on the way back to the hotel, knowing her job search seemed to be over.

'Oh darling, you're not still writing that stuff, are you? I thought you had something literary on the boil?'

As if, Jet thought.

What her mother considered artful or clever writing was a million miles away from the blood-thirsty werewolves, vampires and witches Jet usually wrote about. Having mused once about writing a novel that might fit with her mother's standards, it seemed that she and Gwendoline — her mother's Head of Editorial and Jet's godmother — were poised for her opus to drop onto their next Super Thursday list any moment.

Their faith in her was comforting, she had to admit, but their lack of belief in her chosen genre rankled.

Despite working in publishing in her twenties, Jet hadn't wanted to use contacts to publish her work. Instead, the industry knowledge she'd gained had given her the confidence to go it alone, with dreams of her own indie publishing house one day. But a failed attempt at self-publishing during the Kindle boom had horrified her mother and contracts had soon mysteriously arisen out of thin air offering Jet an editor and a spot on the catalogue for a small indie press in Camden called Vivigi Publishing.

It was minimal exposure, made her mother proud-ish, and kept Jet with a regular release spot every October for her supernatural series. The editor at Vivigi claimed to genuinely love her work. Mai knew more about her characters than she did sometimes.

'I've got a deadline to hit, Mum. Mai wants next year's book asap. I didn't run away to create my ultimate masterpiece, you know that.'

'Ah well,' her mother sighed. 'I guess that when you eventually finish that series and run out of ideas, you'll be old enough and wise enough to produce something spectacular. Something to land you a big deal, so you can finally write full time. Just make sure you do it before either I or Gwennie retires.'

'I'll bear that in mind,' Jet deadpanned.

'See that you do. Anyway dear, must go, there's a programme on at eight that I've had on reminder for weeks, I can't miss it.'

'OK Mum, tell me all about it next time. Love you.'

'You too, darling! Ta ta.'

Hearing her dad profess his love for their only daughter before the line went dead made Jet smile and shake her head as she tossed the phone onto the bed.

Tugging at her jumper with a sound of disgust, she began to peel it away from her skin.

Wandering back into the bathroom, she noted that the rail for the shower curtain was the only suitable place to attempt to dry anything. It would have to do.

With a shiver, she reached out to turn the shower on before she shimmied and wrestled her way out of her wet clothes, dumping them on the floor to be dealt with later.

Stepping into the shower, she sighed contentedly as the hot water hit her back even though it made her chilled toes tingle and sting.

Rachel had asked her to meet her back at the office at 6p.m. When she stepped out of the shower she had two hours, but she still barely made it back to the lobby in time.

Completely overthinking the situation, Jet forgot it was an after-work drink and up-ended the entire contents of her suitcase to pick out a black shift dress. She'd packed it purely for attending interviews where even gumption wouldn't get you through the door in jeans.

'Now I believe you belong here, just not at Virgo,' Leroy cooed as she re-entered the lobby.

As she looked up to reply she found he'd changed out of his uniform shirt and into a hooded sweater with a purple t-shirt underneath, emblazoned with the words

"Unicorns have more fun" across his chest in rainbow colours.

'Keep that cute little number for dates, honey. You might even pick one up looking like that.'

Blushing slightly, Jet smiled.

'Don't go blushing on me,' he warned as he put his coat on and dumped his bag on the desk. 'Redheads are hot, and you all know it. I dyed mine red once. Biggest mistake I ever made.'

'Why?' Jet asked curiously as Rachel appeared from the elevator, hood already up.

'It went orange,' Rachel teased. 'He had an orange afro for an entire morning until he ran off on his lunch break to shave it all off.'

Jet winced.

'See, she gets it.' Leroy motioned to Jet but threw daggers at Rachel.

'I've had some hair-dye mishaps of my own.' Jet bit her lip.

'Don't you dare tell me you tried to cover that.'

'Couple of times. I once dyed it black for a party.'

It was Rachel's turn to wince.

'Been there, done that,' she sighed. 'College. Shall we? Shelley is already over at the bar with a couple of the tech boys.'

'God, yes, get me a beer.' Leroy dove out from behind the desk and led the charge through the front doors.

'You'll be sitting opposite Shelley when you start next week.' Rachel smiled as they followed. 'She's lovely, she moved here from Atlanta eighteen months ago.'

'I'm a little over dressed apparently.' Jet fidgeted with her dress.

'The nerds will love it. I'm front of house, I have to make an impression.' She spoke with the same pride her posture portrayed. 'It terrifies some of them.' She grinned maliciously, her eyes sparkling with humour.

'But only some of them,' Jet grouched.

'That sounds like a story in need of a beer.' Rachel shot Jet a conspiring glance as they exited onto the street in time to see Leroy disappear into a sports bar up the block.

'Or several.' Jet smirked back.

Linking arms, they hurried across the street together.

'So, are you guys always this keen to hit the bar on a Friday night?' Jet asked a couple of hours later as a waitress placed their fourth tray of beers down at the booth.

'Who says it has to be a Friday night?' Leroy returned.

'Ignore him, he doesn't work for us.' Rachel shook her bob out of her face as she selected a beer and raised the glass to her lips.

'He kinda does,' Shelley pointed out with the scowl of someone who was considering whether they'd already had too much to drink. Jet wondered whether any of the Virgo staff had eaten since lunchtime, realising with concern that she hadn't thought to line her stomach either.

'Thanks, babe,' Leroy said as he raised his glass.

Tossing her long black mane of hair, Shelley blew him a kiss.

'It's more a tradition than a burning desire to escape, I promise.' Tom waved it off. 'It's usually the same old usual suspects: Rach, Shelley, Leroy, me and Brad.'

'The freelancers often pop along too,' Shelley said coyly.

'That's a good point, wasn't Daryl in today?' Brad shot Shelley a teasing grin.

'Was he? I didn't notice.' Shelley feigned ignorance while everyone except Jet laughed playfully.

'He and Tina are untangling the mess I made with the VR headset,' Tom admitted awkwardly from behind his beard and beer.

'We should ban you from playing with that thing man, that's the second time this month.' Brad shook his head but laughed fondly.

'The client wants what the client wants, it's not my fault the tech isn't fully up to it yet.' Tom narrowed his eyes at his junior developer.

'So, you're saying you're breaking it by being too good a programmer for the hardware?' Jet raised her eyebrows in Tom's direction.

'Something like that. Fuck, ouch, I'm going to have to watch you.' Tom looked Jet up and down.

'Hot shot tech boys get no sympathy from me.' Jet laughed, remembering some faces from her past. 'In my opinion, you shouldn't be able to break anything that badly.'

'I'll remind you of that when you're IM'ing me to tell me you broke something next week.'

'Oh, there's Daryl now.' Shelley suddenly pointed to

18

the bar.

Curious to know what kind of man would make Shelley practically fall out of the booth like a drunken teenager, Jet followed the line of her finger to the only recent newcomer at the bar. Though she'd been people watching throughout the evening, Jet had been too busy fighting her case with Tom to see him enter.

There at the bar, in the same coat, jeans and boots as earlier, was the guy from Starbucks.

He was glancing around the bar for her colleagues as he waited to be served, which caused the beer Jet had been drinking to swirl around her empty stomach in an unsettling manner.

Jet froze as she watched him, forgetting to breathe as his name echoed through her brain. That was who he looked like, that was the connection her brain had tried to make before, but that Daryl was fictional.

A figment of her eighteen-year-old imagination.

Before he spotted the table, Rachel tapped her glass against Jet's making her jump out of her seat.

'Hey, if you're new in town, where are you staying?'

'I've got a hotel until the end of the month. From there, I guess I'm looking for recommendations,' Jet answered, grateful of the distraction.

'There's bound to be someone looking for a roomie, I'll ask around,' Rachel offered.

'Wasn't Daryl thinking of renting a room out at his place?' Brad asked Shelley.

'Like I'd know,' she countered too quickly, shifting in her seat.

'If he was, I'd have been in it already,' Leroy teased, then suddenly downed the rest of his beer and dove out of the booth.

'Does he do that often?' Jet asked.

'He'll have seen someone he knows, or he's been on Grindr, Tinder or whatever the latest in vogue app is.' Rachel shook her head with a smile.

'All the more room for Daryl,' Shelley said brightly as he approached the booth, beer in hand.

Shooting a look at Shelley that suggested he knew all too well about her infatuation, Daryl paused.

Jet presumed he was deciding whether to sit next to or opposite his potential stalker, but when she looked up, he was staring at her.

'Daryl, this is our newest recruit, Jet. She'll be working with Shelley from Monday,' Rachel announced, barely noticing the discomfort as Jet wished the booth would spit her out the back.

'I'm joining as a content writer.' Jet raised her glass, hoping the shaking in her voice wasn't too obvious and that she didn't sound as flustered as Shelley.

'You have my condolences,' Daryl commented and slid himself into the opposite side of the booth.

'She's just got here from London,' Shelley explained unnecessarily, Daryl's eyebrows had disappeared into his shaggy hairline as soon as Jet had opened her mouth.

'Were you still looking for a roommate, dude?' Brad asked him.

Shaking his head Daryl locked eyes with Jet. 'She

wouldn't want to be all the way up town anyway.'

'It works for you.'

'Virgo isn't my only client,' he answered, his voice deepening as he shot Brad a look.

Attempting to ground herself in the moment, Jet flexed her fingers around her beer and forced a shrug.

'It's fine. I only landed the job today, I'm in no rush to find somewhere.'

With a little shiver she hoped no one noticed, Jet turned her attention back to Rachel and ran her fingers through her hair, ruffling the curls a little to separate them.

Daryl was gawping at her again, this time as though he'd seen a ghost.

'Have you guys met before?' Shelley asked suddenly, having watched the whole exchange with interest.

'I don't think so?' Jet shook her head and dared to meet Daryl's gaze again.

The bar was dark, everyone was lit in hues of red and blue, which caused the aquamarine of his eyes to come alive.

He looked away quickly.

'I've never been to London,' he said dismissively.

'My dad's from New York, I used to have family here. Did you grow up in the city?'

'We haven't met.'

'Wow, things are feeling electric over here!' Leroy reappeared suddenly with a bright blue lipstick mark on his cheek.

Glancing behind him, Jet found Leroy to be

accompanied by a figure in a sea-green mermaid dress, wearing smeared blue lipstick to match the coloured scales shaved into an immaculate buzz-cut.

'Gotta run!' Leroy grinned and shot Jet a wink as he retrieved his bag, grabbed his date by the hand and made a bolt for the door.

'OK. Who wants another round?' Rachel broke the tension by pressing a service buzzer on the back wall.

FOUR

'What was that last night?' Rachel's bright eyes sparkled over the top of her sunglasses as she reached for her coffee.

'I have no idea.' Jet shook her head and leant back in her seat, enjoying the warmth of the sun on her face.

Having taken her number as they were all leaving the bar the night before, Rachel had called to ask her what she was doing with her first weekend in the city.

Despite the writing deadlines, Jet had been keen to get out of her hotel room as soon as she'd seen it had stopped raining. When she'd answered the phone, she was already halfway up Broadway drinking in the sights and smells of the Big Apple.

She hadn't had a particular destination in mind, so when Rachel suggested lunch in Central Park, she'd happily accepted.

Effortlessly glamourous on her days off as well as in the office, Rachel had arrived in a fitted pair of Levi's, what Jet presumed to be a designer T-shirt of some kind, not that she had a clue which, and stilettos.

'The way Daryl looked at you . . . he barely gives anyone the time of day unless he's working with them,' Rachel said with a dreamy grin.

'He's usually that rude in general then?' Jet huffed, though between the staring and the way he'd dismissed her enquiries, she wasn't sure rude covered it.

'I wouldn't say rude, not deliberately anyway, though he can be blunt for sure. He just keeps himself to himself. I'd almost hoped you were an old flame from college or something, so you could, y'know, dish a little dirt. Or at least tell us something about him.'

'He can't be that anti-social to have turned up at the bar?'

'I always got the impression that he comes along because he has nowhere better to be,' Rachel said, her eyes narrowing. 'The tech gang have a monthly poker night. They've tried inviting him along, but he always declines.'

'Maybe he's got a gambling habit?' Jet offered with a smirk.

'Huh, maybe.' Rachel fell back in her seat and pressed her bottom lip thoughtfully, then glanced over her shoulder to see whether her salmon salad was on its way.

'You mentioned you run. Where do you usually go?' Jet asked as a pair of Lycra-clad men pranced past.

'Here actually.' Rachel also watched them go, paying particular attention to their rear-ends. 'There's loads of hot guys out in the mornings.'

Turning back to Jet, she raised her eyebrows suggestively.

'It's something I'd like to get back into myself.' Jet squirmed in her seat, not wanting to admit how long it had been since she'd last run a 5k.

'I go with my roommates. The three of us share a broom closet-sized apartment in the Upper, Upper West Side. If you get a place near the park you should come with us!'

'I think I'll have to. I'm too British and too new to the area to turn down the portions around here,' Jet said, eyeing up the difference between Rachel's salad and her own burger as the waitress appeared over Rachel's shoulder.

'You're not a tourist anymore, you can't live off that stuff for long.' Rachel pointed her fork at Jet before loading it with salmon.

'Best make the most of it while I can then.'

'I'm guessing you're single?'

'Mmm hmm,' Jet mumbled through a mouthful of food, though she swallowed hastily. 'I've had enough of dating in my thirties. I'm a walking dating disaster. I might just have to admit defeat.'

'Are you kidding? You're in the land of Sex and the City now . . . you're old enough to have watched that, right?'

'Pretty much.' Jet nodded.

'My mom used to love that show. Though ironically, she was too old for it and I was too young to understand it.'

'The last season aired while I was at university, I'm not THAT old.' Jet laughed. 'Anyway, Carrie Bradshaw never had to swipe left or right.'

'Simpler times,' Rachel sighed.

'I'll bet we've both got some horror stories to tell.'

'My roommates think we could make a million dollars selling our dating horror stories.' Rachel shuddered as she reloaded her fork.

'Well, if you ever want to turn those stories into a book, let me know, maybe we could make it happen.' Jet's eyes widened playfully.

With Rachel's words in her head, Jet walked around the park for some time after they parted. Rachel had left for a Fifth Avenue shopping date with another friend. Her imagination wanted to run away with the possibility that Daryl had been as intrigued by her as she was with him. Especially if he was anything like the book character he resembled. Telling herself not to be so ridiculous, Jet sat herself by the Bethesda fountain until the spring sunset grew too cold to bear.

Smiling fondly, she did a lap of the fountain before she left, knowing she could return whenever she pleased. She'd first fallen in love with the water feature during Sunday walks in the park with her grandmother. Little Jet would always get a penny in her pudgy little hand to throw into the pool whenever she flew over with her parents for a visit. Every penny had been spent on the same wish.

I want to live in Manhattan someday, like Grandma.

As an adult, she took solace in the sound of water

playing in a fountain. On hot summer days when London asked nothing of her, usually after a meeting with Mai, Jet would take a coffee or a milkshake down to the Shakespeare fountain in Leicester Square and sit for hours watching people, mostly children, dice with the water jets in the paving and listen to the buskers and street performers.

A saxophonist had been playing near the steps when she'd arrived, but he'd packed up for the afternoon long before Jet realised she was losing sensation in her fingers.

It wasn't that warm yet.

This was no balmy city day, though she looked forward to experiencing the dense, even smelly, city heat. It had been too long.

Exiting the park through Artist's Gate, Jet held her hand out for a cab, already deciding that if one hadn't stopped before she could count to five, she'd walk.

Pleased when none of them pulled over, she chose instead to head for Times Square.

She suspected that most New Yorkers avoided the tourist hotspots on a Saturday night in much the same way that her London friends never "went into town". It was an attitude she'd never understood.

Sure, it was busy, and crowded, and full of directionless, clueless people looking to spend their foreign currency wherever their guidebook told them to. But such places were full of life, full of adventure for innocent eyes, and in many cases, full of spectacle.

A quiet sun-kissed pub garden in Muswell Hill was

lovely too, but Jet had always found joy in both. She drew the line at overcrowding, however. When there were too many people, no one was having any fun.

Having started walking, Jet kept going, straight down to 34th Street, around the front of Macy's for the hell of it, pausing to stare up at the Empire State Building while she considered whether to pick up some food or choose another restaurant for dinner.

Eventually she found herself in a grocery store buying random snacks to take back to the hotel room.

Wandering up and down the aisles as she listened to the radio, Jet soon had an arm full of sugary snacks. She paused when she found a range of paperbacks. Having yet to find one of her books in any store smaller than one of the big UK chains, Jet wasn't surprised to find their urban fantasy selection full of names she knew, but not her own.

She resumed her quest for treat food in a small ice cream freezer at the back of the store before deciding she had finally exhausted all the options.

It was only once she approached the male cashier who looked her up and down with curiosity, that she realised how much junk food she was cradling. Though, with an inward shrug, she loaded it all onto the conveyor anyway, when he heard her accent, he'd think she was just a tourist mesmerised by all the American candy.

She made a mental note not to shop there too often while staying in the financial district. Or at least to make sure her next visit didn't involve anywhere near as much sugar. It was easy to get a reputation with overly familiar shop staff.

The wind was picking up as she approached her hotel, the threat of more rain on the way. Ignoring the gusts that nipped at her heels as she entered the lobby, Jet headed for the stairs, some additional exercise couldn't hurt before she munched her way through a pack of chocolate pretzels.

Slinging her rucksack full of goodies onto the bed, Jet located the remote and turned the TV on before nudging her laptop back to life where she'd left it beside the bed.

Two hours later, she fell asleep propped up amongst the pillows with her laptop open on her knee, a half-eaten bag of M&Ms at her elbow and the weather channel talking to itself.

FIVE

'You horrid little . . .' Jet muttered to herself as she leaned closer to the monitor, as if that would help her work out why the program wasn't working.

Barely three days in and Jet already understood why the joke was on her.

'Mornin',' Shelley sighed as she fell into her seat opposite.

Glancing at the time and then up at Shelley, Jet's first thought was coffee, then Shelley raised a bright pink travel mug to her lips and chugged the last of what Jet hoped was exactly that.

'Rough night last night?' Jet paused what she was doing to peer around her monitor.

'I don't want to talk about it,' Shelley grumbled.

'Hang on, didn't you have a date?' Jet lowered her voice. 'Was it a bit shit?'

Having discovered that she swore an awful lot more than her colleagues, Jet was trying to tone it down and, so far, failing.

Brightening, Shelley's eyes widened, then her shoulders began to shake as she attempted to suppress the laughter that escaped through her nose.

'I love the way you say that.' Shelley attempted to replicate Jet's accent, 'Yes, it was a "bit shit",' she paused, 'Didn't stop me going back to his though, idiot that I am.'

'Ah.' Jet nodded in understanding, though personally she could barely comprehend sleeping with a stranger on the first date. Her date-to-bed speed record was second date and even that had only happened once. 'I hope the sex was better than the date.'

'It only half made up for it.' Shelley grinned. 'I'll keep his number for emergencies only, let's put it that way.'

Unscrewing the lid of her travel mug, Shelley inspected the last few drops in the bottom and, with a glance at the front door of the office, stood up.

'Coffee?'

'Sure.' Jet collected a collapsible mug from her handbag and followed Shelley across the open-plan office. As they walked, she inspected the amount of fluff that had gathered on the silicone from inside her handbag and on arrival at the sink gave it a thorough rinse.

'How are you finding it so far?' Shelley asked as she turned from the coffee machine cradling her newly refilled mug in both hands and sniffing the wisps of caffeine infused steam as they rose around her chin.

'Happy hump day!' Brad said brightly as he wandered into the kitchen and began rifling through the cupboards for his regular mug. It was shaped like a Nintendo Gameboy. 'Jet, I think I fixed that bug you found on the CMS, drop me an IM if you're still having trouble with it.'

'When did you fix it?'

'Last night, before I left.' He peered around the cupboard door

'Then it's definitely still broken,' Jet said as she took her turn at the coffee machine. 'None of my content is saving.'

'Damnit,' Brad hissed. 'Better make this a double.' He stood behind her at the machine ready to leap at the espresso button.

'Can't you get Daryl on it next time he's in?' Shelley asked, with a grin of mock-innocence.

'I can handle it,' Brad grouched. 'Besides, since Jet scared him off and needs it fixing today, I'll have to do.'

'What?!' Jet squeaked, eyes wide.

'I'm joking, chill.' Brad laughed, running his fingers through his hair as his coffee poured. Jet thought about glaring at him but could tell it was friendly, he struck her as sweet, but too laid back for his own good. 'He sometimes starts late and stays into the depths of the night, if he's in today you'll see him about lunchtime. Tom would know.'

'Want me to find out what Daryl's issue is?' Shelley offered, raising her eyebrows hopefully.

'No, it's fine, let's just drop it,' Jet said quickly and led them out of the kitchen.

By the time lunch rolled around, her new job had

already given Jet a headache. Brad had all but given up on the glitch and Tom had been in a client meeting all morning.

Shelley was working through lunch to make up for being late and was poking around a courier-delivered pasta pot like it was gruel. Jet could tell it wasn't helping her hangover at all and that the caffeine come down had well and truly hit.

Opening their in-house instant messaging app, Jet pinged Rachel.

Jet: "Coffee?"

Rachel: "Would love to, but Leon has asked me to refresh the flowers in reception. Share the elevator?"

Jet: "Sure, be right out."

Patting her pockets to ensure she had her key fob and wallet, Jet got up and peered over at Shelley.

'I'm going to run to Starbucks. Want anything?'

'Iced skinny, double shot, caramel latte please,' she replied gratefully.

Tugging her phone out of her other pocket, Jet made a note of the order whilst nodding.

'Won't be long.'

When Jet made it to reception, Rachel was already at the elevator, Judy from accounts covering her desk.

'We're a tech company, do you really have to go out for flowers?' Jet teased.

'I prefer to pick them myself, all too often the courier squashes at least one of the displays when I order online,' Rachel explained. 'I'm also faster. There's a little florist two blocks away.'

'Fair enough,' Jet said and reached out to press the lobby button as they boarded the elevator.

'You should come hang out with me and my friends tomorrow night. My roommates found an open mic night in the Village they want to go to. Have you spent much time around there yet?'

'Not yet. What kind of open mic night?' Jet asked with caution.

'Comedy, I think.'

'So long as it's not poetry, sure,' Jet agreed.

'It's going to be music if it's not comedy, knowing the girls. Has Shelley forgiven you for stealing our freelancer's attention on Friday night yet?'

'Define forgiven.' Jet glanced at Rachel. 'We're cool, I think. I'm feeding her hangover with coffee, so I'm hoping that'll help,' Jet said as they entered the ground floor lobby and waved to Leroy, who was on the phone, on their way out.

'You have to admit, though.' Rachel turned to Jet as they were about to go separate ways. 'Having someone as attractive as Daryl Burnes staring at you that intensely can't be all bad?'

'Burnes?'

'Yeah, do you think you really have met him before?' Rachel's eyes lit up as Jet's face twisted in recognition.

Only in my dreams, Jet thought.

'In another life maybe,' Jet said before hurrying off to Starbucks, leaving Rachel looking puzzled.

Another world really.

By the time Jet shoved the door open at Starbucks and blindly joined the back of the long lunchtime queue, her mind was alight with questions. How did a guy who looked like a fictional character rock up in New York with the same name as said fictional character? Not just any fictional character, either. One she had cut from her first novel when he no longer fit the direction she'd taken it in.

A character born out of a lonely teenager's heart.

Jet hadn't been exaggerating when she said her dating history was disastrous. Echoes of shame and humiliation threatened to bubble through her core. Taking a deep breath, Jet swallowed them down.

Her perfect man only existed on paper. The world had already taught her that. There was no way he was merrily wandering around Manhattan.

Taking a step forward as the line moved ahead of her, she felt her cheeks flame to think of the attention her colleagues were giving the situation. As usual any idea that someone found her interesting or, god forbid, attractive, had made her baulk and brush it off with laughter and a self-deprecating joke.

Her brain repeated his name loudly.

Giving herself a mental shrug, she refused to entertain memories of her teenage self and the very reason she'd started writing in the first place; if you can't meet decent people in real life, make them up.

Besides, she'd grown up.

Lonely teenagers wrote dumb shit. Everyone knew that.

Jet had also proven herself to be skilled in being awkward from a very early age. You daren't get caught staring at boys you find attractive if you want a quiet life. Kids could be cruel.

'What can I get you?'

Suddenly at the front of the queue, Jet jumped and fumbled for her phone as Shelley's order went completely out of her head.

'Erm . . . an iced americano, please, and . . . a skinny iced, double shot, caramel latte. Both to go.'

'Skinny iced caramel latte, double shot.' The barista raised her eyes over the cup she was scribbling on.

Jet played her words back in her head a moment too long.

'Yes! Sorry.'

'Can I get a name for those?' The girl arched an eyebrow to tell Jet she was holding up the line.

'Cassie,' Jet answered quickly.

'Hey Daryl!' the barista responded, already turning to the next customer. 'The usual coming right up.' She batted her eyelashes at him and took his loyalty card.

At serious risk of her blush turning into a hot flush, Jet moved out of the way. She'd been so wrapped up in her own thoughts, she'd had no clue he was directly behind her and wondered how long he'd been there.

'That's not your name,' Daryl commented with a frown as he joined her at the pick-up point.

Great, now he didn't need to think she was odd, she'd gone and given him evidence.

'It's a nickname . . . of sorts,' Jet replied, the words spilling from her lips before she could stop them.

'Is Jet short for something?' he asked, as he reached around her for a handful of sugars.

'Henrietta,' Jet said, trying not to wince.

Nodding, Daryl reached for his express-made coffee as it was placed on the counter by an unimpressed male youth who looked his customer up and down with disgust.

Smirking, Jet watched the barista turn his attention back on the girl at the till. Yes, teenagers could be dumb as fuck.

'Are you heading for the office?' Daryl asked as he removed the lid on his coffee, failing to notice the surprise on Jet's face when she realised he was still speaking to her.

'Yes, I'm the hangover cure delivery girl.' Jet looked pointedly at another furiously busy barista in charge of the iced drinks, which given a further upturn in weather, were proving popular. She was glad of the distractions between them, it helped her tame her weird.

'I'm headed that way. I'll wait,' he said as he rifled through the sugars to find two brown sachets to his liking.

'You don't have to, this could take a while.' Jet watched as the barista dumped a tonne of ice into two blenders and wandered off.

'I'm not in a rush.'

Turning suspiciously, Jet found him methodically adding the sugars he'd chosen into his coffee cup.

With a lack of rain or neon lighting to hamper her vision, it was the first time Jet had managed to get a proper look at him.

His collar-length blond hair had fallen around his face as he'd turned his attention on the beverage. Unbothered by the weather, it appeared softer and she could tell the colour was natural. Despite the passing winter it looked as though it was kissed by the sun daily. Jet flexed her fingers at her side as she itched to run her fingers through it.

'Sorry about the other night.' Daryl suddenly looked right at her with a pair of the most piercing aquamarine eyes she'd ever seen. 'I didn't mean to make you uncomfortable. I'd had a long day.'

He'd shaved since too.

'Don't worry about it.' Jet shrugged.

'We're going to be working together, and if you don't feel comfortable asking me to fix that piece of shit they call a content management system, we'll both be in for it.'

Jet coughed in surprise and glanced around at the other punters.

'Lighten up,' he said jovially. 'You couldn't cost me my job, I'm too important to them.'

'Uh huh,' she deadpanned.

'Seriously.' He sobered quickly. 'The system does suck.'

'I'm only three days in, but I had noticed,' Jet said with

a sigh and glanced around for any management who might be in the coffee shop on lunch.

'Don't panic, they all know it.' He grinned and lifted his coffee to his lips to test it before continuing, 'I've reminded them often enough.'

As a set of Frappuccinos that weren't Jet's order were placed on the counter, they both watched the server pick up the cups with "Cassy" written on the side.

'She's getting there,' Daryl commented.

'I'll go round there and do it myself in a moment,' Jet quipped and realised how impatient she sounded.

'Ex-barista?' Daryl asked.

'Bookstore café. College job.' Jet smiled.

'I see.' He leaned on the counter and dropped another sachet of sugar into his coffee. 'English college, American college, or do you really mean university?'

'Whatever the equivalent of all the above is.' Jet waved a hand in the air awkwardly. 'The manager was happy to let me come back whenever *school* was out for the holidays.'

'Cassy!' The barista suddenly yelled directly at Jet, shooting a glance at Daryl before she headed back for the next order.

'Perhaps we shouldn't be seen together in here too often. It seems the girls don't like it,' Jet teased as they headed back out onto the street, Daryl holding the door while she scooted through with a drink in each hand.

Ignoring the comment and, Jet realised, the looks the girls had given him, Daryl began crossing the road before she had time to catch up. Wondering how often people really were pulled over for jaywalking, Jet skipped into the road to catch up.

In the lobby, Leroy was nowhere to be seen and at reception, Rachel's cover was on the phone.

'I have to sign in, catch you in a bit, I want to bounce some ideas off you regarding the program.' Daryl waved her off as, balancing the drinks stacked precariously under her chin, she reached for her key fob.

Nodding as much as she dare, Jet headed for her desk where she found Shelley half asleep reading an email.

Lifting her head as though it was the heaviest thing in the world, she smiled gratefully but didn't reach for the drink. Pursing her lips to show her disapproval, Jet reached over the partition and placed it in front of her face.

'Thank you.' She pouted, then smiled as she dropped her head onto her palms at just the right height to drink from the straw without having to move it.

'If that doesn't wake you up then the guy in reception sure will.' Jet smirked as she took her seat and unlocked her computer.

Blinking stupidly, Shelley inclined her head as though it was a heavy boulder on her palms.

As Jet opened her mouth to inform her that she clearly meant their resident freelancer, he walked through the door, making Shelley sit up and smooth out her eyeliner smudges as though she'd been plugged into the mains.

Keeping her head down, Jet tried not to laugh as Shelley beamed, her head tracking his journey across the office.

SIX

Running her finger around the edge of the cocktail glass, Jet leant back in her seat and took in her surroundings.

The basement club-turned-open-mic-night was bathed in hues of red, spot lamps pointed directly at painted brick walls. There was a low-level stage set up across the back wall that she could tell was as temporary as the red velvet curtain that had been dragged across the usual DJ booth to hide it rather than for effect.

A tiny pang of homesickness struck as she remembered hanging out in similar clubs back home. That was, until the familiarity of it enveloped her and she lifted her glass to her lips with a smile.

'Oh, here's Tracy.' Rachel beamed up at the person approaching their table.

Until then Jet had only vaguely taken note that Rachel's roommate Sasha had been complaining at the absence of her partner, who apparently was always late.

Veronica and Sasha, Rachel's two roomies, had been Rachel's sisters from another mister (her words) since college.

Despite being identical twins, Jet was thankful they were easily told apart. Veronica wore her hair in embellished faux locs, whilst Sasha kept her hair clipped short.

'What kept you?' Sasha asked, side-glancing her partner as she leant down for a kiss before she took a seat.

'Work. As always,' Tracy scoffed, shooting a suspicious look in Jet's direction as she swept the jet-black pixie-cut fringe out of her eyes. 'Didn't we reserve this table?'

'I did. This is Jet, she's new at my office so I invited her along,' Rachel explained.

'Hi.' Jet offered a nod.

'Oh, right, hi.' Tracy glanced at Rachel but only with her eyes, her head remained locked in Jet's direction.

'Baby, Jet's cool. And she's from London.' Sasha reached out to take her hand.

'That doesn't guarantee anything,' Tracy scoffed, slapping her away.

'Tracy, don't start,' Veronica snapped.

In her peripheral, Jet noticed that Rachel pressed her mouth firmly closed.

'Let's go to the bar.' Sasha pulled Tracy up even as she was trying to shake off the bad mood she'd walked in with.

'Sorry about that,' Veronica said, following the couple with her eyes as they began shouting at each other as soon as they left the table. 'Tracy's boss is a raging homophobe and has a fetish for Asian women. He'll also be the reason she was working late.'

'Ah, that kind of prick,' Jet said with an understanding nod and took a sip of her drink. 'Human beings are notoriously shitty creatures, it can be hard to know who to trust.'

'We keep telling her to leave that place, her boss is an ass. Despite things he's openly said to Tracy, she's convinced part of his problem is that she's dating a black woman. Though annoyingly he's never directly said anything of the sort, so she can't report him,' Veronica added.

'Oh, for fuck's sake.' Jet rolled her eyes. 'Pricks like that have to die out someday, surely?'

'There're more out there than you realise.' Rachel folded her arms whilst staring at her drink in a manner that told Jet if she looked close enough, she'd see a bad memory replaying in her eyes.

'That's the damned truth,' Jet hissed. 'There's a lot to be said for castration. That'd fix the problem, and a few others, in a generation or two.'

'I'll drink to that!' Veronica leant forward with a grin, her glass raised.

Jet raised her own in agreement and the three of them finished their drinks.

'Another round?' Jet asked.

'We've got them.' Sasha reappeared with a tray and began handing out glasses.

When Tracy caught up, she was carrying a pitcher.

'This should keep us going for a while.' Tracy put the

jug down in the middle of the table and shot Jet a calmer look as she sat down.

'If I had a boss like yours, I'd be sinking doubles.' Jet smiled.

'Who says I'm not?' Tracy bit back but a smile tugged at the corners of her mouth.

'Men. Can't live with them, could happily live without them.' Veronica mused in to a freshly poured cocktail.

'Bullshit. What's true for me, isn't so true for you,' Sasha said, pointing at her sister.

'That is what vibrators were invented for, after all,' Jet said with a raise of her glass and wished she'd just kept her mouth shut even as the rest of the table laughed. Damn her mouth, damn the two drinks she'd already had.

'We need to get you out on the dating scene.' Rachel narrowed her eyes thoughtfully at Jet.

'No, we don't.' Jet shook her head. 'I've only been here a week, I'm still living out of a hotel room!'

'Ron, how's your little black book looking these days? Anyone you could set Jet up with?' Rachel nudged Veronica's glass with her own.

'My little black fuck-book?' Veronica sassed and shimmied her boobs in her roommate's direction. 'There are a few of my regular boo-tay callers who have expressed a desire to go steady, if you're looking to date rather than screw?'

'Oh my god, I'm not looking for anything,' Jet blurted quickly, wanting to hide under the table.

'How long have you been single?' Rachel asked.

Feeling like a rabbit in the headlights, Jet glanced at Sasha and Tracy, hoping they wanted to change the subject, but they were engrossed in each other, their spat forgotten.

Shit. How long had it been . . . embarrassingly long, if she could class any of her past encounters as relationships.

'A couple of years or so.' Jet shrugged it off. 'I've been busy and most of my friends are now married, and their friend's friends are married.'

'Damn, that thing will dry up if you don't show it some attention soon.' Veronica snatched up her bag and began digging around in it even as Jet pondered going full *Sex and the City* and returning to the conversation of vibrators.

Feeling her cheeks flush, she focused on her drink again.

'Rachel, didn't you have a date last night?' Sasha suddenly looked up.

'Yeah, he didn't show.' Rachel waved her off with a flick of her wrist like it was no big deal. 'I replaced him with a pizza for one.'

Producing a small dog-eared pocketbook from her handbag, Veronica shot her a look. 'You need this too?'

'I've seen what most of the guys in that book look like the morning after, no thanks.'

'That's reassuring,' Jet mumbled.

'She only said *most* of them,' Veronica pointed out. 'Rachel has a very specific type.'

'And Ron's not fussy,' Rachel teased.

'Ain't that the truth,' Sasha drawled.

'Without having to fight my sister for the good-looking guys, I get to try her quota on for size too.' Veronica grinned.

'There's a guy at my work who's recently divorced, seems like a decent guy, the divorce totally isn't his fault.' Sasha sat up suddenly and reached for her phone.

'Who, Roger?' Veronica snorted. 'Jet doesn't want some other woman's very recent cast-offs.'

'Sounds like he needs a confidence boost. Jet, you don't have to marry the guy, you probably wouldn't want to, but it gets you back into the dating game. What do you say?' Rachel's eyes sparkled with excitement.

'He's on the rebound, he might not want to date either,' Jet replied as evenly as she could manage.

'I'll ask him,' Sasha said as if to mark the end of the topic.

'I'll have a rummage around in this thing and make a few notes.' Veronica waved her little black book around before dropping it back into her handbag.

'Shame Shelley would claw your eyes out, or I'd suggest you pursue a certain someone else . . .' Rachel waggled her eyebrows at Jet as the lights went down and the compére took to the stage.

Draining her third glass, Jet wondered what the hell she had gotten herself into and how quickly she could find something else to occupy her time with. As much as the prospect of dating an American piqued her interest — she wanted to know how they measured up against British men, and not in *that* way — the idea of throwing herself *out there* in Manhattan terrified her.

SEVEN

Puffing out a sigh through pursed lips, Jet leant back in her chair and scrolled up and down the list in front of her.

'Is it broken again?'

Jumping at the proximity of the voice behind her, Jet almost toppled the chair over.

Daryl's sturdy left hand was already setting her straight even as she turned to the cause of the distraction.

'Sorry, I thought the sigh was work related,' he admitted with a guilty smirk.

'To answer your question, of course it's still broken.' Jet watched him take a mouthful of coffee from his travel mug and realised he was only just starting for the day. 'It's the sheer choice of apartments.' She waved her hand at the monitor.

Ducking down to take a better look, he mulled over her search criteria.

'You're searching based on price?'

'It's my only starting point,' Jet sighed and ran her

fingers through her hair. 'I used to have connections to the Upper West Side, but just because that's the only area I remember from when I was a kid, doesn't mean it's the best.'

'You certainly don't want the cheapest either,' he said, his brows knitting with concern.

'No, I guess not,' Jet said, deflating, and realised she was reaching for her mug of tea as he lifted the coffee to his lips again.

Remembering what any self-proclaimed psychologist would say about mimicking behaviour, she left the mug alone, hoping she hadn't blushed in her own realisation.

'I don't know what your budget is, but how far do you want to commute?'

'I don't want to sound like the typical tourist, but I didn't move here to live too far away to enjoy it, if you know what I mean.'

'Brooklyn?'

'Perhaps.'

'New Jersey?'

'Hmm, I'd rather not,' Jet said hesitantly.

'What's wrong with New Jersey?' He shot her a look of mock-insult.

'Nothing. It's just that if I can, I want to fully experience New York city, ideally Manhattan.'

'Didn't you ever have to commute into London?'

Jet shook her head. 'Nope, I got lucky there.'

'Parents?'

'So sickeningly all-out Londoners.' She pulled a face. 'Even if my dad was born right here in Manhattan.'

'Ah, it's a very different city to the one your dad will have grown up in.'

'I know, but a girl's gotta have dreams, right?' Jet sighed and slumped her chin down onto her palm, her elbow on the desk.

'You're in a hotel at the moment?'

'For now.'

'When does that run out?'

'Not until the end of the month, both Shelley and Rachel have offered their sofa . . . sorry, couch, if I need it.' Jet pursed her lips. 'It'll all work out. I'm not worried. My dad said crazy roommates are all part of the experience.'

'Oh really? He actively encourages you to share with complete strangers?' Daryl scowled but didn't look at her.

'Rites of passage, I guess,' Jet said, rolling her head to the side to look at him.

'I guess,' Daryl echoed and stood straight. 'So, what's broken this time? No, don't tell me, let me get to my desk and read your email. I'm not ready for that shit yet today.'

Before Jet could reply, he was already walking away.

Glancing back at her monitor, she closed the browser, checking the clock to see if her lunch break was over yet. She wasn't sure she had the stomach to trawl any more apartment listings without further understanding how each district ticked.

Reaching for her tea and realising it was cold, Jet was glad she hadn't taken a swig in front of Daryl, stone cold tea wasn't something she could stomach.

Scooping up the mug, she stood up, stretched and headed for the kitchen. Most people were returning from their lunch, so the hive of activity reserved for 1p.m. on the dot had dissipated, just a couple of people from the graphics department were sat around a table in the corner while Shelley occupied another on the opposite side of the room, chatting away in Spanish on her phone. She didn't even notice Jet walk in.

Dumping the remnants of her tea in the sink, Jet ran the mug under the tap to rinse it before wandering over to the drinks machine for a fresh brew.

As she pressed the button and boiling hot water began hissing in to her cup, Rachel strutted in behind her and began retrieving the components of a tea-tray from one of the cupboards.

Jet looked up as Rachel tossed a tray onto the side and began filling it with cups, spoons, pots, sugar dishes and cookies.

'Everything OK?' Jet asked as Rachel continued to rummage.

'I love my job.' Rachel looked up with a forced grin.

'Last minute client meeting?'

'Board meeting,' she huffed as she arranged the items on the tray neatly.

Reaching into the fridge, Jet plopped some milk into her tea before passing it to Rachel.

'Thanks.' She smiled. 'How's the apartment hunting going?'

'I hit a dead end.'

'Oh?'

'I don't really know *where* to look.' Jet leant against the counter with a shrug.

'Nothing north of the park if you want to get here in a reasonable amount of time in the mornings, but try to stay on the island if budget allows,' Rachel offered. 'Rental prices are ridiculous in this part of the city though, so you won't be close.'

'They weren't any better in London,' Jet huffed. 'So, I expected that.'

'There's still our couch,' Rachel said as she reached into the fridge and straightened, waving a carton of almond milk about. 'I'll also ask my super whether he knows of any apartments about to come available in the building. There are a couple of one-beds in the block.'

'That's great, thanks. I appreciate it.' Jet smiled and followed Rachel from the kitchen as she sashayed awkwardly through the office space in an attempt to keep the heavy tray level.

On returning to her desk, Jet found Daryl in her seat, tipping back the last drops of his coffee.

'Can I help you?' Jet asked with a smirk.

'You broke it this time,' he announced.

'I highly doubt that.'

'You said the clickable areas aren't working.'

'That's right, they're not.'

'Well, you need to set the clickable area.'

'I did.'

'If you click and drag, it doesn't always save.'

'Well, it should always bloody save. And I didn't click

and drag, I used exact coordinates.' She folded her arms and leant her hip against her desk.

'You can't have done.'

'Trust me, I did.' She scowled as he nudged her mouse and the lock screen woke up.

'Show me.'

'Ugh,' she grumbled. 'You gonna get out of my seat?'

Jumping up with a grin, Daryl gave a mocking bow and held the chair out for her to sit.

'Cheeky fucker,' she muttered under her breath as she fell into the seat and entered her password.

Opening the course they were working on, she scrolled back to the last screen she had been trying to implement.

Leaning forward, and a little too close for comfort, close enough that she could smell his cologne, Daryl peered over her shoulder.

'See, right there, the coordinates are in.' She jabbed a finger at the screen and tried to ignore the heat of his body as he leant closer still.

'Shit.' He expelled a breath. 'OK, I'll sort it.'

'Apology accepted,' Jet drawled as he stood back up, his attention suddenly somewhere else. 'Do you think you know what it is?'

'What perfume do you wear?' He wrinkled his nose as he stared over the top of her head.

'What's that got to do with anything?'

'Never mind.' He turned to walk away.

'Your mug.' Jet snatched up his travel mug and waved it at his back. 'It's Poison by Dior.'

Smiling in what Jet would describe as an oddly shocked manner, he span on his heel to retrieve the mug and with a nod, was gone.

'I really hope you don't get that course fixed any time soon.' Shelley was suddenly lowering herself back into her chair, dreamily watching Daryl retreat.

'Hmm. How long do we keep freelancers generally?'

'He's been here longer than half the staff. The dev boys put up with his odd hours because he's good at what he does.' Leon was suddenly stood at Jet's shoulder.

Glad she'd closed down the property ads, Jet turned in her seat to look up at her manager. Aside from her interview and a welcome chat over a coffee on her first day, Jet hadn't seen much of Leon. Everything was handled through project managers who he held regular meetings with from his office on the other side of the floor.

'After this board meeting, I have a team call with the client. Would you be OK to sit in on the call and explain to them in layman's terms why it's busted? Dorothy tells me you explained it really well to her, but she isn't comfortable repeating it to the client.' Leon placed his hands on his hips as he spoke.

'I only know what Daryl has told me from a technical side,' Jet replied.

'Apparently you relay it better than the developers do.'

'OK. Have you got a meeting room, or is it dial in?'

'I'll send you the invite,' he said, checking his watch

before heading for the board room.

Watching him go, Jet began to understand Rachel's mood.

EIGHT

Rubbing her eyes harder than she meant to as she stumbled back to her desk at 8p.m., Jet yawned as Daryl hurried for the exit. He'd taken his coat and bag in to the meeting room and had been checking his watch every couple of minutes for over half an hour, answering each question from the client in an increasingly clipped tone the longer the meeting over ran.

That he'd taken his bag in with him when the meeting started at 4p.m. told her he'd expected to be late leaving.

Already starting to reconsider her own choices with the job, Jet tugged her phone out of her pocket and checked for notifications. She'd felt it go off several times during the meeting, and remembered she had promised to check in with Mai.

Scrolling through the email notifications and the messages as she sat back at her desk and began closing the computer down, she smiled fondly. Especially at the last message which read:

Oi! You should be off-duty by now, it's nearly midnight here, don't make me wait up!

Biting her lip and wondering whether Mai really would still be awake at what was already 1a.m. on a Friday night/Saturday morning, she sent a quick reply and shoved the phone back into her pocket before sliding into her coat, grabbing her bag and making a dash for the exit herself.

Rachel had told her to head over to the bar for the Friday night ritual whenever she was done with the meeting, but she'd since messaged to say they'd all disbanded.

Friday night looked set to be a Chinese takeout over novel-related emails in the hotel room, with an added dose of whatever passed for Friday night TV on in the background.

Jet rubbed at her yawn-induced watery eyes as she rode the elevator down to street level, that plan sounded good to her. Leaning over to check the bags under her eyes in the elevator mirrors, she knew she'd grow to resent extra hours pretty quick.

'No Larry, I'm running late as it is, I can't possibly cover both!'

Standing up straight, Jet frowned as the elevator doors opened to reveal Daryl pacing around the lobby, his bag discarded on one of the glass coffee tables as he ran his fingers through his hair.

As she stepped out of the elevator, he turned and saw her. Scrubbing the hand that had been tangled in his hair down his face, he stared at her, making her stop.

'Larry, give me a second, I'll call you back.'

'Is everything OK?' Jet asked, curious more than concerned.

'You're a writer, aren't you?'

'Yes . . . but . . .' Jet stopped, wondering what he meant.

'I know you write more than just crap scripts for learning courses,' he said quickly.

'How . . . ? Hang on! Crap scripts? Excuse me . . .'

'Come on, they are, no matter how skilled you are, the clients will always scale them back and change stuff.'

'Not always! I've worked with some brilliant clients!'

'Sure.'

'What is your problem?' Jet scolded as she re-shouldered her bag, ready to leave.

'I'm super stuck.' He calmed slightly. 'How would you feel about taking one of my freelance gigs tonight?'

'I don't understand.'

'I'm also a writer.' The admittance left his mouth on a rush of air and Jet realised that she was being offered a secret.

'Fuck off,' she blurted. 'You can't be that as well.'

'Sorry, what?' He gawped at her.

'Nothing . . . coincidence, I'm sure.'

'Coincidence how?'

'Never mind. What do you write?' Jet shook herself into an interested smile, her mind racing as she tried not to freak the man out. His eyes narrowed suspiciously regardless.

'All sorts really, tonight it's a bit of freelance journalism. I know a guy who gets me to write the odd sport or entertainment reviews.'

'That's why you work such odd hours?'

'Pretty much. Look, he just called to say he's got no one to cover opening night for an arthouse movie in the village at ten.' Daryl ran his fingers through his hair again and looked down at his phone. 'I can't cover both, I should have been at a gig up town twenty minutes ago.'

'How arthouse are we talking?' Jet folded her arms but couldn't conceal the intrigue in her voice.

Trying not to smile in relief, Daryl let out another breath as though he'd been holding it. 'Batshit weird.'

'Sounds like fun. How do I go about getting in?'

'Let me call Larry back . . .' He lifted the phone to his ear again and, as it rang, ran over to the reception desk to grab a compliment slip and a pen. 'Can you write your phone number and email address on here while I . . . Hi Larry . . .'

Thrusting the pen and paper into her hands, he began walking laps around the lobby seating while she dropped her bag next to his and crouched at one of the coffee tables to write her contact information down.

'I work with her, trust me, she can write . . . I'm not doing both.' Daryl walked over and took the slip from her as she stood back up and offered it. 'I can give them to you now . . . yeah, email address too.'

Before she knew it, he was hanging up and retrieving his bag.

'I'll send him your contact info when I find a cab, I've got to run. Any problems, this is my number.' Fishing in the inside pocket of his coat, Daryl produced a business card and handed it to her. Before she'd had chance to pocket it, he was already walking away. 'You're a lifesaver, I'll see you Monday.'

'No problem,' Jet muttered to the empty lobby.

Checking her watch again, she pulled her phone from her pocket to enter his number before she could give herself the chance to lose the card. She had no clue what she was doing or even where she was going.

"You bet your ass I'm still awake. I need the next instalment!" was the reply waiting for her from Mai.

'Fuck,' Jet whispered to herself, feeling suddenly way out of her depth.

Running her fingers through her hair, she picked up her bag again and headed back to the hotel. It was going to be tight, but all she had to do was email her latest chapter to Mai before heading back out.

Tumbling out of the subway an hour and a half later, Jet hurried up the street marked on her maps app and very nearly missed the cinema on the first pass. With little more than a canopy to mark the entrance, it took far longer than she was comfortable with for her to make out the name of the Quad Cinema on the glass door.

Larry had called her directly as she'd been crossing the street in front of her hotel to check that Daryl wasn't pulling a fast one, before emailing her the information she needed, including the name of the guy she would be covering for.

She'd known better than to expect a red carpet, but where Daryl had attempted to gloss it over as 'opening night', this was clearly just a film review for the Sunday edition of the New York Times. Larry had explained that he found hacks for all manner of last-minute small fry reviews. He'd used the term *Agent*, Jet thought *Journo Pimp* sounded better.

Walking into what she had thought would be a lobby, Jet found herself in a trendy café-bar with the cinema's name in neon letters near the window. She'd missed that too.

Pausing to consult her phone, and avoid the hopeful gaze of a man sitting by himself near the window — waiting on his Tinder date perhaps — Jet took a subtle look around. A few pairs of eyes peered at her over glasses of wine and heated debates, but she reminded herself that was natural when someone new entered a public place.

A little research on the venue had informed her that this was a cinema popular with students from NYU for its diverse cinematic offerings.

'Jet!'

Startled, Jet jumped and, feeling like a deer in the headlights, looked towards the sound of her name. It had come from the bar.

Sasha was beckoning to her from a stool while Tracy was ordering drinks beside her.

Sighing in relief, Jet headed over with a smile.

'Hey!' Sasha spread her arms wide for a hug, kissing

Jet on the cheek as she accepted the gesture. 'Are you here for a screening?'

'Yeah, I've been thrown a movie review by a writing acquaintance. He's too busy to do it.' Jet raked her fingers through her hair. 'To be honest, I have no idea what I'm doing.'

'That's what we're here for too, Tracy has to write up a review for her radio station.'

'My boss may be a bigoted moron, but one of the producers likes my opinion at least, she regularly sends us tickets to events,' Tracy explained.

'There has to be some perks, right?' Jet smiled before the bar tender caught her eye and she ordered a beer.

'Definitely, but we've seen some awful movies.' Sasha shot her partner a look.

'Some great bands though,' Tracy pointed out.

'So, you wouldn't have had any plans for tonight?' Sasha grinned, her tongue between her teeth.

'I've only been here a week,' Jet reminded her, catching the eye of Mr Tinder whose hopes visibly fell. 'I'm not on the dating scene.'

She inwardly shuddered.

'You are now. I gave Roger your number, he's up for that date.'

Jet almost choked on her beer, wondering how Sasha had got her number so fast and scowled as she covered the cough and her mouth, remembering that Rachel had it.

'She told him you were British and he could hardly contain his boner,' Tracy deadpanned.

'He's not that bad.' Sasha pouted and collected her cocktail glass as she slid off her stool. 'We need to go and take our seats.'

'I need to collect my ticket.' Jet nodded and let them lead her to the box office.

'See you in there,' Sasha called as Tracy sauntered off in the direction of the main screen.

'Hi there, how can I help?'

'I'm picking up a ticket, it should be reserved for Larry?' Jet replied.

'You're not who we were expecting.' The cashier suddenly looked uneasy.

'You were expecting Chuck. Chuck has had to cancel, I'm the replacement.' Jet leant her hip against the counter.

'But, I'm not supposed to . . .'

'I knew the name of the person who booked them, and who I'm replacing. Don't panic. But also, please don't make me call Larry, this is my first movie review.' Jet pouted playfully hoping to put the kid at ease.

'Maybe I should check with my manager?'

'That really isn't necessary.' Jet smiled. 'I can show you the email I have?'

'Yes, please.'

Placing her beer on the counter, she reached into her pocket for her phone.

'Is everything OK?'

Glancing over her shoulder, Jet found Mr Tinder looking at her intently, his hand poised to tap her on the shoulder. Jet's eyes moved, unimpressed, from his face to the hand and back again. He retracted it quickly, but not before Jet could notice that he was holding two tickets, though sadly, still by himself.

Which made her feel guilty enough to offer him a stupid smile.

'Oh yes, thank you, just need my confirmation email.' Jet waved her phone, realising she sounded like Bridget Jones at her most awkward.

'I have a spare ticket if you need it?' he asked, looking hopeful.

'Thank you,' Jet repeated. 'I do have a ticket.' Was she deliberately sounding like Bridget Jones now? She often mimicked her favourite comedy moments when she was uncomfortable.

It had done the job, either way, he was backing off.

'Enjoy the film.' She nodded at him as he turned away.

Yup, definitely Bridget Jones that time.

'Here's your ticket.' The cashier beamed a moment later, handing her an envelope with the note "For Chuck, on behalf of Larry & NYT" but the Chuck was crossed out and someone had written Jet underneath. Larry had called ahead.

'For f—, thank you!' Jet strained and headed off in the same direction Sasha and Tracy had gone.

When she entered the auditorium, she found Sasha waving at her from a seat right in the middle.

'We saved you a seat!' She beamed as the lights went down.

Sighing in relief, Jet headed down and all but fell into

the seat beside her.

'Wow, wasn't that a pile of shit?' Sasha narrowed her eyes as Jet ordered three drinks in the bar afterwards. 'I almost fell asleep.'

'Why didn't you? You didn't have to watch it like we did.' Jet laughed.

'Tracy wouldn't let me.' She rubbed her shoulder where her girlfriend had spent most of the movie poking her.

'Trust me, no one would've been watching it if she'd started snoring through it.' Tracy grinned.

'Ugh, how the hell are we supposed to write that up?' Jet groaned.

'Tell me about it,' Tracy agreed. 'Though I find music easier to write up in general.'

Jet found herself wondering just what type of gig Daryl was at and whether he'd be out for the night. Though as her colleagues had already told her, he wasn't overly social.

'The guy who gave me this write up was off to a gig up town,' Jet said without thinking.

'Yeah? Where at?' Sasha perked up.

'He didn't tell me.' Jet looked awkward as Sasha sought her second wind. 'Sorry.'

'We should try and find it.' Sasha shimmied her shoulders.

'It could be anywhere,' Tracy pointed out, clearly on Jet's side at the idea of an all-nighter.

'Exactly, he just said up town. From the financial district, that's almost everywhere. Could have been a hidden venue or Madison Square Gardens for all I know. It started at eight.'

'Early for a decent gig.' Tracy pulled a face.

'Who's playing Madison tonight?' Sasha looked around as if the answer would be on one of the movie posters.

'Knowing your luck, Taylor Swift,' Tracy drawled.

As Sasha wrinkled her nose delightedly at the thought, Jet considered how badly Daryl would stand out at a concert like that. Like a sore thumb, she'd wager.

'I should find somewhere to get something to eat.' Jet felt the latest mouthful of beer chill her already empty stomach.

Checking her watch, she wondered whether it was worth eating a meal at midnight, or just snacking on leftover munchies back at the hotel.

'Pizza and beer?' Tracy looked to Sasha quickly, her eyebrows risen in hope.

'In bed with Netflix,' Sasha said, as though it was a negotiation, making Jet smile.

'Deal.'

Fifteen minutes later, Jet was alone again on the streets of Manhattan.

She loved how it never felt late in the city. Shoving her hands in her coat pockets she walked to the end of the block and watched the taxi cabs rush south down Fifth Avenue. That was the way she was going. But it was a Friday night.

Reaching in to her pocket to check her phone again, she saw a bundle of emails and suspected she knew exactly who they'd be from.

Sticking her hand in the air, she waited for a cab to pull over.

NINE

At the sound of her mobile bleeping out a ream of text messages, Jet lifted her head off her right hand too quickly and instantly regretted it. Her neck screamed, her arm fell uselessly to her side when she tried to sit up and her feet only found air as she blinked her eyes open and tried to remember where she was.

The phone bleeped again.

Rolling gingerly onto her back, Jet rubbed at her eyes with the hand she hadn't slept on and wriggled the fingers of the one pulsing with pins and needles.

It didn't take long to remember why she was fully dressed, on top of the bed, with the TV on and sunlight streaming in the windows.

Having wanted to write her review while it was fresh in her head, she'd written and sent it whilst chowing down on a small garlic chicken pizza as soon as she got back to the hotel room.

She had also set herself a word count target for the weekend and decided that the best way to hit it was to write a couple of chapters for Mai to chew on before she went to sleep.

Realising the sun was coming up as she emailed the second of the two new chapters to her editor, she had finally closed the lid on the remains of cold pizza and moved away from the desk.

Wondering whether it was technically wrong to be going to sleep as the sun was rising, she lay down to watch a bit of TV and take a nap before writing another chapter.

It seemed she'd only been asleep a couple of hours and Mai was most certainly awake if the quick succession of messages was anything to go by.

Lifting her arm out in front of her and giving it a shake, Jet got up off the bed and headed for the bathroom where she stripped out of her clothes and cleaned her teeth, furry from a night of chewing on melted cheese.

When she returned to the bedroom, with every intention of going back to bed until at least lunchtime, she threw back the duvet as she passed the bed but continued to the desk by the window to open the curtains a little more and check on her phone.

Five messages from Mai. One from Daryl.

Rubbing her eyes again, setting her computer to sleep mode and reaching for the t-shirt she intended to sleep in, she put the phone down and slipped the t-shirt over her head before ruffling her hair and returning her attention to the messages as she fell onto the bed.

Mai: OMG MORE CHAPTERS?
Mai: Were you up all night?
Mai: Shit, what time is it there?
Mai: I'm totally going to read these NOW.
Mai: But first COFFEE.

'Reads to me like you've already had too much,' Jet muttered with a fond smile.

That easily gave her another couple of hours to sleep. It wasn't like she'd given Mai an opus to read, but enough that she would probably read them more than once, taking her time over her coffee, making notes. There would be a return email by lunch New York time, she suspected.

Having your editor turn into a bit of a superfan had its drawbacks. She never got to send a complete manuscript, Mai was far too impatient for that. She had to admit that it had its perks though. Not only had she grown incredibly fond of her editor as a friend, it also meant that on a professional level, she got her ass kicked on the regular and a cleaner first draft overall.

Nervous energy trickled down her arms as she switched senders to read the other message.

Daryl: Thanks for last night! I totally owe you. Larry was impressed with your writing and that you delivered so quickly. I'll collect your check with mine later.

Eyebrows raised, Jet found herself smiling. Her first freelance gig in New York. A little pang of imposter syndrome crept in when she caught herself wondering whether Larry or Daryl would lie to her whilst secretly getting someone else to rewrite it.

A tiny inner voice asked if she cared when she was getting paid. An even quieter whisper still asked her if she was pleased Daryl liked her work.

Rolling her eyes at herself, she knew that she'd totally care if she actually sucked.

Passing out without replying to either message, Jet slept until noon before her phone woke her with another stream of messages.

'You could just ring, and I could just ignore it,' she grouched as she rolled over and sought the device from the bedside table. 'And I could remember to put the damned phone on silent,' she chastised herself.

A further ten messages were waiting for her from Mai and another from Daryl.

Suddenly intrigued, Jet sat up on the bed with a bounce and swept her hair out of her face, which took three attempts before she should see through it to read the screen.

Daryl: Checks collected, I'm on my way to Battery Park, are you staying near the office?

Frowning, instincts kicking in, Jet found herself instantly wanting to conceal her location. He could be moody sure, but she didn't feel the need to avoid him.

Battery Park was only a few blocks away. Glancing out of the window at the cloudy but dry day, she considered taking a walk to the park herself. She shouldn't sit indoors all day, even if she wanted to get that first draft finished sooner rather than later.

Jet: Fairly close for now, yeah. Want me to meet you at the park?

Ball in your court, pal, Jet thought, doubting she'd hear from him again until Monday at the office. He'd probably been planning on dropping the envelope to hotel reception anyway.

Her phone pinged again.

Daryl: Heading into the subway, be there in 20.

'Fuck.'

Tossing the phone back onto the bed as she scrambled up off it, Jet rushed to the mirror and tussle-checked her hair. Thankful that the lack of sleep meant it wasn't trashed and that she would feel semi-decent in public, she dragged her t-shirt over her head as she scooted to the bathroom and scooped her curls up into the complimentary shower cap.

Twenty-two minutes later, Jet reached the fountains in Battery Park. Before she could dig her phone out of her pocket, Daryl rounded the nearby café and handed her an envelope and a hot takeaway cup.

'I was early, it's tea,' he explained when she blinked in surprise. 'Did I wake you?' His smile evolved into a smirk.

'Thank you, er . . . kinda,' Jet blurted, never having been great at lying. 'I spent most of the night writing.'

'But you had the article delivered by 2a.m.?' He looked

at her suspiciously.

'I have a secret identity.' Jet wrinkled her nose playfully as she brought the tea closer to inhale the vapours. 'Her name's Cassie Huygens.'

'Like the Titan probe?' He frowned.

'Exactly!' Jet felt colour rise to her cheeks even as they stretched into a grin. 'Wow, no one ever makes that connection.'

'So my Spidey senses were right about the writing. Pen name?'

'Right again.' Jet carefully slipped her envelope into her bag one-handed, before clutching the cup with both hands awkwardly.

Nodding, Daryl looked around the park, overly interested in anything but Jet for a moment.

'So, what really brings you downtown? My check could have waited until Monday,' Jet asked quickly, before attempting to take a sip of her tea.

Very little milk, no sugar, he'd noticed how she took her hot beverages. She stared at the floor as he continued to be overly interested in a woman walking her dog along the park's edge.

'I have a date with a French lady,' Daryl announced suddenly.

'Liberty?' Jet glanced out across the water to where Liberty Island sat quietly. 'Or none of my business?' she continued when his attention returned to her a little too quickly for her liking.

'Yeah, Liberty.' He tilted his head slightly as he looked at her. 'You been over there yet?'

'Not since my nan died. No.'

'Sounds like a sore point?'

'Not really, just haven't had the chance, I guess.'

'The Crown Café does food.'

'Is that all you're going over there for?' Jet looked him up and down teasingly.

'Pretty much.' He shoved his hands in his pockets and nodded like a child caught with his hand in the cookie jar before relaxing his face and shrugging. 'I go over there every once in a while, I'm sure there's room on the boat for one more if you need to eat at all today.'

'Room on the boat is something that, on a Saturday, may be a problem.'

'I haven't failed yet.' He nudged her with his elbow. 'Come on. I at least owe you lunch for saving my ass last night.'

Before Jet could consider it further, he walked away, as though it was decided. She opened her mouth to scoff, but he was moving too fast to have heard her and she had to scurry to catch up.

Before she knew it, they were leaning over the rail, watching Manhattan Island shrink away from them, Daryl having produced two tickets from his pocket before they'd even reached the queue line.

'Just as well I was free this afternoon.' Jet waved her ticket at him before she tucked it into her pocket.

'I told you. I owe you lunch.' He spread his arms wide. 'I'm sure I could have persuaded some other lonely lady in the park if you hadn't been interested.'

'I'm not lonely.' Jet laughed. 'But I am surprised.

73

Given the look you gave me when we first met.'

'What?'

'You looked like you'd seen a ghost when you walked into the pub . . . bar that night.'

'Something like that.'

'Oh.' Jet leant back against the rail awkwardly. 'Really? Sorry.'

'Yeah, don't worry about it.' He shrugged and turned to rest a hip against the rail himself.

Nodding, Jet could tell he was trying to make up for being a miserable shit, she had done him a favour, after all. Automatically comparing him to her imaginary Daryl, she decided that the fictional version had been written to be a bit too nice at times. Though, she remembered with a secret smile, he had bite when he needed to.

'Did you grow up in New York?'

'It's the only place I've ever known.'

'I used to wish my parents had settled here rather than London.' Jet sighed, letting her eyes drift across the Manhattan skyline.

'I'll bet London rocks,' Daryl said thoughtfully.

'Yeah. Yeah, I guess it does. I doubt I'd have suffered any less at school here anyway.'

'What do you mean?'

'Kids don't take kindly to redheads.'

'Really?'

'Yeah . . . never mind. It was a long time ago.' Jet waved it off. 'You said you've never been to London?'

'Sadly not, I tried once, it didn't end well.'

'Sounds ominous.'

'It was crazy really, a string of errors meant the only time I booked to go it just wouldn't happen. I'll bet London in the summer has quite a charm.'

'A good old British Christmas suits it better, but yes, yes, it does,' Jet admitted.

'Will you miss it this summer?'

'Find me a decent fountain and I'll be fine.' She shook her head enthusiastically.

'Bethesda?'

'Excellent start.' Jet nodded with a grin. 'I've already paid her a visit.'

'Did you have a favourite in London?'

'I love watching unsuspecting tourists getting caught out in the jets around the Shakespeare fountain in Leicester Square. Kids and adults alike,' she said with a smile. 'I find the sound of just about any fountain soothing.'

'I can see where you're coming from on that.' Daryl nodded. 'Sometimes you've just got to switch off to the simplest sounds.'

'What do you listen to, to switch off?'

'Thunderstorms.'

'Ooh, yeah, I love a good storm.'

'Who doesn't?'

'You'd be surprised.' Jet chuckled, looking directly at him, though the breeze from the open water was whipping his hair into his eyes.

Not that he seemed to care. Jet decided she liked laid-back Daryl far more than the grumpy boots version.

'Sounds like you had an ex who didn't like thunder?' He grinned.

'I'm not sure I could call him that. There were many names I did use at the time. However, a dislike of a little summer storm was just one of many hints I didn't take that we weren't suited.'

Daryl squinted as the sun broke through the crowds. 'Sounds complicated.'

'It was a long time ago. Teenagers make everything complicated.' Jet shrugged.

'Do they?' he asked the wind, his voice suddenly quieter than usual.

'Sounds like you know exactly what I'm talking about.' She looked him up and down as the boat began to approach Ellis Island.

When she tried to meet his eye, she found him staring across the deck at the other passengers.

Pushing himself away from the barrier suddenly, he crossed the boat swiftly and began talking to a woman in a wheelchair who was attempting to get into position ready to disembark at Ellis.

Folding her arms and leaning back against the rail, Jet watched with interest as he struck up a conversation with the woman. They were soon laughing about something as the lady gesticulated and flirted with the one person on board who seemed to have noticed she was on her own.

Tilting her head in interest, Jet found herself mesmerised by him. His smile betrayed his appearance. Despite the utility coat and boots that seemed oversized even on a man of six feet in height, his smile, when genuine, was warm and doing an excellent job of comforting someone Jet could tell was incredibly grateful of the attention.

He stayed with the passenger until a member of staff arrived to assist her onto the island before he waved her goodbye.

'Sorry about that,' he said as he returned.

'No problem, she's lucky you spotted her.' Jet gestured to the woman still waving from the shore and felt compelled to offer a wave back.

'I've often seen her onboard, she's not normally alone,' Daryl said as he waved absently.

'Does she usually have a carer with her?' Jet probed, more to prevent an awkward silence than anything else.

'No, her husband. She often says hello, she spots the regulars,' he explained with a shrug. 'She has ancestors who passed through the island and visits regularly.'

Nodding, Jet watched as the boat began to jerk and edge away from the dock.

'He's in hospital.'

'Oh shit, I hope he's alright, is she ok?'

'They're both fine.' It was Daryl's turn to appraise her. 'He had appendicitis.'

'That's good bad news I guess.' Jet smiled.

'Speaking of good bad news.'

'You don't just owe me lunch, do you?'

'Don't be so cynical, it's not quite like that.'

'Not quite like that?'

'Larry wanted me to ask you how you'd feel about

doing more freelance writing for him.' He turned to her at the rail. 'He wants me to give you the hard sell.'

'Is he desperate?' Jet raised an eyebrow.

'What? No! What makes you ask that?' Daryl frowned, genuinely confused and Jet mentally slapped herself for sounding so hard on herself.

'Oh, y'know, the "hard sell" often means they have a bunch of gigs no one else wants.' She pulled a face, attempting to make the raised eyebrow look amusingly sarcastic and realised she'd failed when he gawped at her.

'It's nothing like that. Though with the warmer months coming, he will need extra boots in the field. If you're interested?'

'I might be.' Jet waggled her eyebrows. 'Tell me more over lunch.'

TEN

'Girl, where did you find that apartment listing? Norman's List?' Leroy choked on his laughter, hand to his chest as he fell into the nearest diner ahead of Jet and Rachel.

'I thought we'd never leave alive. What a creep!' Rachel shuddered.

'It didn't look anything like that on the ad, I swear!' Jet held her hands up as they approached a table. 'Right, lunch is on me for putting you through that,' she continued as she slid into a booth, retrieved her pen from her ponytail and scratched the address off the list she had in her hand.

'What a dive!' Leroy carried on. 'I'll bet the landlord lives next door and accesses the bedroom through a secret panel in the closet at night.'

'I'm sure I saw a cockroach too.' Rachel narrowed her eyes as she reached for a menu and signalled to the nearest waitress for coffee.

'I've never seen anything like that. This is a nightmare,

the place I viewed Thursday night was basically a shoebox, and the only exclusivity about the bathroom in last night's viewing was that it was the only one on the same floor as the apartment I viewed.'

'Hey, welcome to Manhattan.' Rachel gestured to the street outside. 'You just gotta find a shoebox you can live with.'

'At least I don't have a lot of stuff,' Jet sighed, thinking of the amount of boxed crap she'd left with her parents while the waitress poured them three cups of strong black coffee before moving to the next table without a word.

'How many more did you find to look at today?' Leroy peered over at the list as he reached for the sugar bowl.

'Just the one at three this afternoon. Potentially a little out of my price range. Upper East Side.'

'How much longer do you have on the hotel?' Rachel asked as she set her menu aside.

'A week. I might be able to extend that to two. Or I'll just find another hotel if it comes to it.'

'You won't be able to do that all summer.' Rachel shook her bob out of her face dismissively. 'Don't forget my offer of the couch. It's not ideal, but it's there.'

'Thank you, but with three, sometimes four, of you there already, I'm sure that wouldn't be ideal.'

'In the short term it would be fine, we've done it before.' She waved a perfectly manicured hand in Jet's direction as the waitress returned for their lunch orders, taking note of a cheeseburger for Leroy, a vegetable omelette for Rachel and eggs and bacon on toast for Jet.

Jet gazed lovingly at the pancakes for all of thirty seconds before remembering the pinch of her favourite jeans as she'd sat down. All the same, Rachel had flinched as she'd ordered her idea of healthier carbs.

'Have you got pictures of the next place so we can vet it before you drag us to our deaths?' Leroy sassed, primly picking up his coffee and taking a testing sip.

'Hang on a sec, I'll send you both the link.' Jet flicked through the sites on her phone and sent them both the link in their house-hunting WhatsApp group. 'There.'

'Is this another sole-let, or have you considered one that actually advertises for a roommate?' Rachel lifted her phone from the table and began tapping at the screen.

After a moment's stony silence, Jet dared look up from her phone.

'Have you even seen the furniture in that dive? It's a bunk bed.' Rachel grimaced.

'What?' Jet scowled.

'Last picture, it's a bunk bed without a mattress, just space underneath for a desk. And the bed covers most of the window, you'd feel caged in that place, honey.' Leroy turned his phone screen towards her.

Scrubbing her hands down her face, Jet growled.

'When I booked the viewing the room was empty, I suspected it might barely fit a double bed, but it looked at least the same size as a pokey hotel room, I could have lived with that to begin with.'

'Cancel it, I think we can safely say a hostel would have a more homely appeal,' Rachel drawled and put her phone down as lunch arrived.

'Ugh.' Jet also put her phone down and caught the waitress looking at her, appalled. 'Oh, not the food, this looks great, thanks!' Jet quickly covered herself even as she felt her cheeks burn.

Hiding behind his burger to prevent from laughing, Leroy fought hard to swallow his first mouthful.

'Let me take a look on that site in a moment, I'll see if there are any realtors I can recommend you keep an eye out for,' he managed as soon as he'd swallowed.

'Thanks,' Jet grouched, miserably cutting into her egg and finding the yolk solid. 'I'm not very good at this, if I'm honest. I've lived alone before, sure, but I hate the whole damn process.'

'Don't rush it,' Rachel suggested. 'You have options, don't you?'

'I can afford another hotel if that's what you mean, but more than another month and I'd be scraping the barrel for all the fees and stuff I'd need to rent somewhere more permanent,' Jet said and resigned her eggs to a smothering of ketchup.

'You said your nanna used to live here, right?' Leroy asked, waving a French fry about flamboyantly.

'I did,' Jet agreed.

'Where did she used to live?'

'The Upper West Side.' Jet sighed longingly. 'She had a beautiful brownstone.'

'Well, whatever happened to it?' His eyes widened as

he popped the fry into his mouth.

Jet blinked and looked down at her phone. 'My dad sold it years ago.'

'That was stupid!' Rachel sat bolt upright. 'Those things are worth a fortune now!'

'I'm fully aware of how much they cost to buy,' Jet grouched miserably. 'It would take a bestseller to get me back in one of those anytime soon.'

Rachel and Leroy looked at each other, perplexed.

'Never mind.' Jet hastily shovelled eggs into her mouth.

'You certainly won't be setting foot in one of those anytime soon with the Virgo wages.' Rachel shook her head sadly.

'Tell me about it,' Jet agreed.

'Tell you about it?!' Leroy said, mockingly affronted. 'Try being a lowly receptionist.'

'I am not a receptionist!' Rachel hissed, pointing her fork menacingly at Leroy, her poise temporarily shattered. 'I'm an office manager.'

'I didn't mean you, darling, I meant me.'

'I thought you were security?' Jet asked tentatively.

'Same difference, in that building they both pay shit.' He waved her off. 'I'll just have to get me a side hustle like everyone else.'

'You've been saying that for years.' Rachel narrowed her eyes at him.

'And as soon as I find something I enjoy, I'll stick with it.' He wiggled his shoulders at her.

'Where in the city do you live?' Jet asked.

'With my mamma over the river in Jersey,' Leroy said as if Jet should have known that.

'But you're such a socialite, how does that work?'

'I have a lot of *friends* in the city.' He waggled his eyebrows suggestively even as his phone offered another notification from one of his many dating apps.

'Speaking of that kind of friend . . .' Rachel smirked suddenly. 'Sasha reminded your date that he still hasn't called.'

'Oh fuck.' Jet winced. 'Her divorcee work colleague?'

'Roger, that's the one. She said she gave him your number and that he'll call you to sort a date. He hasn't already, has he?'

'Not that I'm aware of. Why?'

'I thought you might have told him to . . . how do you put it? Piss off?'

'Probably. Thanks for the heads up.' Jet smirked.

'Did you cancel that viewing this afternoon?' Leroy gestured at Jet's phone.

'Shit, no, I'd better do that.' Shoving the last mouthful of toast past her lips, she sent the email while she chewed.

'Who fancies a mosey around the Guggenheim?' Leroy asked coyly.

'What, so that you can hook up? Ew.' Rachel screwed her face up. 'What a horrid perversion of a house of art.'

Sniggering, Jet watched the thoughts race through her eyes as Rachel tried to think up a fast excuse whilst pretending to check her watch.

'I'll come with you,' Jet offered. 'Strangely, I've never actually been in the Guggenheim.'

'I forgot,' Rachel laughed as she pretended to check her phone and they all started to shimmy out of the booth, 'I said I'd meet Ron at Saks. You don't mind, do you?'

'Not your thing, I get it, hang on a sec while I pay the check.' Jet reached into her pocket for her wallet with one hand whilst grasping her phone in the other.

As Rachel and Leroy shrugged themselves into jackets and tumbled out onto the street, Jet headed for the counter.

Checking her phone while she waited for their waitress to ring up their bill, she discovered an email from Larry with a list of assignments for the week ahead.

Shoving the phone in her pocket as the waitress returned to the counter, she decided she'd deal with that later.

ELEVEN

'How many assignments did you take last week?' Daryl asked under his breath, sliding an envelope to Jet as he pulled up a chair and muscled his way onto her desk with her.

'Only two.' Jet bustled the envelope into her bag. 'Another movie review and a comedy gig.'

'I only took one.'

'They were seriously small fry, he probably thought they would have been an insult to your experience.' Jet sniffed even as she smirked at him. 'Anyway, what else do you want?'

He looked confused until she gestured to the fact that he was making himself comfortable.

'You emailed me.'

'Correction. I raised a Jira ticket,' Jet teased, acutely aware that Shelley had stopped typing to listen in. She'd begun to suspect that her desk mate was getting irritated by the amount of time she spent working directly with Daryl.

Meetings upon meetings with Leon and the client meant she already spent several hours a week locked in superhero titled glass boxes with him. Not alone though, she'd have pointed out to her desk mate if she'd dared to ask rather than shoot daggers from afar.

'Same thing.' Daryl waved at the computer screen. 'Show me.'

'How dare you!' Jet teased.

'Don't be childish,' he bit out but shot her a look that told her he also knew they had an eavesdropper.

Rolling her eyes, Jet switched tabs to show him the latest glitch their software had invented that morning.

'It's determined to lose us this client, I think.' Jet sighed.

'I'm beginning to agree with you, that break is . . . well . . .' Scratching his head in a manner that totally ruffled his already stress-dishevelled hair, Daryl sighed. 'It's crazy, at the very least.'

'Crazy? It's pissing me off.'

'It's pissing *you* off?' Daryl laughed. 'I've never met a platform I couldn't break and put back together. This one is something else. I'll talk to the tech boys and see if there's anything they've been working on behind the scenes, see if they can help explain *that*.'

'Someone needs to,' Jet drawled.

'Coffee?' Daryl asked suddenly.

'Excuse me?'

'Yes please!' Shelley extended her hand, holding her travel mug, over the partition.

Standing, Jet peered over at her and, taking the mug,

placed it back down on her side of the partition. 'The usual?'

'Please. In fact, I could come with you?'

'Who said I was going? He offered.' Jet jerked her head in Daryl's direction as he also stood up.

'Shelley!' Leon called from a nest of desks across the aisle. 'Can I borrow you for a moment?'

Tearing her eyes from Daryl, Shelley deflated as she stood up. 'Sure.'

'Do you know what you want?' Daryl asked, picking up Shelley's travel mug and swinging his chair back under the desk it had come from with the other hand.

'Now I will come with you,' Jet offered as Shelley reached a safe distance.

'I'll meet you downstairs in five,' Daryl said with a smile.

Handing her Shelley's mug, he headed back to his desk as she locked her monitor and headed for reception.

'Coffee, Rachel?' she asked as she breezed through the doors.

'Saviour!' Rachel gushed gratefully as she retrieved her own travel cup and, scribbling her order on a Post-it, stuck it to the lid and handed it over. 'We're going to need it, your client called for a meeting in an hour.'

'Not another four o'clock meeting,' Jet groaned as she headed for the elevator, her shoulders deliberately sagging further as she went. 'Better make mine a double.'

'Woah, wait for me!' Daryl charged after her as the doors opened for her.

'I take it you've heard,' she said flatly.

'Meeting at four?' he growled. 'Yup.'

'Another late night?' Jet asked him as they rode the elevator down to ground level.

'I hope not. I have a game to cover tonight.' He rubbed his eyes one-handed, pinching the bridge of his nose.

'Typical.'

'I was going to ask you if you wanted to tag along.'

'Me?'

'Sure, why not? I always get two tickets, I just never use the spare. You haven't covered a sporting event yet, I'll walk you through my process in case Larry ever has to send you one.'

'Has to?' Jet raised a semi-offended eyebrow, she suspected she knew the reason it was unlikely she'd get a sports assignment. She didn't care for them either, though. 'No women allowed?'

'Oh, there's every chance you'd get one if you wanted one. They're just generally highly sought after, mostly by guys, true, but even the women who put in for them get the gigs over someone who doesn't.' He looked her up and down. 'You got a favourite sport?'

'Of course I have,' Jet scoffed.

'Something you have to leave the house for?'

'Oh . . . no.' She rose to the teasing but felt her cheeks flush.

'Do you even watch sport?' he asked, seriously. 'Because you can also tell me and Larry to fuck off, that you don't want to see the game tonight and never want to write one up either.'

'I'm not against it, I get pretty swept up in anything I get the chance to see, but I don't seek it out.'

'Ah, never mind, forget I asked.'

'You never even told me what it is you're going to watch!' Jet laughed. 'I'll happily take the assignments if no one else is available.'

'It's just a baseball game.'

'Will there be hot dogs? After that meeting, we're going to need sustenance.'

'Hot dogs can be arranged.' He nodded. 'That mean you're in?'

'I'm in.' Jet smiled. 'Just a baseball game?'

'Brooklyn Dodgers.'

'Nice. Oh, shit, what time?'

'Why?'

'I have an apartment viewing at six.'

'Ooh, coffee run?' Leroy stood up from behind the desk as they stepped out of the elevator and waved another travel mug in their direction.

'The usual?'

'Mmm hmm.' He batted his eyelids at her as she skipped over to retrieve the mug.

'Where's the apartment viewing?' Daryl asked as he led the way out of the building and onto the street.

'It's a share in the village. What time's the game?'

'There's plenty of time to do both.'

'Shall I meet you at the stadium?'

'Nah, I'll tag along to the viewing,' He said casually, making Jet almost miss her step.

'You really don't have to do that,' she said, a little too quickly.

'You really shouldn't meet potential roommates on your own.' He scowled down at her as though that was obvious.

'Would it help you to know it's a woman?' Jet scoffed, mildly offended while at the same time her brain appreciated the feeling that someone gave a shit about her safety.

'You've heard of Velma Barfield, Carol Bundy and Aileen Wuornos, right?'

'Should I be worried that you can pluck the names of that many female serial killers out of the air so easily?'

'Should I be relieved to know you recognise the names and therefore got my point?'

'Touché,' Jet conceded with a shrug. 'Just don't do that macho thing of pretending to be my big brother or some shit and come over all protective, I need to find *somewhere* to live.'

'I thought you had an idea of what you could afford and where you were aiming for?' He glanced at her as they crossed the street.

'I did, until I realised that everything in my budget in Manhattan was smaller than my hotel room, which doesn't even have a kitchenette,' Jet sighed.

'Will you be shipping belongings over from England?'

'Probably not, to be fair, I know it's there all the while my parents are, and even after they're not . . .' Jet murmured, trailing off as they entered Starbucks and, finding it fairly empty, dumped all five of their travel mugs down at once and proceeded to confuse the hell out of the baristas.

'What if this call runs over?' Jet asked as they waited at the pick-up station.

'I'll make sure it doesn't,' Daryl answered bluntly.

'Bit arrogant, considering what Leon and this client are like.'

'I've managed it before,' he said, reaching for the sugar.

Jet shot him a look that told him she wasn't convinced.

Two and a half hours later, at five-thirty on the dot, she was following him out of the office shaking her head in disbelief.

'If I let them run over on every call they drag me into, I'd have been fired by Larry a long time ago,' Daryl answered her bewildered look as he opened the door to the cab he'd just hailed for them.

'Thanks,' she said, offering him a twisted smile as she dove into the cab, 'On both counts.'

Riding in silence to the address she had been given, Jet found herself glancing at Daryl often. He seemed to want to keep it that way.

He spent the whole journey checking emails on his phone. Looking up only as they approached the apartment block she was viewing.

'You could do worse, I guess,' he muttered as she paid the driver and he climbed out.

'Seems nice enough,' Jet agreed as she closed the door

behind her, emerging from the opposite side of the cab.

She looked up and down the tree-lined street full of apartment buildings. They'd come up Eighth Avenue, which had been bustling with restaurants, delis, and plenty of cafés. Ever the nerd at heart, she'd gawped as they'd passed an old Port Authority building now home to an internet giant.

'Are you Jet?'

'I am.' Jet turned from the street to an impatient looking woman in a trouser suit waiting on the front steps to her apartment block. 'You must be Constance?'

Nodding, she blew smoke out through her nostrils and looked Jet up and down as she stumped out her cigarette and placed it in a small tin.

'You're early,' Constance observed, gold bangles rattling as she placed the tin in her pocket and shook short blonde curls from her eyes. 'Come on in.'

Looking to Daryl, who was watching Constance with his resting bitch face firmly fixed in place, Jet decided "what the hell" and followed her inside the building.

'I live on the top floor, but the room is furnished, so all that will do for you is sculpt your ass.'

Jet had to stop herself from laughing, if their roles had been reversed, that would have been an icebreaker but looking again to Daryl, who remained stony faced, she realised laughing would have been a bad idea.

'This is me,' Constance announced as she opened the door to her apartment.

Thankful that it smelled mostly of grooming products

rather than cigarette smoke, Jet took in the décor which said nothing of the woman who had greeted them downstairs.

If she'd had to guess, she'd have gone with minimalist chic. What she found instead was a disaster in pink.

Everything was pink.

Different shades of pink.

Even the kitchenware.

'There's the living area, which I don't mind sharing with you if we get on.' She gestured to a den-sized room with a TV and couch on their left. 'Shared kitchen.' She swung her arm in the direction of a pokey galley kitchen on their right.

'Do you work nearby?' Jet asked politely.

'Near enough to be home by six. Yes.' Constance turned briefly to look them both up and down. 'Is this your boyfriend?'

'He's a work colleague,' Jet said, shaking her head.

'No more visitors.' Constance sniffed in Daryl's direction.

This time Daryl did offer her a sideways glance and the judgement Jet had already been forming was replaced by a tell-tale irk. Constance had less than ten seconds to redeem herself or be thrown into Jet's "to be forgotten forever" pit in the back of her mind.

'What if she has a boyfriend?' Daryl asked, folding his arms.

'Then she sees him in public or at his mother's dinner table. I'm not running a brothel for unmarried sinners.'

Yup, that did it.

If it wasn't for the fact that she hated being rude, Jet would have walked out there and then.

'This is you.' Constance pushed a door open to the back of the property.

Unfortunately, the room was the best part of the apartment. Neutrally decorated, a bed, chest of drawers, wardrobe and desk with a chair that she could have written at for hours without ever having to be granted permission to enter the TV room.

'You have sole access to the main bathroom as I have an en-suite.' Constance folded her arms. 'When will you confirm?'

'This is the first flat-share I've viewed, I have others booked,' Jet said in a non-committal manner.

'Cancel them, or stop wasting my time,' Constance sneered.

'Wow. OK,' Daryl said when Jet found herself too stunned to respond. 'We're leaving.'

'I thought she wasn't your girlfriend.' Constance's eyes darkened as Daryl placed his hands on Jet's shoulders and began steering her towards the door.

'She isn't . . .'

'Then take your hands off her.'

Daryl began to move them towards the front door faster as Jet mouthed, 'Wow' herself.

'That's it, get out!'

'He can touch me if he wants, and anyway, I'm an atheist!' Jet threw back over her shoulder too outraged to instantly realise her words.

'You just had to go there.' Daryl bundled her into the

hallway and slammed the front door.

'What. The. Fuck?' Jet began laughing as they headed for the stairs.

Behind them, the door to the apartment re-opened.

'Just go, go, go.' Daryl also found himself laughing as they ran from the building.

'Well, that was crazy,' Jet breathed through her laughter when they tumbled out onto the street.

'You wanted to live in America,' he said, catching her and pointing her in the direction of the nearest subway.

TWELVE

'This one is on me.' Jet waved Daryl off as he reached into his pocket when two large sodas and two hot dogs were passed their way. 'As a sorry for dragging you to that flat viewing. At this rate I'll run out of people to pay off with food.'

'Woah, last of the big spenders,' he teased before taking a large bite out of his hot dog. 'It was nothing, but man, dealing with crazies sure gives you an appetite,' he said through chewing.

'I'll buy you real food after the game if you're still famished.' Jet smirked.

'Real food?! What do you call this?'

'Oh yeah, I'm dealing with a man.' Jet snarked playfully as she began following him into the stadium.

'Have you really got more booked?'

'No,' Jet admitted as she shook her head, partly to get her hair away from the lashings of ketchup. 'It's not that there aren't any suitable, it's that I'm . . .' Jet stopped herself.

'You're what?'

'I'm stalling over the idea of living with a stranger.'

'Thought your dad said it was all part of the process?'

'Doesn't mean I have to like it,' Jet grouched as he began edging down a row of seating. 'I'm not foolish enough to think this will be like one of those sitcoms where my roommate will become my best friend. Even *Friends* came to an end.'

Jet looked up to see him nodding as they stopped and he pointed to the seat beside her.

Sitting down, she took another bite of her hot dog before placing her coke at her feet.

He ate the rest of his in silence, so Jet did the same, realising that he needed moments without conversation and not finding it as uncomfortable as she'd have thought on first meeting him.

'So, I lied the night we met,' Daryl announced suddenly as he rolled his napkin into a ball and shoved it in his coat pocket when he'd finished.

'Great,' Jet said, nonplussed as she shoved the last bit of bread roll into her mouth. 'About what?'

'I had been looking for a roommate.'

'But you changed your mind? Or just didn't like the look of me?' Jet scowled, trying not to feel as offended as she wanted to.

'I'd already rescinded the advertisement. I don't really need one and I knew nothing about you, I guess I'm a bit like you on that front, I don't like the idea of inviting a perfect stranger into my living space.' He looked out across the playing field. 'You'd been in town all of what…?'

'Not even forty-eight hours at that point,' Jet agreed but stopped herself from asking him his point for fear she'd burst the bubble.

'If you want one of my spare rooms, you're welcome to come give it a go, even if you'd prefer a trial basis?'

'*One* of your spare rooms?!' Jet gawped. 'Where do you live?!'

'Your favoured Upper West Side.' He met her eyes briefly, though his face remained neutral. 'In a town house.'

'Fuck off!' Jet grinned.

'Excuse me?!' He frowned.

'I'm trying to cover how excited I might be by swearing at you.' She tried to calm and relax her face but failed. 'It's probably nothing like what I'm picturing in my head, but just the chance to see inside one of those properties would be amazing!'

'Just one condition. Before you even come and see it.'

'What's that?'

'Don't tell anyone at work.'

'That's gonna be a little difficult, I'll need to change my address with HR.' Jet returned.

'Damn. Good point.' He looked down the row as if he was looking for an exit but the stadium was filling up fast. 'Fine, but don't mention it until you've seen it.'

'Sounds fair.'

'Can you come over tomorrow night after work?'

'Are you in the office tomorrow?'

'No.'

'That makes it easier, there will be no witnesses, tomorrow will be fine.' Jet took her phone from her pocket. 'What's your address?'

'I'll text it to you in a bit. Game's about to start,' he said brightly and relaxed into his seat.

'Great. Thanks.' Jet smiled and glanced at her phone anyway, finding a text message from a number she didn't recognise.

Unknown: Hey Jet, it's Roger, Sasha's colleague. Would you be up for going for a drink Saturday night?

'Shit,' Jet muttered quietly as the crowd cheered the players onto the pitch.

'What?' Daryl looked down, concern on his brow.

'Nothing. Well-meaning friends, that's all,' she bit out and looked back to the phone for several moments more.

What could it hurt?

He wasn't a total stranger. Sasha and the girls knew him.

Pursing her lips at the idea of living in Daryl's house and dating . . . she shook herself off. It wasn't like her dates ever went anywhere anyway.

Realising she was making excuses, she huffed out a sigh and replied.

Jet: Hi Roger, that sounds great, when and where?

She read the message more than fifteen times before pressing send, was it too blunt? Too keen? A bit rude?

A bit uninterested? She didn't want to come off desperate when she wasn't even certain she was ready to date ever again.

Maybe he'd think she was stupid for asking when. He'd already stated Saturday night. Should she have specified that she meant time?

After she'd pressed send, she realised with a sinking feeling that she was due to check out of her hotel on Saturday and hoped that he wouldn't ask to pick her up.

Saving his number, she tried to focus on the game rather than being an antisocial twat on her phone.

Roger: Hi Jet, shall we meet by the ticket booth in Times Square, say 7p.m.?

Inwardly rolling her eyes she wondered whether he considered her knowledge of the city to be so limited that she'd only know how to get to Times Square.

Deciding she was being harsh about someone she hadn't met, she confirmed quickly and put the phone into her pocket, forgetting about it for the rest of the evening.

THIRTEEN

'You live here?!' Jet gawped up at Daryl as he opened the front door to his house.

'Hey, you found it ok then?' He smirked, having seen her gaze of wonderment as she'd drifted up the front stoop to press the bell.

'This is gorgeous!' She drank in the beautifully cared for mahogany staircase and hardwood flooring.

'Thanks, I do my best to keep it in good condition.' He awkwardly ruffled the hair at the back of his head.

'How many floors?'

'Five.' He closed the door as she drifted into the lounge towards the original fireplace with a sizeable mirror hanging above it. 'Diner and den, or library, on the ground floor, basement beneath that with a mini wine cellar and gym. Lounge and kitchen are on this floor. Master is second floor and two additional rooms are on the top floor.'

'Let's start in the basement then.' Jet beamed.

Nodding, he returned to the hall and headed towards

the back of the house before dropping down the staircase.

Glancing in at the kitchen as they went, she spied more traditional fittings including a Belfast sink and large solid oak table.

Her jaw dropped when she saw the library and dining room on their way down to the basement. An orangery style conservatory led out to the garden beyond plush reading couches and very full floor to ceiling bookshelves.

'It was pretty much a shell down here. There was a family room which had an old TV and couch, that was pretty much it. Laundry room is right down the back.' Daryl pointed when they reached the lowest level.

'Should wine be stored this close to a treadmill?' Jet asked in awe as she walked up to the glass cabinet, which was lit inside, against exposed brick. Racks upon racks of wine bottles lay within, waiting patiently for the right moment.

A lick of paint wasn't all that had smartened the basement up, the design — albeit a little man-ish — was, in its own way, just as beautiful as the restoration work that had clearly been a labour of love upstairs.

'Let's head to the top and work our way back down.' Daryl headed back to the stairs and led her all the way to the third floor.

'You can have either or both of these rooms, they're connected by a Jack and Jill bathroom in the middle.' He led her into the back room first, causing her to move straight to the window and peer down at the garden.

It was completely decked with built-in bench seating, inbuilt lighting and a fountain integrated into the back wall.

'You have a fountain.' She smiled down at it.

'Oh? Yeah.' He joined her at the window and looked down at the garden. 'I've replaced and fixed as much as I could over the years, but the garden had to be completely re-landscaped. A professional did all that for me.'

'Does it still work?'

'Of course.' He raised both eyebrows, affronted. 'There's a king-sized bed in each room, you might find it a bit quieter with the garden to the rear.'

'I don't really sleep in silence.'

'There's little more than the bed in either room, so it would be totally your choice. I don't tend to have guests, but I didn't want to leave the rooms empty either.'

Jet opened her mouth to ask whether family ever came to stay but he turned and opened the bathroom door and the words died in her throat.

'A roll top bath!' she gasped. 'This house has it all.'

'Well, it would be solely your roll top bath. I have a bathroom downstairs in the master,' he said as he carried on through the bathroom to a door on the other side, opening that onto the front bedroom. 'There's a desk in here, so you'll have a workspace whichever room you choose,' he called back.

Drifting through the bathroom to the front bedroom, Jet felt as though she was walking on air.

It was her dream house.

Ornate wood decorated all the rooms, all stained a homely deep mahogany. A fireplace in almost every room, also carefully restored to the point of seeming new.

'You've done an amazing job with this place. I mean, I have no idea what it looked like whenever you moved in, but it's really . . . special.'

'You're moving in then?' He chuckled, taking in the wonderment on her face.

'If you're still alright with that?'

'When do you need to be out of the hotel?'

'Saturday.'

'That gives me a couple of days to make sure the room is clean and stuff.' He nodded. 'Fine by me.'

'What about rent?'

'Whatever you were willing to give Constance for the pink palace, let's go with half that.'

'That's a steal, will that even cover bills?'

'If it doesn't, we'll work it out.' He shrugged. 'Coffee?'

'Sure.'

'Great, you can show me how to use my machine properly, ex-barista.'

'Me and my big mouth.' Jet winced as she followed him back out into the hall. 'So where do you work?'

'The whole of this floor is a master suite.' He gestured to the doors on the second floor as they passed. 'Bedroom to the back, bathroom and walk-through closet down the middle, and what was once a parlour at the front. That's where my writing desk is.'

He opened the door to the front section onto a large ornate desk with a small green glass lamp as a nod to its heritage even though the rest of the desk was covered in four monitors all glowing onto the empty chair where he'd abandoned his day's work to show her around.

Having been too amazed by the house, it took her until they were back in the kitchen to realise that he was wearing navy sweatpants rather than jeans and a plain white t-shirt without one of his usual open flannel shirts.

'You worked from home all day today?'

'Yeah, remote client today.' He nodded. 'Less of a nightmare than Virgo's current project.'

Entering the kitchen, which was painted in a shade of green Jet could only describe as olive, she instantly spotted the large coffee machine. It was practically coffee shop pro, certainly too large for one man to be using by himself.

'If you don't know how to use this, why the hell did you buy it?'

'I drink so much coffee when I'm out on jobs, I thought I could benefit from it when I started getting the odd remote client. I gathered it would have been easier to learn how to use than it's proven.'

'It's not that easy to fuck up to be fair, it's pretty straight forward.' Jet began searching the machine for all the parts she knew she'd need.

'Says the person who was trained in how to do it. Everything you need should be on top.'

'Coffee beans?' She glanced over her shoulder and

found him leant against the corner unit by the sink.

'To your left.' He pointed before folding his arms.

'What'll it be, sir?' she asked as she stood on tiptoes to empty the bag of beans into the grinder funnel on top of the machine.

'Why not make it a cappuccino?' He smiled as he watched her work.

'Ah… but do you have chocolate sprinkles?' she asked as she set the beans to grind. 'This thing is borderline pro, where on earth did you get it?'

'Bloomingdales,' he replied. 'The salesman was very persuasive.'

'I wouldn't have had you down as either a keen shopper or a mug,' Jet teased as she pressed the ground beans into the filter and clipped it into place in one swift manoeuvre. 'You know you could probably Google or YouTube how to do this right? Shouldn't you be over here watching me?'

'I never got round to it. I can see what you're doing. For tonight, let's just make sure it works, you can teach me how it's done after you've moved in.'

Setting the espresso cups in place and selecting how many shots she wanted, Jet reached for the stainless-steel frothing jug, glad to see he'd covered all the essentials, before heading for the fridge.

She'd been told you could tell a lot about someone by the contents of their fridge. The milk was standard half-fat. One shelf dedicated solely to beer, another for a range of meat, and a tonne of vegetables. Remembering the gym in the basement, she was surprised to find herself impressed.

He may have looked the type to eat as he worked or on the run, but the fridge said otherwise.

'You like to cook?' she asked to fill the silence, realising she'd need to share the fridge space.

'I try to make something fresh every day. Work doesn't always allow. But I get by.' He glanced over at the fridge as the door swung closed again. 'I'll clear the beer shelf for you.'

'Thank you.' Jet slugged a large amount of milk into the jug before replacing the bottle and testing the steamer to make sure it had warmed up enough.

Happy that it had, she warmed and frothed the milk.

Moments later, she set a cappuccino down on the table for him.

'Like riding a bike… sort of, it could probably be better.' She offered him a twisted smile and set her own mug down on the other side of the table.

While he took a seat at the table and lifted the mug for a testing sniff, she cleaned up after herself, finding a cloth to wipe down the steamer.

'Does it need such a vigorous rub down?'

Stopping abruptly, Jet felt her cheeks flame, the best way to get hot milk off a steamer, she'd found, was to wrap a damp cloth around it and… well, give it a bit of a handjob.

'Um…you just have to get all the milk off while it's still hot, or it kind of dries on…'

Turning in a manner that meant she wouldn't have to meet his eye, she rinsed the cloth in the sink before joining him at the table.

Half expecting him to make another lewd comment, she was pleasantly surprised to find he had already forgotten the question and was taking a mouthful.

'That's pretty good,' he said before taking another sip. 'You can tell it's the machine's first outing though.'

His nose wrinkled as he looked up at her cup.

Taking a tentative sip of her own coffee, Jet found what he meant straight away.

'It's a bit metallic and plastic-tasting, isn't it? I probably should have run the hot water through it all for a bit first.'

'Aside from that it's great.' He sat back in his chair.

'It will probably bed in.' Jet took another mouthful to cover her grimace at her own choice of words.

Again, he didn't seem to notice and reached forward for his cup.

Despite the butterflies at the prospect of living with Daryl, Jet couldn't help the excitement bubbling in her chest at the welcoming atmosphere the house gave her. Relaxing, Jet cupped both hands around her drink and enjoyed the coffee despite the new-machine taste.

Leaving him a little while later to get a couple more hours work in, Jet left Daryl's house in search of food just after seven.

She'd walked as far as the American Museum of Natural History, hoping the walk would help her stomach decide what it wanted, when her phone rang.

'Hi, Mum,' she said as she brought the phone to her ear. 'Is everything OK?'

'Hi, darling, oh it's fine, fine! Just thought I'd check in.'

'It's midnight there, right?'

'Well, of course it is, we're aware you work, you know. Thought we'd check in before turning in. Have you found somewhere to live yet?'

'Just. I've just left a beautiful house that I'll be sharing with a colleague from Saturday.' Jet looked up and down the street.

'Not some nut job then?'

'God, no. Not like the one I met last night.'

'That's good, dear. I told your father that was an awful idea.'

'Mum, where was your apartment when you lived here?'

'Oh, we were Chelsea, darling.'

'That's where I was last night.'

'Didn't you like it?'

'The roommate was the problem,' Jet reminded her. 'I thought Dad was Upper West Side when you met?'

'No, that was your grandmother, his bachelor pad was on the East Side.'

'I can never remember where Granny's townhouse was.'

'No idea. Your father will have to dredge that one up out of his memory.'

Jet could hear the kettle boiling and the sound of teaspoons against bone China in the background.

'He's making you tea to take up to bed?'

'Ovaltine, we're both on the Ovaltine at this time of

night. Do you want a quick word?'

'Sure…' Jet trailed off, realising she'd already been handed over.

'Hey! How's my city?' Her dad beamed down the phone, she could hear it.

'Looking as pretty as ever. I'm up by the park, I'm moving in with a colleague who lives Upper West. Mum thinks you were Upper East, but I thought you told me your first apartment wasn't that far from Granny's.'

'It wasn't, the old bat has it wrong, she spent enough time there for Christ's sake. Yeah, my studio had a view of the Hudson. Different times then. You had to take a share then?'

'Yeah, with someone from work though, the lady I met last night was batshit.'

'Ah, but that's the fun part.'

'It got ugly, she all but kicked me out.'

Roaring with laughter, her dad stirred their drinks and tapped the spoon on the rim of each mug as he did so.

'Where was Gran's house, Dad?'

'Don't you remember?' He sounded surprised.

'She moved out of it while I was at uni. I'd know it if I saw it, right?'

'I hear it's been renovated by the new owner. You might not.'

'It would be nice to go see it.'

'What…? Yes, yes, I'm coming.' Her dad sighed. 'Sorry darling, your mother wants her Ovaltine before it gets cold.'

'You just made it.'

'She's already gone up to bed, I can hear her stamping around above my head, so I've already taken too long. You find the house, take a picture and send it to me. Speak to you at the weekend, love you!'

And with that he was gone.

'Love you too,' Jet said to no one, before looking skywards. 'I still don't have the sodding address.'

A parking attendant walking in the opposite direction looked at her strangely before giving her a wide berth.

With a sigh she reached into her pocket for her earbuds and, connecting them to the phone, set her favourite walking playlist and headed for downtown, deciding she'd get bored or hungry enough eventually to pick an eatery and a subway station.

FOURTEEN

Rounding the corner of the ticket booth on Saturday night, Jet checked her watch and on seeing she was early, took a moment to catch her breath. Check out at 10a.m. seemed like it had been yesterday, her day had gone so unexpectedly crazy.

Glancing around, she was certain Roger hadn't arrived yet. Rachel had shown her a photo the night before in the bar, but whether his divorce had caused a total makeover or not, she couldn't see any solo early-forties white men hanging about.

Daryl had slipped her a set of keys on one of their coffee runs so that there could be little chance of anyone getting suspicious at the after-work drinks. She had to wonder why it was such a big deal to keep it as calmly casually secret as possible, but at the same time wanted to respect his privacy. He was her new landlord, after all.

She hadn't expected him to ring her as she'd been handing her key card in to tell her he was going to pick her up. It had come as even more of a surprise to discover that he'd meant in a car. He pulled up ten minutes later in a battered old Jeep.

'Figures,' she deadpanned as she threw her bags in the back and climbed into the passenger seat.

'What?'

'Who has or needs a car in Manhattan? Really?'

'I like to go exploring at weekends,' he said as he waved an arm across the dash.

'How often do you do that?' she asked, wondering whether it meant frequent time alone in the house.

'Why, you want a road trip?' He shot her a smile that caught her off guard.

'I can be partial to a bit of a road trip. Don't go regretting that offer,' she warned.

'Noted. But if I'm going anywhere you have a deep desire to see, I'm sure we could work something out.'

'OK,' Jet agreed hesitantly. 'Anyway, why the need to get the wheels out today?'

'I need to pick up a few things, it's grocery day, there are a few home comforts you might need too, given that I never have guests. How about a mini road trip to the Walmart in North Bergen?'

'Why there?'

'Why not?'

'Gotta love a Walmart,' Jet agreed and started making a list of things she might need in her head. High on the list were her own towels and bedding, especially when Daryl admitted he had no idea how old the ones in the guest bedroom were.

They needed a trolley each and the backseat of the Jeep to get it all home.

'Where'd you put the beer?' Jet asked as she began loading her groceries into the fridge.

'Well, I drank some of it. The rest is with the wine in the cellar.' He grinned.

With new bedding ready to sink into, Jet wished she hadn't had to go back out.

Checking her watch, she realised she'd been stood in the pre-arranged meeting place for twenty minutes and no one even resembling a Roger had appeared.

'Typical, stood up on my first date in NYC, that's me all over,' she muttered to herself, then checked that no one had heard her.

Daryl had laughed when she'd told him Rachel's housemates had set her up on a semi-blind date. He'd laughed even harder when she'd told him where they were supposed to be meeting.

Then he'd given her a confused and twisted smile when she'd told him she was only going in order to be polite to all involved. He fell short of patting her on the head and telling her to have fun, though she'd felt like he'd wanted to before he took a coffee to his office and left her to head out.

Tugging her phone from her pocket, she checked for missed messages.

Nothing.

Well, now who's being rude, she thought.

He could be underground, she reprimanded herself, wondering where he was coming from. She had presumed Brooklyn, but couldn't remember whether Sasha had told her that or not.

Deciding she'd give it another ten minutes, she glanced around for inspiration, what would she do with herself on a mild Saturday evening in Times Square if left to her own devices?

She could act like a tourist and go shopping, she decided. Especially now she had a place to stay.

Angry with herself for going along with the pathetic theatrics that was dating, Jet called it a night at 7:30p.m.

Deciding to stay close in case he'd got the time wrong, and knowing she could be a right sucker, she meandered in and out of a few of the clothing shops, checking on the ticket booth and her phone every time she left one.

At eight, she gave in and bought herself a super large I heart New York hoodie to hang around the house in. A couple of t-shirts also fell into the bag before she found herself in a candy store breathing in the familiar smells of the global chain and reliving some old memories.

Not that she bought anything, tempted as she might have been, she'd already slipped a couple of bags into her shopping when she'd thought Daryl wasn't looking.

Still no sign of a message from Roger when she finally left the store, she glanced back at Times Square and considered a last lap around the ticket booth before the tell-tale prickle of shame and anger made her turn on her heel and begin walking back to the house.

Heading straight up Seventh Avenue, she paused

outside the Christmas Shop with a smile. It was way too early to go in, summer was only just beginning, but she did a quick lap regardless, to cheer herself up.

'That can't have gone well,' Daryl commented, appearing from the kitchen when she walked in the front door.

'He didn't show.' Jet shrugged.

'Are you OK?' He folded his arms in what Jet hoped was anger at another man's uselessness considering his voice suggested he gave more of a shit than his stance did.

'Fine.' Jet shrugged again. 'Didn't want the fuss anyway, did I?'

'Regardless, it's fucking rude and you should tell Rachel straight away.'

'I will. Have you eaten?'

'I'd just been staring into the fridge for inspiration when I heard the door.' He turned back into the kitchen, making her follow. 'Despite going shopping today, it's more tempting to order a pizza. It is Saturday, after all.'

Digging into her pocket for her wallet, Jet rummaged at the notes.

'I could go for pizza.'

'Oh hell, I'll order in, I'm not going out for it.'

'I didn't mean that.'

'Oh, right, sorry.' He rubbed the back of his hair awkwardly and pulled his phone out of his pocket. 'What can I get you?'

'Where do you order from?'

'Just add your choice to the app.' He handed her his

phone before retrieving a beer from the fridge.

Tapping in her stone baked chicken delight preferences, Jet handed the phone back before reaching for one of the beers she'd added to the stash.

'You're not all that bothered that you've just been stood up, are you?'

Looking up, Jet caught Daryl watching her with curiosity.

'Not really.' She took a swig of her beer before shaking her head. 'To tell you the truth it came as something of a relief.'

'Why?'

'Oh, it's all so much effort isn't it? Meeting strangers in the hopes that you'll like them enough to want to see them again. Then needing to want to see them again enough for feelings to develop.' Jet grouched and leant a hip against the fridge.

'Have you ever been in love?' he asked, his voice softening.

'I've loved. But I've never been IN love.'

'Ouch.'

'Don't get me started.' Taking another swig, she wagged a finger at him.

Raising both hands in a gesture of peace, he reached for his beer again.

'What about you?'

'As you've discovered, I like my privacy,' he said dismissively, gazing at the ceiling as he emptied half the beer bottle in one slug.

'OK, we won't go there then.' Jet lifted her beer in a

toast. 'Either of us.'

'Good plan,' he agreed. 'Speaking of which. What are you up to tomorrow?'

'No plans. I might go for a walk in the park if the weather holds.'

Nodding, he looked down at his phone. 'Pizza will be here in the next half hour. There's cable in the next room if you want it.'

'Thanks.' Jet nodded but stayed where she was as he walked towards her, then left the kitchen.

'I'll be back when it gets here.'

Watching him cross the hall and head up the stairs, she felt dread and relief all at once. Getting used to living with someone who preferred their space was going to be awkward, but it was a handy awkward if it gave them both room to breathe. She really didn't want to spill her dating life story to anyone on the island. Though she had to wonder how he'd come to a similar position.

By the time Daryl returned from his study, Jet was wearing the hooded sweater she'd bought, her hair up in a bun, in front of the television with a second beer.

'It's got a cinema package, I've been meaning to watch the latest Tarantino, have you seen it?'

Having heard him jog down the stairs, Jet was less surprised by his presence than she was the mere suggestion of socialising and her wide-eyed peer over the back of the couch said as much.

'I haven't seen it. But I am a fan,' she admitted, sitting up and folding her legs underneath her as he entered the room to put a fresh beer down on the table. 'I could go for that.'

'Pizza's here.' He looked across her at the front window and disappeared from the room again.

Unfolding herself just as quickly, she followed him out.

'I think I can manage pizza.' He chuckled.

'I'm sure you can,' she snarked back as she dug in her pocket and handed him a fistful of pre-counted notes. 'Here's my shout plus the full tip, and I'll get us a couple more beers.'

Without letting him argue, she went to the kitchen as the doorbell rang.

'Alright, alright,' he hushed, turning from her retreat to the door.

Listening to the door and the pizza exchange, Jet reached into the fridge and, grabbing a beer each, let it swing closed as she crossed the kitchen and opened the pair. As her socked feet slid across the tiled floor slightly, she considered the change of plans to have worked in her favour.

She much preferred slouchies and the couch on a Saturday night any time.

'One fresh beer,' Jet said as she re-entered the lounge and put the two bottles on the coffee table.

'Thanks,' Daryl said as he peered into the top of three boxes. 'This one's yours.'

Passing it across, he then lifted the remaining two boxes with a scowl.

'Why are there three?' Jet asked, suddenly curious

herself.

'I have no idea. What did you order?'

'Only the pizza.' She pointed at the box on her lap.

Opening the top box, he frowned again. 'Well, this one's mine.'

'Did we get a free something?' Jet asked, curling up on the couch with her pizza box as he took to the armchair beside it.

'Maybe. Well, I mean, it is now, however you look at it.' He smirked and, swapping the boxes, took a look inside. 'I think it's yours.'

'I really didn't order anything else.'

'Sure, but what makes getting stood up feel even better?'

'It never being mentioned ever again in such a sarcastic manner?' Jet deadpanned as she lifted the first slice of pizza towards her mouth.

'How about a pizza-sized cookie for dessert?' He smirked and tilted the box slightly for her to see.

'Fucking hell,' Jet spluttered. 'That's a big cookie. Did you order that?'

'No.' He shook his head with a genuinely confused laugh. 'We must have triggered a deal or something.'

'Split it with you.' She shot him a narrow-eyed side-glance.

'You can have it.' He shook his head and, closing the lid, popped it onto the table.

'I'm not planning on eating a cookie that size by myself unless you have a vomit-inducing aversion to them.' She shook her head and took a bite of her pizza.

'No vomit was ever induced whilst eating a cookie.'

'That's settled then. I also bought ice cream today.' Jet nodded. 'You want to get this movie started or what?'

'Yes, ma'am.' He nodded and reached for the controls.

'Why did you ask me what I'm doing tomorrow?'

'I might go for a run in the park, if you're a runner you can come along, I'll show you a good route. It's taken me years to work out the quietest times and places.'

'After this lot, that'll be a good idea.' Jet waved her beer in the direction of the calorie fest on their laps. Not that she had run for years, she hoped he wasn't expecting anything like a 5k from her. 'You run in the park even though you have a gym downstairs?'

'If the weather is nice enough, I prefer the fresh air.' He nodded. 'Are we ready?'

'Go for it,' Jet agreed, deliberately ignoring her phone, which she had placed faced-down on the arm of the couch furthest from her.

FIFTEEN

'Oh my god, Jet, Roger told me what happened Saturday
night!' Rachel suddenly appeared in the kitchen, her eyes
wild and stunned, making the group Jet was sat with all
look at her in alarm.

Her colour turning an unflattering shade of tomato,
Jet ran her fingers through her hair.

'Not now, Rach.' Jet shot what she hoped was a
meaningful look at the table where, thanks to a lack of
meeting room availability, she was sat with Daryl, Tom,
Brad and Tina.

'Can it wait, Rachel? We're trying to hold a meeting
here,' Daryl said in his least-friendly manner without
meeting Jet's eye.

'What happened Saturday night?' Brad lit up as he
kicked back in his chair, hands behind his head at the
chance to get off-subject for a couple of minutes. 'We're
only trying to fix the impossible here. I could do with a
temporary distraction.'

'Don't even . . .' Jet went to stand up and drag Rachel

away.

'I set her up and he stood her up.' Rachel clutched her hands to her breast dramatically. 'I feel awful! Why didn't you tell me?'

'Because I don't fuss over assholes,' Jet said bluntly, making Tina gasp.

'What happened?' Tina asked gently, trying to inject some sympathy back into the situation.

'He didn't show. I waited an hour. Then went shopping. It's fine.'

'It's not fine!' Tina gushed, making Tom roll his eyes and Daryl get up and retreat to the coffee machine.

'She went shopping, she said it's fine!' Brad held his hands up. 'I wish all girls were as laid back as you.'

'He told you why, right?' Rachel folded her arms.

'I got nothing.' Jet shook her head with a shrug.

'He got there ten minutes late and ran into his ex-wife. Words were said apparently, then he got cold feet,' Rachel explained. 'She makes him look about an inch tall, I've seen her do it.'

'He was right there, and he left anyway?' Jet blinked in a slightly crazy way to cover her annoyance and caught Daryl watching her from the coffee machine.

'He said he'd like to make it up to you, but only if you'll let him,' Rachel said.

'If he can't even text me to tell me that himself, then no, thank you,' Jet said with a smile, making Rachel back up slightly.

'The poor bastard was probably nervous as hell.' Tina glanced at Rachel.

'He's had two days to recover.' Jet shrugged. 'He clearly isn't ready to date again.'

'But . . .'

'Tell him that when he is ready to be a grown up, and willing to come to me directly, then I might consider it. I'm nowhere near interested enough to want to hold his hand while he clambers back into the dating saddle,' Jet said quickly before Rachel could speak. 'I could text him that myself if you prefer?'

'No, it's fine, I'll tell him. You might scare him off women forever,' she grouched pitifully.

'Sounds like his ex-wife has already done that.' Jet glared up at Rachel. 'Sorry, Rach, I rarely give second chances anymore. They're just not worth it.'

'Ouch.' Tom pulled an awkward face as Rachel nodded and left them to their meeting.

'I don't date babies.' Jet explained as Daryl re-joined the table.

'All men are babies.' Tina smirked. 'Some of them just hide it better.'

'That's not fair, we can't all be useless. Look at Daryl, I pity the woman who tries to smother him,' Brad grumbled.

'Seriously? Grow up,' Daryl said quietly with a pointed upwards flick of his eyebrows. 'Now, let's get back to fixing this piece of shit.'

Nodding, Jet met his eyes briefly.

'Ugh, I don't know that we can, not without completely rewriting the code.' Tina reclined in her chair and massaged the back of her neck.

'So, rewrite the code.' Tom grinned.

'It might just be possible,' Daryl agreed, then looked at his watch. 'I'll have to shoot in about an hour, but I'll give it a go on my home system tonight.'

'Thanks, man.' Tom tossed his pen down and scratched his beard. 'I don't want to be the one to tell Leon we could miss a deadline.'

'Just leave it with me,' Daryl said, his brows knitting as he stared through his notebook in thought. 'I'll report back in the morning.'

As the developers all left the kitchen, Jet glanced at the drinks machine and, pocketing her phone, picked up her mug. Crossing the kitchen to make herself a hot chocolate, she breathed in the silence and let her mind go blank as her drink poured.

Daryl would be out most of the evening, he was leaving early to attend a charity event at one of the museums. She considered turning her phone off there and then for the rest of the day and making the most of the peace.

Instead, she dug her earbuds out of her pocket and spent the rest of the working day wearing them.

Her music was still her only company as she climbed the front stoop.

Finding the house empty as expected, she danced to the music all the way to the top floor of the house, changed into some suitable attire and headed for the basement.

Daryl had already shown her how to use all the equipment after the Sunday run had had to be cancelled due to further bad weather.

Jet had the choice of the treadmill, cross-trainer, bike, rowing machine, weights or punchbag. Having never really liked weightlifting, she decided to take the day's frustrations out on the punch bag.

The conversation with Rachel had played on repeat in her mind whilst she'd ridden the subway. All the games, speculation, tittle-tattle of dating, was exactly what she hated.

Hitting the bag with a testing jab, Jet remembered every batshit crazy date she'd ever been on and with every blow a different face appeared before her, each with a different reason for making her self-loathing rise to the surface.

After she'd run out of men to pretend to hit, the faces of various women she'd known over the years replaced them. Snide comments, cruel comments, pitiful comments all played over the music in her head.

When her arms felt too much like jelly to lift anymore, she screamed in frustration and, hugging the bag to steady herself, slid onto her butt on the floor.

Pulling the earbuds free and setting them on her thigh, she listened to her breathing, the only sound in the room, until she had cleared her mind and calmed down.

If she didn't clear her mind, it could run away with her, usually creating some unrealistically perfect hero who would swoop in and rescue her from herself before she hogtied the image into her next book.

One rogue tear slid down her nose and dripped onto her ankle before she swept her hair back decisively, grabbed her earbuds and stood up.

'That's quite enough of that,' Jet muttered before returning to her room.

Sitting on the bed for a moment, eyes closed in the silence, she paused before slowly peeling all her clothes off and heading for the bathroom.

While the bath filled, she tied her long curls into a high bun, put her gym gear in the laundry basket, and collected her giant hoodie and some fresh underwear. Placing them on the closed toilet lid for when she was out of the tub, Jet set her phone on charge in the bedroom, turned it up loud enough for her to hear and instead of music for the bath, switched to an audiobook.

With the bath only two thirds full by the time she'd done all that, she stood in front of the mirror, poking at the softer areas of her body curiously until the water reached the level she preferred.

It wasn't until she slipped into the foaming bath water and her stomach grumbled that she realised she hadn't eaten since before the meeting that afternoon.

Running through the delights of the fridge in her head and considering what she could be bothered to cook when she was out of the bath, it wasn't until Jet heard the bedroom door open and close below her that she realised Daryl was home and that she had been on the brink of nodding off.

The audiobook had stopped too.

Listening to Daryl moving around downstairs as she remembered that he'd promised to work into the night,

Jet checked her fingers to see how wrinkly they were. She had no idea how long she'd been in the tub or even what time it had been when she'd run the bath.

With a sigh, she pulled the plug with her toes and climbed out of the water.

Yawning as she slipped into her clothes, she listened for movement downstairs as the bath drained. Jet hadn't expected Daryl to be home before she went to bed and had planned on wearing the sweater like a dress. It wasn't quite decent enough to do that with her housemate home, so if she wanted food, she needed sweatpants.

With another yawn, she hopped into a pair of leggings and headed for the kitchen.

Treading softly as she passed Daryl's office, the sound of furious typing drifting out from under the door, she wondered whether he'd need a coffee. Shrugging to herself, she carried on downstairs, he might have already had one, and the more disturbances she created, the longer it would take him.

Jet had sunk two slices of bread into the toaster and the retro kettle she had bought in Walmart was starting to whistle on the stove when Daryl walked into the kitchen. His hair was mussed up and the shirt and tie he'd worn to the event were unbuttoned and hanging loose.

Jet found herself wishing she'd seen the dressed-up article before he'd left the house.

'Good event?' she asked through another yawn, glad it prevented her from gawping at him. 'Sorry.'

'It was OK,' he said, stifling one of his own in response. 'Pretty basic really, drinks, canapés, speeches, some art for auction and the elite networking and breadcrumbing over which of their existing pieces they might bring to the next event now they've bought more than their walls can take.'

'Do you want a drink?' Jet asked as she reached for the kettle.

'Yes, but I'm fridge-bound,' he said, reaching into the double-doored monstrosity and retrieving a beer.

Nodding, Jet prepared herself a hot chocolate to go with her toast.

'Evening snack?' he asked as the toaster popped.

'Dinner,' Jet said guiltily. 'I forgot to eat.'

'Are you alright?'

'I'm fine,' she said quickly, without looking up. 'I hit the gym when I got in, then went for a bath. Time disappeared, that's all.'

With a shrug, she lifted the mug to her lips and, after a gentle blow, tested the hot chocolate before placing it on the table and moving on to the toast.

'You *hit* the gym? Are you sure everything is OK?' He had moved to the door but paused uncertainly. When she looked like she was going to pretend he hadn't spoken, he continued, 'Rachel was out of line today. No one else needed to know your business like that.'

'Yet people like her can't stand to see me single,' Jet said in an exasperated whisper.

'I know we said we wouldn't talk about it . . .'

'Then don't,' Jet mumbled, refusing to meet his eye by

busying herself with buttering the toast.

'But, if you need to let off steam about real-time shit like that, then go for it.'

'I did.'

'Is the gym still standing?' he asked, a gentle smirk on his face when she finally looked up.

'The punchbag is very resilient,' she agreed.

'It's clear you don't take any shit. That's good to know.' He gave her a meaningful look from beneath his ruffled hair.

'It's never worth it.' She leant back against the counter, buttered toast on the plate in her hand and lifted a slice to her lips to take a bite.

'Speaks the voice of experience.' He lifted his beer in salute before taking a mouthful.

'Hmm,' Jet hummed dismissively before swallowing her first mouthful. 'You're not going to be up too late working are you?'

'No,' he scoffed. 'I know exactly how I want to break that software and roughly what I need to do to do it now I have permission.'

'Can I help at all?' Jet asked before taking another bite.

'You already have, our various conversations have helped me plan this breakage. It should be fine.' He waved his bottle about.

'OK.' She nodded and decided to take a seat at the table to finish the second piece of toast and drink her hot chocolate. 'I can't guarantee I'll be awake much longer anyway.'

'Do you have anything from Larry this week?'

'I have a comedy night to review on Thursday. Nothing else this week though,' Jet said through another mouthful of toast. 'You?'

'Only tonight's gala, but he hinted that there might be more when I spoke to him on the phone,' Daryl said thoughtfully. 'We'll just have to see what comes in, if anything.'

'Do you need extra assignments this week? I've got a squeaky editor on my case for the next novel, so I should probably look at delivering something to her too by the end of the week.' Jet drummed her fingertips against the side of her mug. 'If he asks me, I can hand them over?'

'Not specifically, I thought you might want the extra experience.' Daryl shrugged and turned to leave.

'I need the extra experience, but Mai is being particularly pushy this week.'

'Aren't deadlines fun?' he said with a hint of mischief Jet found herself surprised to see. 'Speaking of. . .'

'Yes, go, don't spend all night on that bloody software.' Jet waved him off before scooping up her mug to sip at the hot chocolate in silence until it was gone.

Once she was finished, she washed, dried and returned everything to their correct homes, then made her way slowly up the stairs to her room.

Glancing at her laptop on the dressing table she was using as a writing desk, she considered turning it on and getting at least a thousand words written. But as the machine blurred through further yawn-induced tear-duct leakage, she realised she was unlikely to get anything of use ready for Mai.

Deciding to climb straight into bed, she promised herself and her distant editor that she'd aim for five thousand words the following day. She'd have to, to make up for taking Thursday night off.

SIXTEEN

'Where are Sasha and Tracy?' Jet asked as Rachel and Veronica appeared out of nowhere and began to take a seat at the table that had been reserved for her for the comedy gig. 'Didn't you say they were coming?'

'They're trying to, something came up,' Veronica explained, handing Jet and Leroy a shot each. 'They call it a Quickie.'

'I'll bet they do!' Leroy laughed outrageously.

Realising what she'd said, Veronica also snorted a surprised laugh. 'I mean the drink!'

'You'd better drink it in the same fashion, they're vile,' Rachel complained. She was still holding her shot at arm's length on the table in front of her. 'Ron's idea of a starter drink.'

'Everything else tastes amazing afterwards.' Veronica beamed. 'Ready?'

Lifting her glass, they all followed suit and drank their drinks down together.

'Fuck,' Jet garbled through the afterburn. 'I don't need

to know what was in that.'

'I'm sorry for telling half the office about your date the other day,' Rachel wheezed as she shook from head to toe after her shot.

'So you should be!' Leroy chastised. 'If you'd done that to me, I'd have slapped you.'

'That's not necessary,' Jet soothed as Leroy looked set to demonstrate.

'He would have, though,' Rachel agreed.

'I have a reputation to uphold. You never know who's admiring you from across a crowded room.' He waved flamboyantly at the room around him.

'Is it another open mic night?' Veronica asked with expert timing.

'Sort of, it's international night. Some of the comedians have been invited to perform, there are two from the UK, one from Italy, one from Japan, another from Australia and a Canadian,' Jet said. 'The owners post on social media for any acts that might be passing through.'

'Hey, it's New York, they're always passing through. Like randy sailors.' Leroy stole another searching gaze around the room, trying to spot who the tourists among them might be.

'This is their third month, the first month went so well that they did it again, and now it's caught the attention of the guy I freelance for.' Jet smiled.

'I'll pretend I didn't hear that.' Rachel winked.

'It's just a writing gig, do you think Virgo would have a problem with it?' Jet asked, wide-eyed.

'Only if it interferes with your day job. Especially if it affects a client meeting or delivery. Otherwise, I'm sure just about every other creative at Virgo has a side hustle, most of you lot do.' Rachel shook her hair out of her face. 'But no one talks about it.'

'Noted.' Jet grimaced playfully as the compére climbed onto the stage.

After the third act, the lights came up for a short break as Jet was assessing the drinks situation and preparing to go to the bar. Rachel sighed.

'That last guy, oh my god.'

'He was hilarious!' Jet said, surprised as she stood, wiping a laughter tear from the corner of her eye as she did. 'More wine?'

'God yes!' Leroy nudged the ice bucket in her direction. 'I couldn't understand a word that last dude said. What language was that?'

'Drunk Glaswegian,' Jet said so fast they barely caught that either.

'See, I don't even understand it when you say it.' Rachel shook her head.

'Sasha just text, they're going to make it for the second half.'

'Cool, I'll get two bottles then.' Jet nodded and began winding her way between tables to the bar.

On returning to the table, she found the group complete but looking shifty.

'Hey guys.' She smiled, putting the bottles down, one in the cooler. 'What kept you?'

Glancing in turn at all of them as Leroy dramatically

folded his arms and shot Rachel a look, Jet spotted an extra chair at the table.

'Well, someone needs to tell her before he gets back,' Leroy sassed.

'Before who gets back?' a man's voice asked as, returning from the bar, Roger reached for the empty seat.

'We ran into him,' Tracy explained quickly, telling Jet she was more annoyed than shifty, 'and Sasha opened her big mouth.'

'Jet,' Roger said awkwardly as he placed his beer down and fidgeted with his right arm, as though he was considering whether to shake her hand or not. 'I'm so sorry about the other night. I'd like to explain.'

'Later maybe, I'm actually working here.' Jet turned in her seat so that she was facing the stage as the compére returned.

'Sounds like he basically followed them here.' Leroy leant forward to mutter into her ear as he poured himself another glass of wine. 'Because that's not creepy at all.'

Turning her head to catch his eye, Jet raised her eyebrows in agreement, acutely aware that Roger was staring at her as though he'd spotted a celebrity crush or supermodel.

Focusing on the compére, she tried to remember she had a job to do. She hadn't failed to notice that Roger wasn't dressed in a manner that suggested he'd been bumped into on the street. His smart jeans, shirt and suit jacket would have been more at home on a date.

Clenching her jaw and taking a deep breath, Jet tapped her pen on her notepad and tried to concentrate around the creepy vibes.

Jotting down as many notes as she thought might help her remember the second half, Jet shoved the notebook in her bag and made a dive for the bathroom as soon as the last act drew applause.

A little tipsy, she sighed and paused, her forehead against the door of the stall, before heading to the sink. Washing her hands in slow motion, she looked up into the mirror as if to ask herself what the hell she was going to do next, when Tracy walked in.

'I can help create a diversion if you want to escape?' Tracy asked, meeting her eye. 'Sasha told me what you said to Rachel, I don't give second chances lightly either.'

'Leroy said he invited himself along,' Jet stated questioningly, turning off the tap and moving to the hand towels.

'As soon as Sasha said we were meeting you he acted as though we'd invited him. It looks more suspect than it is, he's not that dodgy.' Tracy smirked. 'At least, I don't think so.'

'OK,' Jet sighed. 'Because this isn't awkward at all.' She offered Tracy a twisted smile and headed for the door as Tracy locked herself in a stall.

Returning to the table, Jet was temporarily relieved to see that Roger wasn't in his seat. Though, she quickly discovered he was back at the bar.

'How much have we got left?' she asked the table as

she lifted the last of their wine bottles out of the cooler.

'Enough for a short top up, but I'll be calling it a night shortly. Save my strength for tomorrow night.' Leroy grinned.

'What's so special about this Friday night?' Rachel asked as she held out her wine glass for Jet to pour out the remaining wine, sharing it between them.

'I have a date,' he admitted, pouting ever so slightly as he raised his wine to his lips.

'A real one?' Rachel teased. 'Not just a booty call.'

'No.' He gasped dramatically, then grinned. 'That's just how we met.'

'A booty call wants to see you again?' Rachel scowled.

'They often do.' He squirmed playfully in his seat.

'It's ok for some,' Rachel drawled as she downed the last of her wine.

'What's up your ass?'

'It's more what's not. She's going through a dry spell,' Veronica said pointedly.

'Who is?' Sasha asked as she returned to the table with Tracy and Roger.

'Our roomie,' Veronica said quickly as Roger looked to Jet with eager expectancy. 'You didn't get more wine, did you?' She changed the subject.

'No,' Sasha sulked. 'Tracy wouldn't let me.'

'We all have work in the morning,' Tracy said pointedly.

'But it is a Friday.' Sasha pouted.

'And mine plans to be a busy one,' Tracy reminded her.

'Oh yeah, sorry.' Sasha smiled and reached for her partner's hand.

'I'll have to head off in a moment, anyway,' Jet admitted as she rolled the stem of her glass between her fingertips. 'I'll have to write this review up before I call it a night.'

'Can I walk you to the subway?' Roger asked her directly.

'Only if you have to go to the same one anyway,' Jet said after a moment in which the whole table seemed to hold their breath.

'We're all going to the same subway station.' Rachel pointed out but her eyes met Jet's in a manner that suggested she was trying to be helpful. 'We'll all go together.'

Roger opened his mouth to argue with Jet, but when she nodded in agreement and met his eye, he thought better of it.

She wondered whether Rachel had told him what she'd said, either directly or through Sasha. The brief attempt to negotiate Rachel's terms with Jet directly told her he had no idea what he was dealing with.

As if Rachel had declared that they were leaving with her suggestion, everyone began draining their glasses and shrugging jackets on. Swallowing the last mouthful of wine, Jet followed suit and stood at the same time as Leroy.

'I'm going to disappear before this gets even more awkward.' He held his arms open for a hug and as she grinned and obliged, squeezing him tight, he pecked her on the cheek. 'Fill me in in the morning, yeah?'

'Of course!' Jet smiled. 'Get home safe.'

'Girl, that might be the most British thing you've said to me since you got here!' He laughed good-naturedly and with air kisses to the rest of the group, pranced out of the venue.

Being furthest from the door meant that as the others filed out, Jet found herself at the back of the group and Roger waiting to bring up the rear with her.

'Have you had a good night?' he asked as she insisted that he went up the stairs to street level ahead of her.

'Mostly,' Jet replied bluntly, instantly chastising herself for sounding ruder than she'd intended. 'Comedy is usually fun, having to take notes disrupts the laughter a little.'

'How long have you been writing?' he asked sweetly, in a manner usually reserved for small talk on the date they hadn't had.

'Twenty-two years,' she responded flatly, aware he probably wasn't expecting such an answer.

'That's cute.' He glanced back with what he must have thought was an encouraging smile.

Waiting until he'd turned back around, Jet rolled her eyes as hard as she could.

Once out on the street, the group paired down, with Jet and Roger at the back, in order to walk to the subway. Rachel and Veronica held the middle and both kept glancing back to make sure they kept together, which Jet found herself grateful for.

'I really am sorry for standing you up last Saturday,'

Roger said after half a block of painful silence.

'It takes time to be ready to get back into the dating scene.' Jet shrugged. 'Maybe you're not ready.'

'Oh, no I am!' he answered quickly. 'I'd like to make it up to you.'

'You really don't have to do that.' Jet shouldered her bag to cover a second shrug. 'You've apologised. Though I'm still confused as to why it took you five days.'

'I… yeah, that looks pretty shitty whatever I say,' he agreed.

'So, what were you doing out late enough tonight to run into Sasha?' Jet asked, aiming to divert the conversation and glancing again at the smart jeans and suit jacket, realising he was carrying a satchel and wearing a pair of green Chucks.

'Working,' he said brightly, swinging the satchel. 'Client dinner.'

'What do you do?'

'I'm an accounts manager for the advertising agency Sasha works at.' He glanced across at her and she noted that he wasn't much taller than her, not that height bothered her. 'Client portfolios. I'm not an actual accountant.'

Smirking in spite of herself, Jet appreciated his attempt at humour and wondered whether she should burst his bubble by telling him one of her favourite people was her accountant. In the end, she decided that would be too mean.

'So, what exciting activities would we have been doing

had you not bottled it Saturday night?' she found herself asking, genuinely curious.

'I was going to see if there were any last-minute Broadway tickets available,' Roger admitted, looking at his feet as they walked. 'If not, show you any sight you hadn't seen yet, your choice.'

'My dad grew up here, there aren't many I haven't seen,' Jet said gently.

'Oh, right!' he exclaimed, surprised and awkward all at once. 'You're dual nationality?'

'Yeah. I'm all for a bit of cheesy tourism, though. I went shopping in Times Square when you didn't show.'

'You didn't buy an I love New York t-shirt did you?'

'To go with my other twenty or so? My nan used to send me a new one whenever I grew out of the last.' Jet laughed. 'No, I went for a hooded sweater this time.'

'Got to keep up tradition, I guess.' He chuckled in response as they neared the subway. 'I'd like to find out more about your love of this city. Let me buy you dinner one day next week?'

Aware that they were about to have the *this is my station* conversation, Jet mulled it over for a moment, still uncertain that it was a good idea to get in anyway more involved.

'OK, but let's not call it a date.'

'O… K…' he said slowly.

'Takes the pressure off.' She pointed out as they all drew to a stop. 'How about next Friday?'

'I've got a few client meetings next week. I'll check my diary and let you know.' He smiled with a gracious nod.

'Sure.' She nodded hesitantly.

Expecting not to hear from him again and for the charade to drag on, Jet resisted the urge to tell him to shove it, instead she moved into the middle of the group just in case he was a hugger or cheek kisser.

'You're Brooklyn, right Roger?' Veronica asked pointedly.

'Yeah, I'm going east, you girls all going north?' he asked as they all drifted down towards the platforms.

'We're all on the same line,' Rachel agreed. 'Night, Roger.'

As they parted ways, Rachel linked arms with Jet as Roger looked set to say something else.

'Jeez, are you alright?' she asked as they reached the turnstiles and uncoupled.

'Yeah, he wants to take me to dinner next week but doesn't yet know when he's free.' Jet puffed out an annoyed breath.

'Well, that's useful,' Veronica drawled. 'Creepy and flaky, just what you want.'

'Just one of the many reasons I don't date.' Jet ran her fingers through her hair, relieved to be going home.

'Sorry. If he doesn't call you this time, I'll make sure you never have to see him again.' Sasha hooked Jet by the neck for a playful hug.

SEVENTEEN

Falling in the front door as her phone rang for what felt like the fiftieth time that day, Jet growled in annoyance and began marching up the stairs. Mai had been so insistent that they needed a call that she'd been unable to join the others for the traditional Friday night drinks. Though that hadn't stopped her hanging around the lobby long enough to see how Leroy emerged from the cloakrooms ready for his date.

When he went all-out he was a bigger stunner than most of the women she knew, and he knew how to wear makeup better than most of them too.

Mai had been sending her emails about her deadline all week, and knowing she was falling behind, she'd been ignoring them since Tuesday.

As it was, she had only planned to allow herself one drink before getting back to her chapters for the night, and probably most of the weekend so that there would be something for London to view first thing Monday. But for some reason Mai had been calling ALL DAY.

It would have been irritating if she'd left a bunch of messages, but no voicemails had been left. Jet wasn't sure whether to be concerned that something was wrong or prepared for an utter bollocking down the line.

Dragging her work-weary self up the stairs to her room, she stripped off all her clothes and put something comfortable on while her laptop booted up. If she was going to be on a conference call with her editor, she expected it to last at least an hour, and she decided she was going to be comfortable at least.

Sitting at the desk with a heavy sigh moments later, Jet plugged her headset in and started skimming the emails as the app-based phone rang.

Most of the headers in her inbox were simply "Call me", one said something about contracts, another about new opportunities. She tensed right through her core at the idea of adding more projects to her workload.

'Where the hell have you been this week?' Mai squeaked when they finally connected.

'Trying to catch up, sorry!' Jet blurted, though she was trying not to laugh at the outraged editor, whose squeak was certainly worse than her bark and mostly only audible to dogs.

'Catch up?'

'You wanted five more chapters by the close of today for you to read over the weekend, I only have three at the moment,' Jet admitted. 'I was out last night.'

'New York making you sociable? Surely not?' Mai harrumphed playfully.

'Sort of, I was with friends, but working, of sorts.'

'Working how?' Mai asked slowly.

'Writing reviews here and there. It's nothing really, just a little side gig that might lead to a bit more freelancing.'

'May I remind you that I already gave you a side gig? Besides, how is doing three jobs at once ever going to get me more material?'

'Well, if I can go freelance with the review writing, I can jack in the day job,' Jet pointed out smugly.

'You might be able to do that anyway…' Mai trailed off cryptically.

'What have you been up to?' Jet tried to hide the grin from her voice, wondering just what it could be.

'We do want to sign you on for the next batch in the series, but . . . we've also been approached about film rights.'

'You're fucking kidding?' Jet squeaked after a moment of gaping like a fish as she fell back in her chair.

'No,' Mai said sharply. 'Dead fucking serious.'

'By who? What for?'

'For the first book in the series at the moment, they're tentative, but it could be series wide if they get a good feeling about it. The query came in to the rights team over the weekend but of course we didn't even catch up with ourselves until the beginning of the week.'

'What happens now?'

'They're LA based, but they want to meet to throw some ideas around. They're even willing, in this technological day and age, to send someone to New

York to talk to you.'

'I have no idea what to do!' Jet gave a squeak of her own. 'I haven't worked with film rights before.'

'That's why I'm going to fly in with the rights manager and meet them with you,' Mai squawked excitedly. 'Netta could probably dial in on her own, but I've sweet talked the money our side. I haven't been to New York in years, I'm totally overdue a visit!'

'That will be amazing! I'll have to see if I can get a day off while you're here or something. Any idea when that will be?'

'Their people are talking with their people and we're talking with our people, don't expect it to move too fast, but that's basically where we're at! Can you imagine?!'

'No... I mean, yes, but just... wow.'

'Seriously, don't get too far ahead of yourself, even if they buy the rights, they may never make the film.' Mai reined herself in to talk some sense.

'Yeah, I'm aware enough of that.' Jet sighed even though her cheeks were starting to hurt from grinning. 'I think you're excited enough for both of us!'

'You kidding? I just want to see who the hell they're going to cast for some of the roles! I mean, drool, right?'

'Depends how big the company is, I guess.'

'I thiiiink it's a biggy.' Mai sounded coy down the line. 'But I'm not going to confirm or deny that until we get progression.'

'Alright. Wow.' Jet gazed out of the window at some of the town houses up and down the street. Maybe, just maybe, one day she'd be the owner of one. 'I can't wait to see you!'

'I'll just have to book myself a long weekend city break in the summer if it doesn't happen. Don't you have any plans to pop back to the UK?'

'Not now I'm working, there isn't anything… besides this… big enough to get me back just yet. And anyway, I love the way you say "pop back". It's a seven-hour flight on a bad day. I wouldn't call that popping out for lunch exactly.'

'Bigwigs do it all the time,' Mai huffed.

'You know how much my last book made. I'm no bigwig.' Jet laughed.

'Yet,' Mai sang.

'Yeah, you keep working on that,' Jet teased.

'I intend to!' Mai sassed. 'How are things with the housemate?'

'OK so far,' Jet said quietly, even though she hadn't heard Daryl come in from the after-work drinks. 'We manage to keep ourselves to ourselves without it being too awkward or overbearing.'

'I can't wait to see what he looks like up close, how did you describe him? A Chris Hemsworth body double after a bad day at the office?'

Jet grimaced, when she first updated Mai on her living arrangements she'd gone for the closest description she'd thought Mai would connect with.

'Something like that,' Jet admitted through gritted teeth, hoping those words were never repeated in front of him.

It was kind of true, though.

'See, now whenever I think of you in that house alone with him, I think you have a brooding Thor roaming the halls,' Mai said dreamily.

'His hair isn't quite that long if you're thinking early Thor rather than Ragnarok Thor. It's somewhere in the middle,' Jet pointed out.

'Jesus. Even better. Is there any way you could talk him into attending the meeting? Surely we can find a use for him?'

'My god, I don't think I want to unleash you on him, ever.' Jet rubbed her forehead. 'I need somewhere to live, I like this house, and you'll only be here for a long weekend…'

'Maybe a week if I can swing it by adding to the budget personally.'

'Regardless, I intend to stay here much longer than that.'

'Does he act?'

'I know what you're thinking and NO,' Jet exclaimed through laughter.

'Maybe we should swing it that you need to be in on the casting. Then I'll change my job and become your PA so that I have to attend.'

'You'd better be planning on staying in a hotel.'

'Thought you had another room on your *floor*?'

'It's not my house, remember. I can't go inviting guests to stay for a week! It's not a hotel and my landlord likes his privacy,' Jet said forcefully.

'Oh alright, I'm quite fond of the Wellington anyway,

I'll just share with Netta.' Mai calmed herself down. 'Anyway, tell me all about that date you were supposed to go on last weekend.'

'Oh god, where to begin.' Jet ran her fingers through her hair and reclined as far as she could in the chair.

'Spill,' Mai commanded, stifling a yawn. Jet looked at the clock and, working out the time difference, realised Mai might be content with the short and sweet version.

Two hours later, as she heard Daryl enter his room below her, Jet finally managed to sign off with her sleepy editor.

'If I promise to write you something more to read tonight, will you go to bed?'

'The full five chapters?'

'Four if you want it in the morning.'

'It's early enough there, surely?'

'It's nine, which means you've made it to two in the morning, if I make it to the same time, I might make it to five. We'll see, you'll get the full five, maybe even more, by the end of the weekend, I promise.'

'Send what you have in the morning. The weather is being typically British, and I have nowhere else to be this weekend. Indulge and entertain me, please,' Mai whined.

'Alright, alright, but you have to go to bed, or you'll get nothing.'

'Gone, babe. Speak soon!'

'You bet. Night, hon.'

Mai mumbled something along the lines of a goodnight and cut the call off. Chuckling to herself, Jet pulled her earbuds from her ears and stretched upwards, then sidewards as she reached for the desktop lamp. A few hours extra work had been promised and a few extra hours she would need to produce.

Glancing around the room, she listened for sounds of movement downstairs before getting up from the desk to put the bedside lamps on and close the curtains.

Knowing it would prove to be a late one, she moved all the clothes she'd thrown on the bed to the wingback chair in the opposite corner so that she could fall into bed once her eyes could no longer see the keyboard.

Reaching over the back of the desk chair, she pulled up her novel in progress before leaving the room. Mai's urgency had meant she'd forgotten to eat again. Deciding it might have to be toast and coffee, she rolled her hair up into a bun, fastening it with the hairband around her wrist, and headed down to the kitchen.

A fire engine roared up Central Park West as she descended the stairs, but that hadn't prevented Daryl hearing her. As she passed his bedroom door it flew open and his head popped out, he was still tugging a white t-shirt down over his hips as he fully emerged when Jet stopped.

'You missed the celebrations.' He smiled. 'The project was delivered this afternoon, just before you left.'

'It's a day for good news then it seems.' Jet grinned. 'We'll just have to hold our breath for the client amends.'

'Don't burst the bubble. Have you eaten?'

'I've only just got off the call with my editor, so no,

have you?'

'Not yet,' he answered, raking his fingers through his hair to smooth it back out. 'Celebratory Chinese?'

'Hmm,' Jet hummed thoughtfully as she folded her arms and leant against the banister. 'I have got a lot of writing to do this evening.'

'So have I,' he admitted. 'You up for ordering in?'

'Better that than cooking I guess.' She narrowed her eyes. 'What happened to all the healthy eating you claimed to do?'

'We both have work to do, I've had a few beers, it's getting late.' He folded his arms as he leant against the doorframe and yawned.

'Coffee while we order?' Jet asked, yawning in return.

'You making?'

'Sure.' She smirked as she moved passed him and started heading down the stairs.

Closing his bedroom door, Daryl followed.

'What are you working on?' she asked as they entered the kitchen and she switched the coffee machine on while he began rifling in a drawer.

'Well, now the software from hell seems to have been temporarily tamed, I've found I have a little headspace... before the beers,' he paused to rub his face, 'to consider taking on some new projects. Larry has me writing a tester article, I might get a regular column.'

'On what?' Jet asked, yawning again as she leant back against the counter, the coffee machine whirring in her ear as he produced a delivery menu from the drawer.

'Techy stuff mostly, he needs a proposal and a sample. I've got a few ideas, a few angles, I'll work it out.'

Opening the leaflet, he turned the pages and checked the reverse before tossing it back in the drawer and taking his phone out of his pocket.

'Not the right one?' Jet nodded to the drawer as she turned back to the task of coffee.

'It is so out of date, it would be pointless to use it, the app is better,' he muttered as he sat down at the table and began adding dishes to his order online. 'Have you got cash?'

'Not this time, no,' Jet admitted as the espresso cups filled. She leant against the machine, edging closer to the cups in order to sniff the aroma in the hope that inhaling the fumes would start to wake her up.

'You get the next one,' he suggested.

'Sounds fair,' she agreed, crossing the kitchen to the fridge.

Finishing their coffees as he distracted himself with the wonder of the extensive menu, Jet worked in silence until she placed two cups down on the table. Looking up in surprise, he sighed and handed his phone over.

'If I order any more, I'll be eating leftovers all weekend.' He lifted his cup as he sat up in the chair. 'This is just beer-induced ordering.'

Running through the list quickly as Daryl tried repeatedly to drink his cappuccino before it was cool enough to do so, Jet added a noodle dish, chicken dish and a duck dish to the basket and handed it back.

'Looks like delivery is going to be around an hour,' she

said as he appraised the order.

'Yeah, around that.' He repocketed the phone. 'Cooking would have been quicker.'

'Probably,' she agreed, still stood next to the table. 'Maybe time to get an hour's extra work in before it arrives?'

'Oh, you're one of those writers?' He laughed as he stood slowly. 'A bit of a slave driver.'

'Hardly. You've seen how much procrastinating I've done this week.' She smirked. 'It's different when I have a deadline.'

'You've had that deadline all week.' He frowned as he followed her to the stairs.

'Yeah, but now it's almost here. Which is how I've always done my homework. Last minute.'

'Editor cracked the whip?'

'A little, she likes to read it as I go along, she's just about the only person I know who is addicted to my characters.' Jet glanced over her shoulder to give him a twisted smile. 'See you in an hour.'

As her witchy lead character set off to wander the sewers in search of her missing demonic lover, Jet rubbed her eyes and checked her watch. Food had to be imminent.

Setting a new chapter ready for her return, she saved the document and a copy before standing from her desk and stretching first up to the ceiling, then down to her toes.

She didn't bother to check her phone, there was little

point when the UK was asleep. Though, when she had a book on the go, that was how she preferred it. Peace and quiet was golden, even though she knew there were many who would disagree with her choice of city for such reverie.

Returning to the kitchen, Jet found herself a beer in the fridge and, moving to the cutlery drawer, dug out a couple of forks. Finding chopsticks as well, she pondered whether Daryl used them or merely saved them from previous deliveries. Not wanting to presume either way, she lay out a set anyway.

Hearing his footsteps on the stairs, she turned in time for the doorbell to chime.

'That was good timing.' She raised her bottle of beer as he brought their dinner into the kitchen. 'Want one?'

'I think I've had enough of that stuff for one night.' He glanced up and shook his head as he began opening cartons and splitting them out.

'Are you struggling to concentrate?'

'Yeah, a little, I'm hoping food will help. Did you get much done?'

'One chapter down, at least one more to go.'

'Do you have them planned out? Or do you wing it?' Opening the last carton and plucking a chunk of chicken from it, he straightened to look at her as he popped it into his mouth.

'I make a list of plot points, bullet points, and work my way through them,' Jet said as she reached for one of the containers he'd slid her way. 'They tend to change though as I go along, often a better idea will slide in at random, or an extra scene.'

'I do something similar when I write, but one of the benefits of non-fiction is that the bullet points lay themselves out and pretty much stay as they are.' Reaching for the chopsticks, he took a seat at the table. 'What was the other good news you said you had?'

'What?' Jet frowned as she watched him and, wrestling with the plan she'd had to take her food upstairs, decided instead to join him and sat opposite.

'You said it was a good news day all round. What did your editor want?'

'She had some news about a potential rights deal on my first book. I can't say much more though in case I jinx it. It's early days, but it might mean she has to pop over here for a meeting.'

'Would you write full time if you could?'

'Isn't that the dream for every writer?'

'That depends. I write to inform, in all my writing, even the programming. Most write to entertain. Except you.'

When Jet looked up from digging around in her noodles, he was looking right at her. Swallowing a mouthful of chicken, she raised a questioning eyebrow.

'You do both,' he stated simply, though he was looking at her with an intensity she found unsettling.

With his eyes fixed as though he was trying to work something out, Jet found herself glancing around the kitchen uncomfortably.

'My publishing deal doesn't exactly pay for a London or Manhattan lifestyle. You could say I have expensive taste. Luckily, I found copywriting, like writing content for training courses, it's a way to use my other skills to do something useful,' she said carefully.

'I'm not sure many of those subjected to e-learning would agree with you on that one.' Daryl laughed.

'True, but that comes with the job.' She reached for her beer and took a swig. 'Why don't you write full time? Especially if that's your opinion of electronic training.'

'Because I'm good at it.'

'Spoken like a true developer.' Jet snarked.

'Tech pays the bills, you're aware of that, writing is just something extra to fill my time, a side hustle, a hobby.'

'You work all the time,' Jet said slowly, realising that though they'd only lived in the same house a week, he only emerged from his study to exercise, eat or go to one of his client's offices like Virgo.

'So do you.' He shrugged, his expression relaxing.

'I have a deadline.' Jet pointed at him with her fork. 'But when your hobby also makes you money it does take up more time.'

'So why not let mine take me to gigs, games and premiers?'

'Touché,' Jet agreed, sensing he had never aimed to talk about himself and deciding to push it. 'Do you ever just get out for fun?'

'The gigs, games and premiers are fun,' he said quickly, staring into the carton in his hand.

Narrowing her eyes while he wasn't looking, Jet watched him shut down in front of her. She'd never cared much for a social life, there was always another book to be written, but that didn't mean she didn't enjoy spending time with friends and family.

The guys at work had warned her that he was very private, he had warned her that he was very private. But she knew what it was like to try to be too private and fail.

'Oh, I forgot to tell you,' Jet said brightly, changing the subject deliberately before the atmosphere had the chance to get awkward. 'My non-date from last Saturday invited himself to the gig last night to publicly announce he was sorry.'

'He did what?' Daryl's eyes blazed as he looked up.

'He ran into Sasha, one of Rachel's roomies that he works with, and when she told him I had got them tickets to the comedy gig, he decided to tag along.' Jet widened eyes again, playfully.

'Fucking hell, is that how modern dating is?' He shook his head. 'What did you do?'

'Praying he'd fuck off wasn't going to help me much, so I told him to wait until the end of the night because I was working.' She grimaced. 'He wants to make it up to me with dinner. But doesn't know when he's free.'

'I thought you didn't give second chances.' He narrowed his eyes suspiciously.

'He kinda cornered me. However, I fully expect to not hear from him again.'

'Well, if you do and you go, I'll make sure I'm about. Text me.'

'Hopefully it won't come to that, but thanks.'

EIGHTEEN

Waking suddenly, face down and still clothed on her bed, Jet spluttered out a mouthful of duvet and rolled over, wondering what had startled her.

Patting the duvet to see if a puddle of drool would suggest choking on the cotton had woken her and finding it dry, she sighed and, grabbing the corner of the duvet, tugged it around her ear as she turned again towards the bedside table. It was light, but the city wasn't buzzing too loudly outside her window, suggesting it was still early.

The dawn chorus being performed by the birds in Central Park suggested it was little past sunup.

Turning her phone towards her, she snorted in disgust when she read 6a.m. on the display. The snort soon turned into a groan as she realised she had five missed calls and three text messages — all from Roger — from the night before.

To avoid distraction, she had left her phone next to the bed faced down whilst she'd cracked out three more chapters before finally crawling to the bed at 2:30a.m.

The missed calls would have been enough to irk her as it was, no one called to arrange these things anymore, but five calls was insistent. She wondered what the hell he could possibly have wanted to talk about.

The texts themselves were, in the first instance overly cautious, in the second uncertain and questioning, and by the third borderline desperate because she hadn't responded. The guy seriously needed to pull himself together in Jet's opinion, she wanted to meet him just to tell him as such almost as much as she wanted to tell him there wasn't a chance in hell of seeing her again.

Flopping onto her back with a sigh, Jet checked her emails, specifically the sent folder, to make sure she'd delivered on her promise and sent Mai all the hard work she'd done. Smiling when she found an illegible response filled with excited capital letters to have received more than expected, Jet put the phone down again, intent on getting a couple more hours shut eye before getting up for a gym session.

She hadn't realised just how hungry she'd been when the Chinese had been delivered the night before and had scoffed all three cartons and an extra beer before returning to her room around eleven.

Wondering whether Daryl had worked as late as she had, Jet closed her eyes and willed sleep to return.

Ten minutes later, she heaved herself into a sitting position to look at the texts from Roger again. He wasn't just *going* to be a problem, he *was* a problem. But if he was already that shy and unsure, her telling him to fuck right off wasn't going to help him in the long run.

She could almost see one of her lead characters folding her arms and telling her that it wasn't her job.

No, it wasn't.

With a sigh, she considered how she'd feel if it was the other way around.

You mean when it was the other way around? Her imagination laughed at her.

'I've never been desperate,' Jet whispered to herself. 'It's not a good look.'

Not that the opposite had ever done her any favours either.

Attempting to block out the unwanted thoughts of self-loathing that often followed such thoughts, Jet growled, tossing the phone to the sheets and bouncing out of the bed.

Fictional conversations with her imaginary friends never got her anywhere. Much like Alice, Jet and her character entourage, though rarely in Wonderland, often gave each other very good advice, but she very seldom followed it.

Seeking out her earbuds from the desk, Jet snatched up the phone and rummaged around for her gym clothes.

'Time for a run,' she said to herself decisively as she opened the bedroom door.

Aware of the early hour, she was as soft footed as possible descending the stairs but found Daryl's bedroom door wide open as she approached. Peering in as she passed, she found all the curtains drawn back and the bed made. When he'd said he liked to run in the park, she'd never dreamed that he might go little after sunup.

However, she suspected that was the best time to go to avoid crowding. Unless of course, that was trendy in itself.

Stopping by the kitchen to grab a water bottle, she paused a moment to breathe in the smell of a fresh late-spring morning seeping into the cooler room.

Bouncing down the stairs to the gym, she heard him before she saw him. Daryl wasn't out for a run, he was battering the crap out of the punchbag.

His focus was so set that he continued to box the guts out of the bag, head down, sweat sodden hair swinging across his forehead, for a minute or so more before he realised he had company.

Stopping suddenly, making Jet flinch and realise she'd been staring, he gripped the top of the bag to stop it swinging as he caught his breath.

'Did I wake you?' he panted.

'Possibly,' Jet admitted. 'Unless something woke us both up.'

'I woke myself up… that might have woken you up.'

'What did you do? Fall out of bed?' Jet sassed.

'I haven't been to bed,' he muttered. 'But something like that.'

'Are you alright?' Jet asked, realising there was more to his workout than calorie burn.

'I'm fine,' he bit back as he straightened and slicked his forearm across the sweat on his brow.

'Has something happened?'

'Nothing new,' he sniped, his voice deepening.

'If you need space, I can run in the park,' she offered gently.

He looked her up and down in a way that made her defences prickle. She almost expected him to scoff.

'I do need space. I'll go to the park.'

'I can come back later,' Jet offered, but her voice betrayed her annoyance.

'It's fine. I was going to go anyway,' he said, turning his back on her as he started to unwind his hand wraps.

'Would you rather I didn't go to the park?' Jet asked aggressively.

'It's not about that,' he answered, chucking the wraps into a bag on the floor. 'I didn't get the chance to show you the routes like I promised.'

'It's a park, I'm sure I'll cope,' Jet bit out through ground teeth even as she stared at his sweat sodden t-shirt, especially where it was clinging to the strong structure of his back.

The main character still lurking in the back of her mind also fell silent in recognition.

'It's fine,' he repeated as he turned.

Their eyes met briefly before he set his gaze on the wall behind her and, walking towards her, he aimed to pass her without another word.

'It's not fine, this is your house, I am a guest and I can bloody well look out for myself. I'm sorry I disturbed you, but I won't pussy-foot around your brooding temper. Be straight with me and I'll be straight with you.'

'I had a rough night. I'm going to go run it off.' He glanced down at her before moving around her. 'That's all there is to it.'

Shooting him a look over her shoulder as his footsteps retreated up the stairs, she caught him looking back, that same confused expression fixed on his face that he'd worn the day they'd met.

With an aggressive sigh, Jet shook herself off and moved to the treadmill.

She ran for an hour. Longer than she usually would but once she hit her usual five kilometres, she slowed to a jog and let the scenes she needed to write that day play out in her head.

Finally making her way upstairs on wobbly legs, earbuds still in place, she collected an array of brunch items and snacks to take to her room with her.

Daryl's door was still open.

With enough breakfast and lunch goods to see her through to the afternoon, she knew she could avoid him all day if she needed to.

Much calmer from the workout, despite the clash with Daryl, Jet text Roger back to confirm that Friday night at eight would be fine. She also included in the message that he would need to at least text her the name of the restaurant he wanted her to meet him at, deciding that wherever he chose, she'd eat there regardless of whether he turned up or not.

NINETEEN

'Jet?'

Peering over her desk at the questioning tone from Shelley, Jet found her floofing her glossy mane of black hair in a pocket mirror.

'Yes?'

'You have been working with Daryl a lot, yes?'

'We were both working on the delivery that went out last week,' Jet returned and went back to her computer. She had a new assignment while they awaited the client's feedback, she was writing a two-minute animation about the benefits of a market-leading toothpaste as part of the parent company's onboarding program. There were worse ways to spend a Monday.

'Does he ever talk to you about anything other than work?'

'Not really,' Jet said honestly. Most of their discussions were around work, even when they were orbiting around each other in the house. 'He's very focused on what he does.'

Saturday had been quiet. He'd retreated as much as she had, and they hadn't crossed paths again until Sunday by which time they'd both slept better and cooled off enough to pretend nothing had happened.

'Maybe I should just ask him on a date,' Shelley said questioningly.

Raising an eyebrow behind the monitor, Jet stayed quiet.

'What do you think?'

'You won't know until you try, I guess,' Jet drawled, fairly sure Shelley was about to make the workspace far more awkward for herself.

'Won't know what?'

Flinching, Jet turned, almost expecting to see Daryl stood behind her, until she remembered he wasn't due in that day and the voice hadn't matched.

'Whether Daryl will go on a date with her,' Jet said simply.

'Yeah, good luck with that.' Leon scowled, though it was clear he didn't care. 'Jet, I have a client meeting tomorrow evening that I need you to sit in on.'

'What time?'

'Seven. It's the new medical practice safety training. You said you've worked on medical.'

'I'm sorry Leon, I can't make seven tomorrow,' Jet said as evenly as she could manage, hoping he wouldn't ask her why. 'Is there any other way I can help?' she continued quickly in a bid to stop herself looking too evasive.

'You're contractually bound to attend client meetings

where necessary. Whatever else you have, reschedule it,' Leon said, unimpressed, and walked off before she could dare answer him back a second time.

'Shit,' Jet whispered.

'Do you have a date?' Shelley stood up to peer over at her desk mate, grinning from ear to ear in expectation of gossip.

'Not exactly,' Jet huffed, digging into her pocket for her phone.

Jet: Leon has hit me with a meeting tomorrow night at seven. I can't make the game

Daryl: Who the fuck has a meeting at 7? I'll cover it and save you a seat

Jet: Guessing a company down the west coast

Daryl: If you're going to be stuck on a client down the west coast you might have to inform Larry

Jet: Bollocks

Daryl: I'm serious, he will scratch you off the list if you mess him around

Jet: I gathered. Bollocks in this case = Oh Fuck

Daryl: Noted

Smirking to herself, Jet popped the phone back in her pocket.

'That look tells me it is a date,' Shelley gushed.

'Private joke, that's all,' Jet said as she got up and snatched up her mug to head to the kitchen. 'I was just being a tourist. I'd managed to get Knicks tickets for tomorrow night. I haven't seen a basketball game yet.

Coffee?'

'Sure.' Shelley pouted in disappointment as she stood from her desk.

Reappearing suddenly, Leon followed them into the kitchen where Tina was sat.

'Tina, is Daryl in today?'

'Not today, chief,' she sang over her coffee. Tina had little respect for Leon, he wasn't her line manager and his short-notice meetings often caused hell with her childcare arrangements.

'Is he in tomorrow? I need him on a meeting.'

'I think so, but he's leaving early.'

'Why?'

'Who knows, he does his own thing, just said he had tickets for something and would be working an early shift.'

Tensing up, Jet turned her attention on the exchange whilst keeping half an eye on Shelley who either hadn't heard or was pretending not to.

'I bet he's taking some bitch to a musical or something,' Shelley sniped as she waved a bangled wrist about before swearing under her breath in Spanish.

'None of my business,' Jet said simply as they exchanged places at the coffee machine, wondering whether Shelley was trying to trip her into admitting something.

Returning to her desk, with Shelley close behind, Jet hoped that would be the end of Shelley's obsessing for the day. A workplace crush was a dangerous thing. Daryl was lucky he was a freelancer.

Ten minutes later, Jet's phone lit up. She'd moved it to the desk to listen to music, and on seeing the display, instantly regretted it.

Grabbing it quickly, she read the message.

Daryl: Did you tell Shelley we're going to the game tomorrow?

Jet: No! I told her I had a game. Tina then told Leon you had tickets for something tomorrow night. He wants you on the meeting

Daryl: Shelley just emailed me asking if I have a spare ticket for tomorrow. They're both shit out of luck

Jet: I think she suspects we're up to something. Serves you right for checking your mail

Daryl: Bad habit. I'll throw her off the scent

'Who is that?' Shelley asked, reappearing from the bathrooms.

'My date for Friday night,' Jet answered smoothly, hatching a plan.

'Oh.' Shelley grinned. 'So, you do have a date!'

'Someone Rachel's roomie set me up with.' Jet nodded. 'He's a bit odd.'

TWENTY

'This should be fun,' Jet sighed as she rode the elevator down to the lobby with Daryl.

'I can't believe you're going.' He smirked. 'And straight from work.'

'Friday at eight didn't really give me much time. As it was, today's delightful meeting barely gave me time to get changed.' She sighed again and checked her makeup in the mirrored wall. 'Why aren't you at the bar already?'

'I had something to finish up before closing down for the weekend,' he said, looking at her. 'Which dress did you go with?'

Having found time to start panicking about going on her first proper dinner date in New York, Jet had focused her anxiety on what to wear to what might be a fancy restaurant in Manhattan. After suggesting Daryl stick around at the week-end drinks long enough to throw Shelley off the scent, he'd asked her whether she was going straight from the office. Which had made her realise she would need to change there too.

Untying the black dress coat she was wearing, she opened it to show him just as the doors pinged open, giving Leroy the perfect opportunity to get the wrong idea.

'I know he's romantically challenged, honey, but you don't need to flash him!' Leroy hollered.

Blushing furiously, Jet leapt out of the elevator, her coat still open.

'I didn't realise you were still here. I'm trying to get an opinion on this dress.'

'A little black number suits you.' Leroy appraised her. 'You look fabulous. What's the occasion?'

'I have a date,' Jet admitted sheepishly. 'With Roger.'

'I didn't think you wanted anything to do with that weirdo, let alone actively try to impress him?'

'She's more worried that New York will reject her British modesty,' Daryl said bluntly. 'You headed for the afterparty?'

'Yes, but I'm surprised you are. Shelley is on the prowl.'

'I'm aware.' Daryl shot Leroy a look. 'I'll handle it. Walk with you?'

'Sure, I just have to change my shirt.' Leroy dove into the office behind the desk.

'You look wonderful.' Daryl lowered his head to mutter in Jet's ear. 'Text me if you need me.'

'Thank you.' Jet smiled shyly, glancing over her shoulder at him quickly before Leroy could return.

He gave her a subtle nod. 'Time you were in a cab.'

Checking her watch, Jet realised he was right.

'Leroy, I have to run. Catch you later!'

'Go! Manhattan *needs* to see you in that dress.' He grinned, sticking his head around the office door.

'Gone, babe!' Jet giggled as she turned and headed for the street.

Roger had chosen what Rachel had informed her was a relatively up-market restaurant, in Greenwich Village. Not the type that had a waiting list the length of Broadway or required a hefty backhander to get a table on a Friday night, but still likely to be busy.

When the cab pulled up, Jet found Roger waiting at the door, hopping from foot to foot nervously. Feet that were still wearing sneakers.

Feeling vastly overdressed, Jet took her time paying the driver and sliding herself out of the cab.

'Wow,' she heard Roger exhale as she closed the car door behind her. 'You look stunning.' He smiled.

Crossing the sidewalk to meet him, Jet smiled back. 'Thanks.'

'I assumed you'd come straight from work.' He reached for her upper arm, laying his hand on her shoulder so tentatively she barely felt it as he leant forward to kiss her on the cheek.

'I did,' Jet confirmed. 'But you don't wear the kinds of things I wear to work on a date.'

What, Chucks? she asked herself, glancing again at his feet. If it was good enough for him, then it would have been good enough for her. His attire was the same as the week before, smart jeans and shirt, tucked in, tieless but a suit jacket over the top.

'Ah, well, this is me, day in, day out, work, dates, weekends, weddings, bar mitzvahs.' He spread his arms wide. 'Shall we?'

'Lead the way.' Jet smiled pleasantly.

'Hi Steve, my usual,' he said to the concierge.

'Your usual?' Jet asked as a waiter led them to the corner table in the window.

'I eat here every Friday night after work,' Roger admitted, laying a hand on her back. 'I'll take the seat by the wall, if that's OK with you.'

Realising he was steering her into the opposite chair so that he could scoot around her, Jet released a heavy breath through her nose.

'I bet you say that to all your dates,' she said lightly, her tone mocking.

The waiter paused to push her chair in but didn't offer to take her coat. Sitting quickly, she shrugged it off onto the back of the chair.

'You're the first woman to agree to accompany me.'

'You never brought your ex-wife here?' Jet asked archly, raising an eyebrow.

'Oh.' He deflated. 'No. I've only discovered it since the divorce.'

'Sorry. Sasha told me about the situation with your ex-wife,' Jet explained, feeling mean.

'It's alright. At least that way, I don't have to.' He looked up for the waiter, who came straight over with a bottle of white wine. 'Glass of wine?'

'Sure,' Jet said slowly as the waiter began de-corking it.

Teasing the menu between her fingertips, she shot a glance at the bottle. A Sauvignon Blanc. Just as well she didn't prefer a red.

The waiter poured Roger's glass first then Jet's, barely a half measure in each glass. Jet decided to bring her Bridget Jones out of the closet.

'Oh, don't go pouring half measures. Fill her up!' she said, and slathering on some extra accent, Jet lifted the glass to give the waiter better access.

Doing as he was asked, albeit with a look of disdain, the waiter then poured an equal measure into Roger's glass before placing the bottle into a cooler and leaving it with them on the table.

'Ah yes, you Brits love a drink.' Roger laughed and, raising his glass, toasted hers before she could take a large mouthful.

'Especially after a long work week,' Jet agreed. 'So, what do you recommend?'

'That you keep drinking,' he said, a smarmy glint in his eye.

'I meant on the menu,' she replied darkly.

'I was joking. I'm not the type to take advantage of a hot drunk redhead.' He laughed. 'Not on the first date, anyway.'

'That's good to know,' she said before taking another mouthful, her eyes on the street outside in longing.

Looking him up and down as he lifted his menu, she took in the all-American boyish grin he shot her from beneath a mousy-brown short back and sides, the bit at the top swept sideways with gel, and wondering whether it was all his own hair, decided she could just break a couple of his fingers if he tried anything.

He'd gone from lonely desperado to sleezeball in less time than it had taken the maître d's eyebrow to raise. Realising she was profiling him based on other slimeballs she'd met, she took a smaller sip of wine and tried to offer him the benefit of the doubt.

Arseholes got nervous too, right?

'Their main selection is pretty basic here, but the specials make this menu,' he announced suddenly. 'I can highly recommend the duck. They only bring it out once a month.'

'The pesto chicken looks great,' Jet said, reading from the main menu.

'A woman of simple tastes, huh?' He grinned.

'I like cooking with basil myself.' Jet smiled though inside she bristled.

'Bayzil.'

'Excuse me?' Jet blinked.

'You said Bahzil, it's Bayzil.'

'In your accent it is.' Jet snarked.

'It's adorable.'

'British expats your type?' Jet asked.

'And redheads.' He nodded in agreement, attempting to inconspicuously check out her tits. He failed miserably.

When she chose not to rise to his window shopping, he let his gaze settle on her cleavage for a full minute.

Get a good look, Jet thought, *this is the most you'll ever see.*

'So, how are you finding the New York dating scene?'

he asked suddenly. 'We'll both have the pesto chicken.'

The waiter, who had been making his way towards them, nodded and turned on his heel to head back to the kitchens.

'I . . .' Jet watched him go, realising there was no chance of asking for a side of garlic bread and that she was too shocked to be outraged. Her date ordering for her was a completely new level of absurd. 'I didn't move here to date.'

'But here you are?'

'Sasha is to blame for that.' Jet laughed in awe at the sheer craziness of the situation. 'What is it with women determined to set up their single friends?'

'You can't tell me you've never meddled in a friend's love life?'

'Not like this.' Jet shook her head. 'Perhaps a different kind of meddling . . .' She inclined her head with a look of mock-innocence as she watched a couple walk up the block hand in hand. 'No blind dates though.'

'I'd probably have let my dry spell last another year if it wasn't for Sasha . . .'

'You still might.' Jet whispered into her wine glass.

'She knows how lonely I've been since my wife left.' He sighed, his bravado dropping a couple of points.

'Loneliness is an avoidance of finding peace with yourself,' Jet replied.

'Wow, that's deep. You been married?'

'No.' Jet rolled the stem of her wine glass between her finger and thumb. 'I'm used to my own company.'

'Picky?'

'Writers don't get out much. We make our own company.' Jet rolled one shoulder back nonchalantly in a half shrug.

'We can soon sort that out. I have plenty of hobbies.'

'It doesn't need sorting out. Writing is my job.' Jet looked up, locking eyes with him.

'There's plenty of time to pick it back up again once the kids are grown up.'

'The what?!' Jet exclaimed, a little louder than she'd meant to.

'You must want kids, and soon, you're what? Late thirties?' he asked just as casually. 'I'm not afraid to have the kids talk. I've always wanted kids. It's wise to discuss these things early on, isn't it?'

'I don't want to have the kids talk,' Jet bit out, glancing to her right to make sure the nearest table wasn't witnessing their conversation.

'Oh . . . right, sensitive subject? Sorry.' He grimaced and glanced at the window himself. 'Moving on?'

'Yes.' Jet took a deep breath, wondering if he considered that a strike against her and whether she could bring herself to walk out before the main had arrived. She'd never done it before because she considered it to be rude to the restaurant.

Damn her British half.

'So, what are these hobbies of yours?'

'One second, I'll be back.' He held up a finger to stop her and sliding out of his seat, made a dash for the men's room.

While he was away, Jet pulled her phone out of her

purse three times in an attempt to write an SOS to Daryl. But she couldn't bring herself to do it. Damn her manners. He had agreed to help. She willed herself to get up.

No one is coming to save you, you can walk before he comes back from wherever he's disappeared to, she thought.

Also, you can handle this, food is ordered, eat, be polite, leave, block his number.

Jet lifted the wine glass to her lips again in agreement with herself, at the same time realising she was drinking too fast.

Roger finally returned ten minutes later, just in time for their main course.

'Well, this looks better than I'd expected, good choice.' He beamed as he cut into his chicken. 'So, you wanted to know my hobbies? Maybe one of them could be our second date?'

'That depends on the hobbies,' Jet humoured him.

'I enjoy hiking, rock climbing, and I'd love to take up Salsa dancing. Want to try out some dirty dancing with me?'

'No. Been there, tried that, still traumatised.'

'OK, not that.' He chuckled, spearing another piece of chicken.

As Roger continued to list of a range of things he either already did or wanted to try, Jet patiently listened and enjoyed her meal. The homemade pesto really was the best thing about the evening.

Laying her knife and fork across her plate, having

eaten without being allowed to say another word, and reaching for her wine glass to drain it, Jet nodded vacantly as Roger continued to list off all the musical instruments he'd tried to learn over the years, determined, he said, to master one of them.

'So, you can probably tell, I'm pretty handy with my mouth.' He waggled his eyebrows suggestively as he put his own fork down and dabbed his lips with his napkin.

Lost for words, Jet couldn't have been more relieved to see Daryl suddenly peering in the window next to them. It wasn't raining but his hair was soaked and sticking to his forehead, giving him a slightly crazed look.

Tapping at the glass, he pointed to her then to the door.

'Who the hell is that?' Roger asked taking in the size of Daryl as he glanced between them.

'That's my housemate,' Jet said slowly, genuinely confused. 'Excuse me, it must be urgent.' Getting up, Jet headed for the entrance to meet him.

'What the hell happened to you?' she asked looking at the state of his hair. 'What do you want?'

'I've burst a pipe back at the house, we have to find alternative accommodation for the night.' He glanced at the concierge. 'I'm really sorry to interrupt.'

'Shit. Well, can I go back there to get my things?'

'Plumbers are there now trying to shut the water off. We'll know more in the morning but it's OK to go back for essentials.'

'Fuck. Alright. Wait here. I'll be right back.' She left

him leaning against the wall.

Rushing back to the table, she scooped up her coat and bag.

'I'm so sorry Roger, the dumbass has burst a water main at home and I'm going to have to go.'

'Why? Can't he deal with it?'

'We need to find alternative accommodation overnight. I have to go.'

'You could always come back to mine?' he suggested quickly.

'I have to go. Do you want to split the bill?'

'If you don't mind. But I'll stay, I always have dessert and a coffee. My night isn't over quite yet.' He reclined in his seat, shooting daggers at Daryl. 'A fifty should cover it.'

'Fifty?' Jet staggered, she'd seen the cost of her main.

'The wine. You had a rather large glass.' He picked the bottle up to inspect what was left as she plucked her purse from her bag, thankful she'd grabbed more cash just in case.

Jet never expected a bill to be paid for her on any date, especially if she didn't plan on seeing the guy again. To eat and run wasn't her style.

Dropping a fifty-dollar bill onto the table, Jet turned sharply and left the restaurant, making Daryl scramble to catch her up.

She walked to the end of the block without a word before stopping.

'Why do you smell of beer?' she asked wildly as she turned on him.

'Because that's what Shelley threw all over me when I turned her down.' Daryl held his hands up in surrender.

'Wow, that's one fiery temper she has.' Jet laughed awkwardly as she tried to calm down.

'She's not the only one.' Daryl looked her up and down without judgement, which almost made her heart melt.

'Oh my god, thank you.' Jet sighed, relieved, before her eyes narrowed. 'But I didn't call you.'

'He looked like a loser,' Daryl teased as he looked over the top of her head back towards the restaurant, avoiding her eye.

'You have no idea!' Jet pinched the bridge of her nose before sliding her coat back on.

'How about I buy you a milkshake and you can explain?' Daryl smiled as he stuck his arm out to hail a cab.

'You still haven't explained either, what are you doing here?'

'Didn't you text me?' he asked with an innocence she didn't buy.

'No, I didn't, and who says I want a milkshake?' Jet folded her arms and raised an eyebrow.

'You need to cool off.'

'I'm fine. Really. Whatever made you decide I needed rescuing, thank you.' Jet sighed to calm herself and followed him to a cab as it pulled up.

TWENTY-ONE

'This is exactly the situation I try so hard to avoid. Smiling politely through strange behaviour, then feeling useless for putting up with it, even for an hour,' Jet whined. 'Why do I always find or get set up with the strange ones?' Her eyes widened.

'Have you ever set yourself up on a date with someone you haven't met online or through a friend?' Daryl laughed after Jet had finally stopped ranting about the way Roger had flipped the switch from Dr Joke to Mr Asshat.

'There needs to be booze in this.' Jet peered into her strawberry milkshake, almost sliding off the glittery pink stool she was sat on.

'There is.' Daryl chuckled, glancing at the waitress as he lifted his beer bottle off the chrome counter and took a swig. He'd tipped her extra to add a double shot of vodka when Jet had wandered off to find the toilets, grumbling something about alcoholic milkshakes as she went. 'You didn't answer my question.'

'Yes, I've made the first move,' Jet snapped. 'A couple of times.'

'Didn't they go any better?' he asked, his eyes alight with amusement as she swayed on the stool.

'No. In England it seems that, as a heterosexual female, if you make the first move with a heterosexual male, you're either desperate and terrify the fuck out of them or some slut who needs to get some too badly to even wait for or deserve the dodgy pickup lines first. I almost prefer scaring them off, the second type try to take advantage.' She ran her fingers through her hair and chewed on the straw before taking another sip.

'You didn't honestly think American men could possibly have more gentlemanly manners than British boys?' Daryl teased.

'I at least expected to be called ma'am before one tried to cop a feel.' Jet laughed.

'We're not all called Donald.' Daryl rolled his eyes.

'I bet even he doesn't wait 'till the girl is asleep before grabbing himself a bit of . . . never mind.' Jet stopped herself. 'We promised not to parade our pasts in front of each other.'

'Sounds like yours has been particularly . . . unusual, and maybe even in an illegal way.' Daryl's eyes were thunderous when she looked up.

'My tale may not sound like a happy one, part of that is my fault, but I have never actually come to any harm at the hands of a man.'

'I wouldn't be so sure of that.' He maintained eye contact as he finished his beer.

'Not physically anyway, others aren't so lucky,' Jet said quietly as she turned back to her shake and finished it.

'Do you want another, or shall we head home?'

'I couldn't drink another shake, but if you want another beer, I'll order something else next round.' Jet reached for the menu but stopped herself. 'You're still covered in beer and haven't told me why.'

'I did tell you why,' Daryl answered. 'Shelley.'

'Let's go home so you can get a shower, we don't want you getting arrested for being stinking drunk in public.'

'I'm not drunk.'

'You don't smell like it.' Jet smirked.

'How far can you walk in those shoes?'

'We are NOT walking home from here,' Jet hissed.

'It's not that far.' He grinned.

Glancing out of the window of the diner towards the Empire State Building a block over, she shot him a wide-eyed glare. 'It's nearly sixty blocks.'

'Sixty-one,' he corrected her.

'Fuck off,' Jet said bluntly as she slid carefully off the barstool.

'It is a nice evening, though.'

'And you're covered in beer,' she reminded him as they left the diner and she started trying to hail a cab.

'You suck at that,' he said, sticking his arm out and getting one immediately.

'Worked earlier,' she groused as he opened the door for her before stepping out into the street to get in the other door.

'Hey, one of you two got beer back there?' the driver

asked in alarm.

'It's in his hair not in his hand,' Jet explained.

'You have great aim.' The driver glanced in the rear-view mirror.

Jet glanced across at Daryl and couldn't help but giggle. Where the beer had dried, his hair had gone sticky and straw-like in the front.

'It wasn't me,' Jet said sucking in a deep breath as she spoke to stop herself laughing.

'You're headed home to make it up to each other, I guess?' The driver laughed.

Expecting Daryl to defend himself, Jet looked over to see him staring pointedly in the other direction.

'The only thing he's getting up to tonight is a shower,' Jet informed the driver.

Thankfully, the driver didn't have time to make the conversation any more awkward, he was soon too busy yelling out the window at a police officer on horseback diverting vehicles around a fender-bender further up.

As the driver rerouted, Jet lay her head back and enjoyed the sounds of a warm night in the city beyond her open window. The buzz of conversation at outdoor restaurants, music booming out of open apartment windows and the rush of warm air as it entered the cab. She waited until they were home and stood in the hall before she spoke again.

'After your shower, do you want a coffee in the garden?' she asked gently.

'I think I might need to just fall into bed,' he admitted, rubbing his eyes. 'It's been a long week.'

'What did Shelley say to you?'

'She told me to stop playing games and take her to dinner already.' Daryl had walked to the foot of the stairs, but turned slowly, his arms folded.

'What did you say to make her throw her drink?' Jet asked curiously, looking up from where she was bent double, trying to get the ankle straps of her shoes unbuckled.

'I told her I wasn't interested in dating at all right now.' He glanced upwards at the mess of his hair. 'She screamed at me, called me a liar, and tossed the drink before walking out.'

'She's probably convinced that you had a date Tuesday.' Jet bit her lip. 'Are you alright?'

'Me? She's the one who made a fool of herself.'

'Sorry. Rachel told me she's been extra jealous since I started working with you. If she asks, I try to avoid getting dragged into what always turns into an information dig.'

'It's where we both work.' He sighed. 'You're allowed to say my name.'

'Exactly.'

'At least I'm not there every day.' He unfolded his arms to reach up and pick at his hair. 'Besides, it gave me chance to leave before . . . I just decided to walk in the vague direction of Greenwich in case you needed me. Are you OK?'

'I'm fine. I'll just go back to my simple, quiet life, writing imaginary romances rather than wasting my energy on trying to live them.' Jet offered him a twisted smile, refusing to meet his eyes as she finally stepped out of her shoes and reached down to pick them up.

After a brief silence, Daryl nodded as if to himself and turned to begin climbing the stairs.

'Thank you,' Jet said as she followed him. 'Not just for being my wingman tonight, but also for not giving me any of the usual bullshit advice.'

'Like, there's someone out there for everyone?'

'Yeah, that.'

'It's not true, is it?' he asked on a sigh, attempting to meet her eye, but she didn't look up.

'Not for everyone,' Jet agreed. 'Though the future's not ours to see.'

Nodding again, to himself, Daryl headed into his room as they both muttered "Goodnight".

As his door closed behind him, Jet heard him remove his belt buckle and clothing hit the floor as he stripped on the way to the bathroom. Glancing back too late, once the door had closed, she chastised herself for looking.

Changing into her oversized hoodie and a pair of leggings, Jet scooped up a book and headed down to the garden to sit amongst the deck lights and listen to the fountain.

Popping into the kitchen for a cup of tea, she considered whether Daryl would let her string some festoon or fairy lights around the garden perimeter to make it even more inviting as summer took hold.

Sitting with her cup in one hand and the book in the other, Jet looked up when Daryl's bedroom light went on. Peering into the remains of her tea, she realised he'd been in the shower a long time.

The angle up to the bedroom didn't offer her much of a chance to see what he was up to, so she went back to the book.

Moments later, distracted by the feeling of being watched, Jet glanced up again.

He was at the window, towel around his hips. She couldn't be sure, but it looked as though the skin of his torso was a little red, as though he'd turned the shower up extra hot.

Before she could think to get a better look, he'd closed the curtains.

TWENTY-TWO

Fighting back a yawn, Jet pressed the intercom buzzer and stepped back to wait. She'd stayed up until her mind had quietened enough to go to sleep, having stayed in the garden until her fingers were too cold to turn the page of her book.

Between the way Roger had behaved and Daryl had shut down on her in the cab ride home, she'd found her mind racing. Not just about the night she'd had, but on the past. Something she knew it was dangerous to dwell on.

She hated herself for how much she'd told him. He didn't need to know her shit. Hell, she wished she didn't know half the crap she'd put herself through with men.

Her brain had still been racing after her body gave in and she passed out as the sun was coming up. Vivid dreams had plagued her sleep to the point that she didn't feel she had really slept at all.

Breathing in the notorious heated-concrete smell that Manhattan had, she smiled to herself and pressed the buzzer again. She wasn't alone, she had friends and family.

'Sorry! Come on up!' Rachel called through the intercom as the entry door clicked open.

Making her way up to the fourth floor, Jet heaved her bag onto her shoulder, wincing when glass rattled inside, and wondered if the girls would be able to tell she was feeling rough. She hated it when people made a fuss.

'Hey!' Veronica opened the door as she approached and pulled her inside. 'Hope you brought your PJs!'

'As instructed.' Jet patted the bag on her shoulder.

'I can't remember the last time I was at a slumber party,' Tracy said bluntly as she wandered out of the bathroom in an electric blue camisole set as they entered the large open-plan living area. 'I might have been thirteen.'

'Oh, lighten up.' Sasha pulled her down onto a mound of cushions and blankets that they'd thrown around the floor and couch.

'This place is amazing, is it an old factory or something?' Jet asked glancing around her at the industrial themed apartment.

Large grid-paned and undressed windows looked out onto the buildings beyond, while metal and brass featured heavily in the kitchen area set against exposed brickwork and old-fashioned filament bulbs hanging from black wires.

'Yeah, it was, though I can never remember what they made here,' Rachel said from the couch, a blanket wrapped around her.

'Shoes,' Sasha reminded her. 'You know, those things you buy just to line your closet.'

'Men's shoes.' Rachel pointed at her, remembering. 'Which is why I file the information away.'

'I brought wine,' Jet announced, plucking three bottles from her bag to lighten the load on her shoulder.

'There's room in the fridge, go get changed while I pour you a glass,' Veronica offered as she took them from her.

'Thanks, I hope everyone drinks white wine?' Jet smiled. 'Where's the best place to change?'

'Pick any room, we won't peek,' Tracy drawled playfully.

Shooting her an amused look of shock, Jet went through the nearest door, which happened to be the bathroom.

Slipping out of her jeans and into jogging bottoms, she kept her t-shirt on and swapped her jacket for a soft cardigan and her sneakers for fluffy socks.

Veronica was holding her glass of wine out for her as she emerged, whilst taking a mouthful from another glass.

'This is good stuff.' She appraised the glass as Jet relieved her of the second glass and they joined the others. 'Where'd you get it?'

'My housemate has tonnes of the stuff. He insisted I took some of it off his hands.' Jet smiled and tasted the wine herself. 'Oh, that is nice. I had to take his word for it.'

'That's a point, where are you living?' Rachel narrowed her eyes in Jet's direction.

'I told you, I found a house share in the Upper West.' Jet glanced in Rachel's direction but hadn't failed to notice that they were all looking at her. 'What?'

'Would this housemate be particularly clumsy with pipes?' Sasha asked, her eyes wide in mock innocence.

'And look like a bit of a jock?' Rachel licked her lips.

'You've heard from Roger,' Jet sighed.

'Yes, I have.' Sasha laughed. 'He messaged me to tell you he never wants to see your fussy as fuck double timing ass ever again.'

'He said that?!' Jet spluttered as she sat forward too quickly and almost spilled her wine. 'Cheeky bastard.'

'He was actually more colourful in tone than that. But as you're bringing wine from a supposedly flooded house . . .' Tracy explained.

'We assume it did not go well,' Veronica interjected.

'What actually happened?' Rachel asked, wide-eyed with excitement. 'And do you really have a fit-to-fuck housemate?'

'I got the impression he was pretty pissed when he made me split the bill.' Jet smirked. 'He wasn't going to get to see my ass, double-timing or otherwise, ever again anyway. But I can see why he might have thought my housemate was competition. They're very different, um… types. I guess you could call my housemate fit, he works out.' Jet laughed.

'Is he single?' Rachel grinned.

'As far as I know. I don't really know him, I just rent

a room.' Jet took a large swig from her glass to cover the false truths.

'Next girl's night is at yours, then,' she teased.

'I'd have to ask his permission on that one.' Jet laughed, planning never to do anything of the sort. 'He came in bloody handy last night though, I've never had to run away from a date before. Or at least, I've never had the guts to be that rude.'

'Honey, if he's going to talk about you the way he did in my texts, he deserves to be single for a very long time. No decent man bad-mouths a woman, or anyone, like that.' Sasha shook her head. 'Let him go to hell.'

'I kinda wanna know what he said now.' Jet frowned.

'You sure about that?' Tracy asked. 'I've seen them.'

'It won't be worse than what I've had text to me directly before.' Jet held out her hand. 'Let me see.'

'Alright,' Sasha said, giving in, and scrolling through her phone to the right messages, handed the device over.

Taking a mouthful of wine for courage as she accepted the phone, Jet almost choked on it straight away.

They all sat in silence as she scrolled up and down the barrage of insults he'd sent to Sasha.

'Wow. Prick. I'm sorry he dragged you into this, Sasha. Will he be a problem at work?'

'Nah, he's in a different department. I don't have to see him either.' She waved dismissively as she took the phone back.

'Good.' Jet nodded. 'And that's exactly why I don't date.'

'What do you mean?' Veronica asked, getting up to retrieve the rest of the bottle she had opened and offered top ups.

'I tend to bring the asshole out in even the best of them,' Jet said lightly.

'Well, you're doing something wrong, I've never seen him talk about anyone quite that way before. Even his ex-wife,' Sasha said jovially but Tracy punched her on the arm. 'Oww, what?'

'It's fine, she's right,' Jet laughed. 'When it happens often enough you have to take a look inwards. No one's that unlucky. It's mostly that I don't like dating and I'm cynical as hell.' She grinned.

Ignoring her inner voice, which told her she was just a scaredy cat, Jet took another mouthful of wine.

'There's a reason I don't want anything more than a good fuck and why Rachel has a type,' Veronica said. 'We're all just as flawed as the partners we seek. No one's perfect.'

'It just takes the right one to see your bullshit clearly enough to tell you it's bullshit and persist,' Sasha said gently, looking at Tracy.

'Ain't that the truth.' Tracy pecked her on the nose. 'So, which horrifically cheesy rom-com are you planning to subject me to tonight?'

'Why not a horror movie instead?' Rachel asked, reaching for a large bowl of popcorn on the coffee table.

'Because we always watch something horrifically cheesy on Skint Saturday,' Veronica pointed out for Jet's benefit. 'It lifts our spirits.'

'Skint Saturday? This is a regular thing?' Jet looked at them all in turn with amusement.

'Last weekend before pay day,' Rachel explained. 'We all throw the last of our cash into a pot and see how many pizzas we can order in with it and stick a "happy" movie on.'

'PJs are usually optional,' Tracy deadpanned.

'It doesn't have to be a slumber party every month,' Sasha soothed. 'That was just our ruse to get Jet here and drunk enough to spill the beans about what really happened last night.'

'Ah, one more glass might just do it. Especially after seeing those texts.' Jet held her glass up to inspect the dwindling contents. 'What happened to the pizza?' She pouted.

'You're looking at it.' Rachel lifted the popcorn. 'We bought snacks instead.'

'We bought frozen and cooked them earlier,' Veronica explained.

'Has your new place got a decent... kitchen?' Rachel asked, fixing an overly interested look on her face as she popped a couple of kernels of popcorn in her mouth.

'The whole house is gorgeous. It's just like the one my gran had but it's been totally remodelled. The kitchen even has a proper coffee machine.'

'Like we have at the office?' Rachel frowned.

'Like they have at Starbucks.' Jet's eyes went wide.

'Fuck, what does your housemate do? Don't tell me he works at Starbucks?'

'He had no idea how to use it. He's obviously a sucker for a salesman, or thought it would be easier than it looked.' She smirked.

'Sounds like an architect or investment banker to be buying that kind of toy.' Rachel gazed up at the ceiling dreamily. 'And those houses definitely have room for a wife and couple of kids as well as a lodger. I wouldn't expect you to move out right away or anything.'

'Gee, thanks,' Jet drawled but smiled as she chose to ignore the question about what he did.

No point digging a deeper hole than necessary, there would be hell to pay if they ever found out who she really lived with.

TWENTY-THREE

'Leon?' Jet addressed her manager as she tapped on the frame of his open office door.

'Hi Jet, what's the problem?' He swivelled in his chair to face her, his legs spread and fingers tip to tip under his chin.

'No problem as such. I just wondered whether I could take some leave at the end of next week?' Resisting the urge to fold her arms uncomfortably, she chose instead to lean against the door, going for casual.

'You're not quite out of probation yet, so you're not technically entitled to any time off, what's it for?'

'A friend of mine is flying in next weekend from London, she'll only be here for a few days.' Jet bit her lip, pausing for thought. 'What if I made the hours back?'

'You can have one day, provided you make the hours up. Which day do you want?' He turned back to his desk and opened his calendar. 'Do we have any meetings booked?'

Swallowing down a snort of derision, knowing Leon never gave them that much notice for meetings in the first place, she took her phone from her pocket and checked Mai's last message.

'Friday would be great, I can easily build the hours into the first four days so that I'm ahead for the week after.'

'Thank you for thinking this through before asking. I like your resourcefulness.' Leon barely looked up at her as he blocked the day in his diary and sent her an email invite to mark it in her own.

As if she could forget what promised to be the biggest lunch meeting of her writing career to date.

'If a meeting does come up, will you be able to run in?'

'If a meeting comes up before I leave for the weekend on the Thursday evening, I will ensure you have all the necessary information and documentation to handle it without me,' Jet answered smoothly and evenly. 'Thank you.'

Turning quickly, able to see that he wanted to answer her back but hadn't quite found the words, Jet walked away before he could go back on his word and, on returning to her desk, accepted the invite and immediately informed HR.

She didn't like the idea that he could call a meeting for the Friday and insist she turn up for it despite having done extra hours, so she emailed herself a copy of his calendar invite.

'What was that all about?' Shelley asked darkly from behind her monitor.

Since the incident with Daryl, Shelley hadn't spoken his name once, not in front of Jet anyway, who had noticed that her attitude towards her had flipped.

No stranger to the blunt questions and being ignored, Jet knew that as far as Shelley was concerned, she was enemy number one. And that was without anyone knowing she was Daryl's lodger.

As suspected, Shelley had put five and five together and made a hundred. The narrow-eyed glances and frequent silences were enough for Jet to build a narrative in her own mind regarding what Shelley probably believed was the truth. The mention of those game tickets had planted the very seed Jet had hoped wouldn't grow.

'I need a day off next week,' Jet replied politely. 'I have a friend coming over from London.'

'A male friend?' Shelley asked quickly.

'No, a female one.' Jet smirked. 'Why, does it matter?'

'I thought you had a date recently, that's all.' She waved her bangled arm dismissively.

'I did. The guy was a jerk.'

'A bit of a jerk? A total player?' Shelley suddenly appeared over the top of her monitor, her eyes narrow and spoiling for a bitching session.

'No, a desperate divorcee.' Jet looked up and held her gaze.

'Oh,' Shelley said as she disappeared back behind her monitor.

Almost able to hear her brain chewing that one over, Jet shook her head and reached for her phone to let Mai know she could make the meeting.

She sighed when she saw three emails had landed since she'd returned to her desk. All from Larry. Assignments for the next week.

Realising she would have to work until at least 8p.m. every night to make up the hours for Leon, she had to turn down two of them instantly.

The third was on the Thursday night.

Mai was arriving at 2p.m. on the Thursday.

The whole week was a write off for Larry.

She cursed under her breath. Daryl had warned her not to piss the guy off.

Taking a deep breath, she composed an email in return to confirm that she would, regrettably, be unavailable all week.

Then she text Mai.

Then she text Daryl in a mild panic that Larry would drop her down the favourability list.

Glad there were no meetings that night, Jet packed up on time and headed for home. She hadn't heard back from Daryl or Larry, though Mai was thrilled enough to make up for both of them.

Her mind took a welcome pause as she entered the subway, knowing none of them could get through to her down there anyway.

'You come here often?'

Pausing as she retrieved her earbuds from her pocket, Jet looked up with what she knew was an overly sarcastic glare.

'Nightly, actually.' She smirked when she found Daryl

at her side. 'You're out early.'

'Actually, I'm out late. I should have left an hour ago, but Tom had me fix something that simply couldn't wait. I could say the same for you.' He looked her up and down as he stepped from foot to foot, his record bag over his shoulder, hands shoved in the pockets of the coat he deliberately wore a size too big.

'I couldn't bear the thought of a last-minute meeting just as freedom was in view.'

'Did you forget I was in the office today?'

'What makes you ask that?'

'You usually DM me, not text me, when we're in the office together.'

'This was about the other work, and no, I didn't think. Sorry, did anyone see?'

'No, it's fine. Dangerous ground with your desk buddy though.' He swayed from side to side as they waited for their train. 'Larry will be cool with you blocking out a week. It might be a little short notice, but it's freelance for a reason, and he has a black book the width of his fist for that same reason.'

'I just don't want to lose the opportunities to write now I have them.'

'So maybe it's time you lost the opportunity to tinker with training courses.' Daryl raised his eyebrows as he pursed his lips.

'Leon is pissed that I asked for time off, isn't he? What have you heard?' Jet screwed her face up as she raised a hand to rub her forehead.

The roar of the approaching train caused Daryl to wait

until they'd boarded to answer her, which only caused a humorous level of panic to appear in her eyes.

'Relax.' He smiled, amused. 'Nothing's been said, but do you really need three jobs?'

'I don't have three jobs,' Jet returned in a mocking tone, but stopped herself. 'The other two don't pay the bills.'

'I hear your landlord gave you a sweet-as deal, could the writing sustain that?' He had been paying attention to those on the train around them, but slid his eyes sideways to her as they took seats for the journey uptown.

'It's not stable work.' Jet shrugged.

'Stop being afraid of yourself, will you?' He closed his eyes as he lay his head back and slid down in his seat.

Looking around the rocking carriage at the faces of many other New Yorkers on their way home from jobs they either loved or hated, Jet eventually settled her gaze on the floor in order to overthink his suggestion.

TWENTY-FOUR

'What the hell just happened?! You never mentioned it was a BIG studio!' Jet screeched at Mai in an explosion of enthralled horror once they were safely clear of the lengthy lunch meeting the company had arranged at the Rockefeller Center.

'It gets better than that,' Mai admitted before biting her lip and shooting her a big brown-eyed stare from beneath her chocolate-coloured curls.

'How can it?' Jet fought the urge to grin.

'If the deal goes ahead, our parent company want to throw more budget my way to increase the imprint's standing and get more books out of you. Which means bigger advances for more manuscripts than we normally contract you for at a time.'

Jet's head snapped sideways fast enough to give her whiplash as she gawped at Mai.

'More books? In the same series?'

'Could you do it?'

'How many are we talking?'

'At least five.'

'They're not going to make ten movies.' Jet shook her head in disbelief.

'But the fans will probably read ten books.' Mai pointed at her. 'At least. And you know what fandoms do. Look at previous big-selling-book-based movie series.'

'Even the someone I think you mean stopped at seven.'

'Last I looked they were still managing to make movies with her name on.' Mai smirked. 'You never know.'

'True. Though the first movie could flop, we both know all it takes is a terrible cast and the whole thing will be yesterday's stale popcorn.'

'Lighten up will you.'

'I'm being realistic.'

'Well, start getting excited enough to at least take me shopping.'

'What happened to the wild celebrations?' Jet smirked.

'We did too much of that last night.' Mai rubbed her head.

Jet had to agree with her on that one. In the excitement of a reunion in Manhattan, they had trawled all the bars in the vicinity of the Wellington for a catch up and way too many cocktails. The jetlag and booze had hit the rights manager, Netta, extra hard and she'd gone back to the hotel earlier than Mai with the excuse of prepping for the meeting.

After the meeting ended, she offered to head back to the hotel to write up the meeting notes and inform the UK office of next steps.

'She wants a nap.' Mai had laughed after she'd left. 'I've told her to meet us when she feels ready. Though I wouldn't be surprised if that's not until dinner now.'

'Where do you want to shop?' Jet asked. 'Up Fifth Avenue and Bloomingdales? Or down towards Macey's?'

'Where's Tiffany's from here?'

'North, not far from Bloomingdales.'

'Let's go north, we can do Macey's after breakfast tomorrow and work our way back up.' Mai grinned.

'Is that all you want to do while you're here? Shop?' Jet sniggered.

'Like you, I've done the touristy bits, this is a business trip and so I feel that's the perfect excuse to waste all my spare time melting my credit card.'

'What time is your flight?'

'Midnight tomorrow night.'

'Ouch.'

'Yeah, the deal isn't in the bag yet, I could only swing for two nights hotel stay. They want us back in the office ready to negotiate from Monday, so back we go.' Mai sighed. 'I'll just have to come back for a holiday.'

'Yes, you will.' Jet grinned as they began heading up Fifth Avenue.

'Don't you just feel like Holly Golightly?' Mai said with a whimsical smile. 'We even look the part.'

Jet considered her fitted black shift dress and Mai's

maroon number of a similar cut and decided that they did indeed look like the kind of career girls movies set in the city loved to portray.

'Ooh, Saks!' Mai suddenly cooed, dragging Jet to the crosswalk.

'It ain't no Camden Market.' Jet sighed as they stepped into Saks. 'But it will do.'

'Ah, Camden misses you too.' Mai glanced at her with a playful pout as she headed for a display of bags. 'Will you pop back soon?'

'Let's see how it goes.' Jet resisted the urge to touch a particularly pretty midnight blue bag when she could see it didn't have a price tag. 'I'll bet that bag costs more than my last advance.'

'One could buy everything one's gothic little heart desired in Camden for the price of just one of these bags.' Mai's eyes widened. 'But that's not the point, is it?'

Her fingers drifted over the shelf, barely daring to touch even that.

'Depends.' Jet grinned. 'I've never really fallen in love with a label enough to spend four figures on a single item.'

'Neither have I, yet. Let's see if I can't break that habit today. But maybe not in here,' Mai said wistfully. 'Let's do a lap of each floor though, just for the hell of it.'

'We have all day. Or at least until Netta catches up with us.' Jet spread her arms.

'Her loss if she doesn't, she'll just have to make herself a shopping list for tomorrow.' Mai pouted. 'You should at least pop back for your birthday in August.'

'I have a job, popping across the pond might not be something they look favourably on,' Jet pointed out. 'Let's start at the top and work our way down,' she suggested, heading for the escalator.

'If we sell these rights, you can tell that job where to poke it. Then you can zip over the pond whenever you like.'

'Steady on,' Jet warned. 'I like it here.'

'There's a bench in Leicester Square with your name on it,' Mai cooed.

'Don't do that . . .' Jet complained playfully. 'Fine. I'll see what I can do about getting a week in August.'

'Yay. Hopefully, we'll be celebrating much more by then too.' Mai dived at her, wrapping her arms around her neck.

'You never know,' Jet said with a whimsical laugh as they reached the top of the escalator and Mai let her go in favour of a rack of dresses.

Following her, Jet realised her phone was ringing in her bag. Expecting it to be Leon, she was tempted to ignore it. Tugging the device free, she found Larry on the caller ID.

'Larry, hi.' Jet beamed as she answered the call with a wave to Mai, though her face fell as Larry began talking.

Mai kept peering over the rack after her attempts at waving dresses in front of her friend had failed to get attention. Jet was nodding and pulling faces and glancing at Mai worriedly.

'I have visitors in the city tonight, but if you can swing

for an extra ticket, I'm sure I could talk them into a change of plans.' Jet knew she was pushing her luck, he'd offered her two as it was, but he sounded stuck.

'What was that all about?' Mai raised an eyebrow as Jet grinned sheepishly at her.

'How do you fancy going to a movie premier tonight?'

'What? How?'

'Remember I told you I've been taking on some reviews? Well, there's been a last-minute dropout tonight and I've managed to swing for an extra couple of tickets to cover it, on the proviso that you and Netta can come with me.'

'Now I definitely need a new dress!' Mai grabbed her arm and gave it an excited squeeze. 'But not in here, I'm not that desperate to melt my credit card!'

'Don't get too excited. Knowing the assignment level I'm at, we're talking C-list celebs at best, it won't be a biggy. Also, it's a Friday night, meaning it's likely to be a preview screening or arthouse more than a red carpet event.'

'Don't spoil my daydream.' Mai pouted and, using the grip she had on Jet's forearm, pulled her back towards the escalators where they made their way back to ground level and out onto the street.

'Couldn't he have given you four tickets, one extra for your housemate?' Mai asked as they once again headed up Fifth Avenue.

'He also writes reviews for this guy, so if Larry had to come to me, he's probably already asked Daryl. He might have another assignment tonight.' Jet shrugged.

'Pity.' Mai smirked. 'You still haven't sent me a picture of him.'

'Because I don't have one!' Jet laughed, exasperated. 'I'm not going to randomly take a picture of him and he's not on social media.'

'He's a freelancer, he must have a website or LinkedIn or something!' Mai asked desperately.

'He has those for professional purposes,' Jet agreed.

'Then there must be a photo. It's unprofessional to have LinkedIn and no photo.'

'He has an image.'

'So, let's see it!'

'It's his website's logo.' Jet grinned.

'Oh, for fuck's sake.' Mai sighed. 'This promises to be a long afternoon. Let's get a coffee.'

'Well, it is practically illegal to pass a coffee shop and not go in,' Jet agreed as Mai steered her towards a Starbucks. 'But if you do that here you'll never get anything else done.'

Looking up the street as they headed into the café, she could clearly see the next in the chain in the distance.

After a power-up in the form of an iced coffee, Mai dragged Jet into every high street clothing store from Saks to Bloomingdales. However, by the time they reached Bloomingdales they each had a new dress, as did Netta who had managed to catch up.

Tucking her small Tiffany's purchase inside the bag holding a collection of dresses, Mai sighed as they entered Bloomingdales.

'I'm about done in,' she admitted. 'But I might have to get me one of their famous bags.'

'The brown ones?' Netta asked. 'I've been told I have to go back with one of those for my sister-in-law's birthday.'

'We'll do a quick scout around, then we should think about grabbing food and getting changed.' Jet nodded.

'Maybe we should have cocktails to start the evening too?' Mai waggled her eyebrows but Netta went visibly green.

'Probably best we don't,' Jet said, coming to the rescue of the rights manager. 'After all the shopping today, we'll be struggling to stay awake during the film as it is.'

TWENTY-FIVE

'Aren't you a bit over dressed for a reporter?'

Startled, Jet looked up at the man who had appeared next to her. He smiled with twinkling brown eyes and offered her his hand.

'I've been to enough of these screenings to recognise the reviewers. I'm Jim, I scored the movie.'

Shaking his hand, Jet found herself smiling back. 'That obvious huh? I'm Jet.'

'I hope you and your friends enjoy the movie.' He glanced over at Mai and Netta waiting at a nearby table, staring at the exchange. He offered them a little wave to let them know he knew they were watching. 'I had a lot of fun composing for it.'

'I would hope so. Aren't you supposed to enjoy your job?' Jet raised an eyebrow.

'It helps,' he admitted with a laugh. 'Don't drink too many of those, you need to pay attention in there.'

Looking back at the three cocktails on the bar as they arrived one by one, Jet found herself searching for words as he flicked a lock of dark hair from his forehead.

'Combining girls' night with work has its occupational hazards, I guess,' she said eventually and reached for the drinks.

'Have you travelled from the UK to see this film?' he asked, stopping her from leaving the bar as he moved in to place his order.

'They have travelled from the UK to see me. I live here.' Jet smirked.

'Really?' His eyebrows raised as he shamelessly gave her a head to toe once over. 'I'd have remembered seeing you around the circuit, surely.'

'I haven't been here long. Just a couple of months now.' She smiled, realising he was flirting and, picking up the glasses, began to turn away.

'Well, hopefully I'll catch you again.' He shot her a flirtatious smile, collecting a beer from the bar before turning in the opposite direction.

'Who was that?!' Mai fanned herself with her handbag as she watched him go. 'And where can I get one?'

'He's the composer for the film we're about to see. And this room is crawling with movie crew, take your pick.' Jet extended her arm in the direction of the hordes of men stood around drinking and congratulating each other.

'They're not all as good looking as that one.'

'Jim,' Jet said, remembering his name. 'I reserve judgement until I've heard his work.'

'Well, this isn't the red carpet event Mai hoped for, as

you warned, but there are free drinks, at least,' Netta piped up, sniffing her drink. 'I'll be OK with one.'

'It's a pretty big theatre though, there were photographers out front, and it's a free night out with a lot of movie-making creatives. Some of whom are very good looking.' Mai grinned as her eyes scanned the room.

'Jim thought we were overdressed.' Jet grimaced.

'Bollocks. There's a group of women over there positively dripping in bling . . . and fake boobs,' Mai hushed her. 'He was just chatting you up.'

Tilting her head with a pout, Jet considered that for a moment, then agreed with a nod. 'They could be actresses, but fair point.'

'Have you met many good-looking Americans since being here?' Netta asked, wide-eyed, over her drink.

'There are good-looking men everywhere, but yes, New York doesn't generally disappoint.' Jet wrinkled her nose playfully.

'Jet doesn't date if she can help it,' Mai informed Netta.

'Why not?!' Netta's eyes widened even further.

'If one of these Americans turned my head, how would I ever get the next book written?' Jet took a mouthful of her own drink but found her eyes wandering towards where Jim was laughing with a group of people.

'She'll be one of those writers who becomes a total recluse and dies at her keyboard aged ninety-something.' Mai shot Jet a look with a smirk. 'They're opening the doors, shall we go bag ourselves some seats?'

'Ooh, complimentary popcorn too,' Netta announced as cinema staff appeared and started handing out small pots of popcorn to those entering the screen.

Allowing herself to be guided by her excited guests, Jet shouldered her bag and followed them towards the doors.

'Will you be attending the afterparty?'

'Do you have a habit of sneaking up on women?' Jet glanced over her shoulder at Jim.

'Only the really pretty ones.'

'Nice line.' Jet smirked up at him.

'Stick around after the show if you and your friends are up for a party.' He winked before slipping back into the crowd.

'We're sticking around after, for sure.' Mai was stood directly in front of Jet as she refocused her attention forwards, causing her to almost walk into her editor.

'Let's not write off your last day with hangovers,' Jet warned as they entered the screen and sought out some seats near the back.

After twenty minutes of back-slapping speeches that put Jet a little on edge with the sheer amount of self-congratulation amongst what was clearly a largely male crew, the film finally got underway.

Realising very quickly that the only thing with more testosterone than the audience was the movie itself, they were all relieved when it only lasted ninety minutes, though despite having had a nap mid-afternoon, Netta managed to fall asleep and needed nudging awake as the lights came up ready for even more speeches.

'Can't we sneak out?' Mai whispered in Jet's ear.

'No one else is leaving and with the house lights up, it will be bloody obvious if we're the first to go,' she muttered back.

The director returned to the stage to a hearty round of applause from many of the other guests, family, friends and press. As he started speaking again, Jet noticed a few other press members get up and start to file out.

'That's our cue.' Jet nodded to Netta, who had the aisle seat.

'What?' Netta looked from Jet to the rest of the audience, confused. 'Oh. Thank god.'

Taking their lead, a few audience members around them backed them up by leaving at the same time.

'Wow, what was that?' Netta asked as they left the screen.

'I hope it wasn't all that bad.' Jim appeared suddenly, returning from the men's room. 'Has Dan got up to give another speech?'

'He has,' Jet responded. 'The music was pretty good though.'

'Pretty good?'

'I'm no composer, but it worked.' Jet nodded and started leading the others towards the exit.

'What about the afterparty?' he called after them. 'You promised you'd come.'

'I never promised anything, we've had a long day, it's

probably best we call it a night.' Jet smiled apologetically. 'I'll see you around the circuit, as you said.'

'Not even for one? They're still complimentary.' He grinned.

'A nightcap, and then a cab wouldn't be a terrible idea.' Mai pouted.

'Alright. One,' Jet said to Mai.

'Wait right here ladies, I'll get them.' Jim steered them back to one of the standing tables in the lobby and headed towards the bar where theatre staff were preparing trays of drinks.

'I hope no one asks me if I enjoyed it.' Netta pulled a face as crew began filling the lobby, the speeches finally over.

'Jim probably just wants to make sure I don't write a shit review.' Jet shot a glance over her shoulder.

'Here we are, ladies.' Jim reappeared with a whole tray of cocktails. 'It's ok, you don't have to drink them all.'

Sliding the tray into position, he handed them each a drink in turn, starting with Jet.

'So, how are you two enjoying New York?' he asked Mai and Netta.

'I love it here. It's a shame it's only a short trip,' Netta said stroppily as she took a mouthful of her drink.

Determined not to drink too much, Jet deliberately only sipped at her drink. She had to write up her notes before going to bed.

'Which hotel did you choose?' Jim asked, sliding a glance Jet's way.

Mai caught the intent behind his question and smirked. 'We're staying at the Wellington. We haven't met Jet's housemate yet so it would have been rude to invite ourselves along.'

'Not one for uninvited houseguests, huh?' Jim laughed.

'It's not a hotel.' Jet shrugged, her words sounding far more blunt than she'd intended.

'Found herself a swanky house share in the Upper West Side, lucky thing.' Netta blinked her wide eyes dreamily. 'I would have liked to see it.'

'Maybe next time.' Jet widened her eyes in warning at the tipsy rights manager.

'It is a nice area.' Jim shoved his hands in his pockets and nodded. 'I'm up that way myself. So, are you going to give me an excellent review, even if you didn't enjoy the movie?'

'I'm going to give it a fair review. It's not my job to be opinionated. One girl's hard watch is another's inspiration.'

'Ooh, quote that. I like it.' Untucking his hands, he reached for one of the drinks and drank it down in one.

'Art isn't made to please everyone, after all, is it?' Jet returned a strained smile.

'This is true.' He clinked his empty glass against hers.

'It still needs to sell,' Mai pointed out. 'If the writer wants to make another.'

'Also, very true.' He tipped his head in acknowledgement at Mai. 'What do you guys do?'

'Well, I'm Jet's editor, and this is Netta, our rights

manager.' Mai smiled.

'Editor for what?' Jim grinned as he turned on Jet.

'Novels. This isn't just a pleasure trip. We all had a meeting today,' Netta spewed the words out before she could stop herself, suddenly sounding tipsy.

'Publishing is our game,' Mai agreed, also looking a little glazed.

'And you both need to be on a flight tomorrow, so I think it might be about time we called it a night,' Jet announced, realising they would both crash out soon if she didn't get them in a cab.

'But you haven't finished your drinks yet.' Jim smiled.

'I have!' Netta claimed, downing the last of hers.

'I've had enough. I want to do some more shopping tomorrow.' Mai took one last mouthful of her drink and put it down, almost empty.

'And I have to write this review and be awake enough to play tour guide in the morning.' Jet had barely touched her drink but took one last sip to be polite. 'It's been lovely to meet you, I'm sure I'll see you around.'

'Well, I'm about done here. Can I share your cab? I'm going your way,' Jim asked quickly. 'I'll just grab my coat and meet you out front.'

'Are you going to be OK going up town with him?' Mai asked, a scowl on her face as they stumbled out onto the sidewalk.

Checking her phone, Jet looked back at the lobby then at her two wobbly companions.

'I'm sure it will be fine. Please drink plenty of water when you get back to the room,' she teased. 'I can't show you shit tomorrow if you're hungover.'

Seeing Jim, jacket on, talking to someone but edging away, Jet hailed a cab and told the driver they would be going to the Wellington first and gave her address before Jim could reach them.

'All in one?' He raised two surprised eyebrows as he moved around to the front seat while Jet got Netta and Mai into the back with her.

'It makes sense,' Jet replied as she used her hip to bump Netta further into the vehicle. 'When we get to mine you can give the driver your onward address.'

Less than five minutes later, she was watching Mai and Netta stumble into the Wellington holding each other up through blurred eyes. Telling herself the other two were just exhausted, she took a deep breath and blinked as her head swam a little.

Aware she couldn't have been as drunk as she suddenly felt on two drinks, she checked her phone again, wondering whether Daryl was home. Not wanting to risk losing her phone, she quietly tucked it back in her purse as the cab began its journey up Central Park West.

As the streets flashed by, she started feeling queasy as the car began to feel as though it was rocking like a boat in stormy seas.

Fumbling for the concealed zip at the back of the purse where her bank card was nestled, Jet took it out ready to pay the fare and gripped it tight for something to focus on until the cab stopped.

'Thank you,' she heard herself slur slightly as she

reached out and tapped the contactless card machine. 'Your turn, Jim.'

Reaching for the door handle as she swayed the other way, Jet found nothing but air and began to fall out of the car until Jim caught her.

Deliberately dead-weighting herself, she parked her butt on the sidewalk and very carefully put her card back in her purse as her heart hammered in her chest.

'Hey, where are you going buddy?' the cab driver yelled.

'I should help her in, I think she's had too much to drink,' Jim said, concern in his voice as he zipped Jet's purse closed for her and placed the bag in her hands before closing the back door of the cab and leaning in the passenger side. 'I can walk from here, thank you.'

'So, walk. I'm fine,' Jet slurred as she crawled to the front stoop and sat on the bottom step.

'You are not fine. Which is it? This one?'

Tugging one of her arms around his shoulders, he helped her up and, letting her lean on him, got her to the front door.

'You've got a key in that teeny tiny purse, I hope,' he said as she slid to her knees to rummage in the bag.

'Yeah, it's in here somewhere,' Jet muttered as she heard the taxi drive away.

As soon as it had, Jim joined her on the ground.

'Come on, I don't think I can wait much longer,' he hissed in her ear as he grabbed her hips from behind and pulled her ass back against his crotch. 'Maybe we should do this right here.'

Hooking his thumbs under her skirt, Jet felt him start to lift her dress, just as she found her key.

Slamming her fist down with more accuracy than she thought she had, she drove her key into the back of his left hand.

Jim let out a roar, but it wasn't enough for him to let her go, instead he headbutted her in the back of the head, causing her to fall against the front door with a bang.

His bloodied fist reached out and grabbed a handful of hair, just as the door was opened by her first confused, then incensed, housemate.

TWENTY-SIX

'What the fuck is this?' Daryl asked darkly.

'This dumb bitch dropped her key.' Jim shoved Jet hard enough to send her sprawling onto the entry mat.

Recovering as quickly as she could, Jet clambered out of the way, into the safety of the hallway.

Jim stood up, as if to follow her in, but Daryl locked his palm against his chest.

'I don't fucking think so.' Daryl looked pointedly from Jim's hand, to his crotch and back to the ugly red mark on his forehead.

'Who the fuck are you, anyway?'

'That's none of your damn business.'

'Come on man, don't let her be a prick tease as well as a drunken idiot.'

Before Jet had had time to process what Jim had called her, Daryl's left fist had connected with Jim's nose, sending him flailing backwards down the stoop and into a heap on the sidewalk.

Getting back to her wobbly feet, Jet fixed her dress

223

and peered in the hall mirror at the state of her face. She turned in time to see Daryl go after Jim.

As Jim continued to insult her, Daryl continued to chase him down the street. Jet listened to them go until she could no longer hear the footfall or the yelling.

Realising she was shaking, Jet shuffled to the door, hiding out of sight but ready to close it for her own safety.

When footsteps approached, she peered around the doorjamb cautiously.

'Are you alright?' Daryl asked as he reached the top step.

'Drugged I think,' Jet slurred. Daryl stopped in the doorway to cup her cheek in his hand as they leant on the same doorjamb. Tilting her head upwards, despite her wince of pain, he inspected the bruise blooming on her forehead.

'He was carrying strong painkillers,' Daryl said quietly as he edged around her to shut and lock the door, the hand on her face sliding to her shoulder. 'I made him empty his pockets, opportunistic bastard. He ran off when I said I'd call the cops. If you got his name, you should report him. You could be in for one rough ass night.'

'Please . . .' Jet reached for her bag which fell open, spilling her bloodied key and phone onto the floor. 'Please text Mai . . .'

'You think he might have drugged you all?' Daryl picked up the phone and did as she asked while she nodded, heavy headed.

'I knew the cab share was a bad idea. I'm so stupid.' She put her head in her hands and slid down the door back onto her ass.

'I've told her to do what I'm about to make you do,' Daryl warned her as he set her bag to one side and reached out to pick her up.

Frowning in confusion, Jet gave in as his strong arms lifted her with ease. He took her to the couch where he set her down before heading for the kitchen.

'At least you're still conscious,' he said with relief as he handed her a glass of warm water. 'Regardless of what was in the drink, that was one hell of a bump to the head.'

'I didn't drink it all,' Jet managed to say before taking a sip of water and instantly spitting it back into the glass.

'Neck it.'

'Why salt water?'

'Because I'm hoping it will make you spew any remaining drink in your stomach before you digest it,' Daryl said as he placed a bucket between her feet on the floor.

'Oh god.'

'Don't be a prude, not now, get on with it,' he instructed forcefully as her phone pinged.

Guzzling the drink down as fast as she could, Jet watched him check her messages.

'Mai has said she'll do as instructed if they feel odd.' Daryl smirked. 'Though I don't think he put anything in their drinks. They've gone back out for pizza.'

'That's a relief,' Jet whispered around the first waves of nausea.

'I'll be back in a second. Don't pass out,' Daryl said softly, reaching out to stroke her hair as he got up.

Shaking her head, Jet took a deep breath and as soon as he was out of the room her stomach let go.

'Wow,' Daryl said brightly, looking into the bucket when he returned. 'Is that everything?'

'For now,' Jet sighed miserably. 'Hopefully that's most of it.'

'I think your breakfast is in there too, if you didn't drink the whole drink you might get away with it,' Daryl said gently as he placed two pint glasses of water on the table in front of her.

Jet glared up at him as she began to slide down the couch but his eyes were worried.

'Will I be OK?'

'Never been spiked before?'

'I don't think so. I've had some pretty wicked hangovers though that might have been . . . I really don't want a wicked hangover,' she whined sadly.

'Let's hope not,' he replied before taking the pungent bucket from the room.

When he returned with the rinsed and emptied receptacle, he slid onto the couch next to her and tucked her up against him. 'How about a movie while we try to prevent you passing out?'

'Sure.' Jet yawned. 'I'm pretty tired, though.'

As Daryl pointed the remote at the television, Jet unconsciously reached for the back of her head and

winced when she found the second bump Jim had left
her with.

'What kind of . . . who does that?!'

Looking up, Jet realised Daryl was staring at her rather
than the TV.

'I'm fine, it could have been much worse,' Jet
parroted, unconvincingly.

'It's not fine. I . . . how did you even end up anywhere
near that asshole?' Daryl glared down at her, making
Jet's eyes swim with tears.

'I told you, I attract them. I don't know how.'

'Surely not every man you attract has to be an abusive
bastard.'

'Then I'm only giving "date me" signals to the bad
boys of the bunch.' She sniffed to make sure her nose
wasn't running. Crumbling in front of Daryl was the last
thing on earth she wanted to do but the drink was
loosening her tongue. 'I didn't even flirt with that twat,
I was polite and with friends and still . . .' At that she
lost it, her tears turning to full sobs. 'I could have put
them in danger too.'

'You need to stop blaming yourself.' Daryl sighed,
calming his temper. 'You also need to realise how
amazing you are.'

'What?' Jet's tears stalled on a hiccup.

His hand slid to her cheek and into her hair again,
making her heart skip a beat, inching closer as though
he could kiss her, he stopped halfway and lowered his
voice. 'If you look for the bad boy in every guy you
meet, you'll always find it. Don't be afraid to hold your

head high and seek what you truly deserve.'

'What if I can't?' A wave of tears blurred him out of her vision. 'What if I've already written myself off?'

'No one is beyond hope,' he muttered, though he didn't sound convinced. 'What do you want to watch?'

'I think I'd rather have a bath.' Jet shuffled out of his reach to stand up.

'OK.' He nodded, turning the TV off and standing with her when she swayed. 'Take this.' He handed her one of the glasses of water.

'Why?'

'You want to walk up two flights of stairs feeling like that?'

'No.' Jet looked him up and down. 'But I can walk if you hold on to me.'

'Just let someone else look out for you for once, will you?' he said before scooping her up into his arms again and taking her all the way to her room.

Sitting on her bed while Daryl ran her a bath, Jet sipped at the water and listened to him fussing about in the bathroom.

'This is about ready if you are?' He reappeared. 'How are you feeling?'

'Better than expected. More shaken up, I think,' she admitted.

'I'll stay with you tonight, if you want? I'll sleep in the other room or something.'

Nodding, Jet stood, less wobbly already, and slid past him to the bathroom. 'Thank you.'

'I'll need to pop downstairs while you get changed, but

I'll be back.' He watched her hesitate at the door.

Turning, Jet met his eyes briefly but only nodded and headed into the bathroom.

Waiting for a moment to make sure she didn't fall over, Daryl headed downstairs to fully lock up and turn everything off. By the time he returned, she was in the bath but had left the door open a tiny crack to listen for him.

Jet heard him lay on the bed, and hoped he couldn't hear her quiet sobs.

When she had managed to dry her eyes and steady her breathing, he got up and tapped at the door.

'I'm OK,' she answered. 'I'll be out in a moment. Could you pass in the PJs on my pillow please?'

Daryl did as requested, before moving back to the bed.

When Jet emerged from the bathroom, still a little woozy, but thankful no more vomiting had occurred, she thought Daryl was asleep. Easing herself into the bed carefully, she turned out the light and pulled her comforter over him.

Turning away and curling into a ball, Jet felt herself relax when he shuffled close enough that she could feel the warmth of his body behind her. Comforted by his proximity, and flooded with relief, she finally let herself pass out.

TWENTY-SEVEN

Jet awoke to the sound of her phone ringing.

Sitting up a little too quickly, her stomach reminded her to be gentle as her head pulsed and swam. Squinting at the time, at the call from Mai, and putting the phone on silent, she chucked it back on the bedside table and glanced over her shoulder where Daryl lay fast asleep, fully clothed, on her bed.

Biting her lip guiltily, she sat still for a moment, hoping she hadn't woken him again.

Though she hadn't ingested too much of the spiked drink, she had woken up around 3a.m. and stumbled to the bathroom to be sick again, waking Daryl up in the process.

While they'd waited for her stomach to settle a second time, Daryl had insisted on emailing Larry for her, writing a tiny review based on her notes, before returning to sit with her until she went back to sleep.

It had been comical to watch him typing, hunched over her laptop at the dressing-table-turned-desk.

Between the events of the evening and what she told him of the movie itself, Daryl had declared it his most cynical review ever.

Reaching for the glass of water next to her phone and draining the last half, Jet checked the time again and text Mai back to tell her she was mostly OK and would attempt to see her, as agreed, for brunch at a diner near Macey's.

'Hey,' Daryl muttered, his voice thick with sleep, as he rolled over. 'How are you feeling?'

'Much better than expected.' Jet narrowed her eyes as she turned to look at him. 'Thank you so much for last night, I realise I owe you big time. I dread to think what would have happened if you hadn't been here.'

'Me too,' he said gently. 'I'm just glad I was.'

Nodding, Jet shuffled to the edge of the bed and got up.

'That is a very interesting tattoo.' Daryl yawned again, catching sight of the pentagram on her right hip as the PJ shorts she was wearing rode up for the umpteenth time since she'd put them on.

'Sorry.' Jet blushed as she fixed the shorts.

'Interesting choice,' Daryl said curiously as he also got up off the bed and moved around the room towards the door.

'Supernatural writer, remember.' Jet grinned.

'Ah yes, of course, that could also explain the black lace it's next to, I guess,' he teased watching the outrage in her eyes turn to laughter as she realised he was trying to lighten the mood.

'At least at the end of the night, you were the only one to see it.' Jet offered him a shrug and a goofy smile.

'How are you? Really?' His eyes narrowed.

'I'm not really sure. Ask me again tonight. For now, it was a lucky escape.' Jet shrugged out a hefty sigh.

'OK, I will,' he said quietly.

'What are you up to today?' Jet suddenly asked.

'Why? I thought you had plans.' He frowned, pausing as he reached for the door handle.

'I do. But they're brunch plans and I at least owe you that.'

'If I recall, this is to meet your publishers for some last-minute shopping before they fly back to London.' Daryl's frown deepened into a scowl as he forgot the door handle and placed his hands on his hips. 'You can owe me this time.'

'Are you about tonight?'

'I'll be in all day. I have a project I want to work on.' Walking towards her, Daryl reached for her shoulders. 'But if you need me, call. I can come and pick you up if it suddenly hits you and you don't want to be alone.'

Releasing her pent-up breath on another sigh, Jet met his eyes. 'That means more than you know.'

Nodding, Daryl held her gaze before looking her up and down with unhidden concern. 'I'll let you get dressed. Will your stomach handle food?'

'Your guess is as good as mine.'

'I'm going to make some breakfast, I'll make you some toast as a tester.'

'Good idea, thanks.' Jet smiled, wanting to hug him,

but he was already backing away so she began retreating into the bathroom. 'I'll be down in ten.'

Showering quickly, Jet kept her focus on her breathing, partly to ensure she didn't feel sick with her eyes closed against the water, partly to prevent herself from overthinking.

It had been a lucky escape.

If Daryl hadn't been home . . .

Rubbing her face harder than she meant to with the towel, she growled to herself as she stepped out of the shower. She'd known something wasn't right as soon as she started to feel drunk.

She shouldn't have waited for Jim to get to the cab before making it drive away. A wave of nausea rushed over her, but not in the way she expected.

Throwing on a pair of jeans and a loose sweater, Jet ran a black eyeliner pencil between her lids and quickly combed some mascara onto her lashes to detract from the puffy lack of sleep look she wasn't rocking.

'I think you look worse now than you did when you woke up,' Daryl commented through half-closed eyes when she walked into the kitchen.

'Thanks,' Jet said miserably as she joined him at the table and tugged the plate with a single slice of buttered toast on it closer. 'So do you.'

'I'll probably go back to bed for a bit.' He yawned. 'Hopefully you'll sleep better tonight.'

'Hopefully.' She stared down at the toast for a moment. 'If my brain let's me.'

'Don't go there.'

'It really could have been so much worse. What if he'd drugged Mai and Netta too? What if there had been more of them? I should have been more careful.'

'You were very careful. You got them out of there quite quickly, all things considered. Could you have avoided having that one last drink with the guy, maybe, could you have known he was dodgy? Not necessarily.' Daryl shrugged. 'You'll probably be more cautious going forward, but don't dwell on the what-ifs when they didn't happen.'

'They could have.' Jet met his eyes.

'They could have,' he agreed, his eyes shifting uncomfortably. 'But he messed with the wrong person. He probably has stitches in the back of his hand to prove it.'

'How do you know that?'

'I saw the state of his hand when I tripped him to the ground at the end of the street. I knew I hadn't done that.'

'Fuck. I'm so sorry.' Jet sighed and felt tears sting the corners of her eyes.

Shrugging, Daryl reached for a coffee he'd poured himself. 'He's lucky that's all he got. Opening the door onto . . . well, seeing someone trying to attack you . . . He's lucky I didn't have a baseball bat or something handy.'

Looking up quickly, Jet found him staring at her intently.

'Don't be sorry. I'm glad I did what I could to prevent him hurting you further.' He toyed agitatedly with his cup in front of him as he spoke.

'Thank you, for putting yourself in that position for me,' Jet said quietly before taking her first mouthful of toast.

'Any time,' he said softly, lifting the coffee to his lips.

Chewing and drinking in silence, they both waited for Jet's stomach to decide whether she'd be allowed out at all.

Once she'd finished the whole slice, she sat back for a moment.

'Anything?' he asked her after finishing his coffee.

'Nothing,' she said thoughtfully.

'You shouldn't have gotten away with that so lightly.'

'Definitely not.' Jet shook her head even as she debated a second slice of toast. 'I didn't hear from Leon yesterday. I take it there were no last-minute meetings I could have been dragged in on?'

'It was actually pretty quiet down there yesterday. There was an announcement just before we all escaped to the bar, though.' He grinned.

'Oh? A bad one?'

'No, though that depends on how keen you are on socialising with your work colleagues on a Saturday. They've set the date for their annual summer party.'

'Oh. Anything super fun and hyper embarrassing?' Jet grimaced.

'Depends on how good you are at sports?'

'I suck.'

'Then not fun and potentially very embarrassing.' He grinned. 'They've hired a softball pitch in the park for the day and will be laying on a barbecue.'

'Interesting way to throw a corporate party. When is it?'

'Second Saturday in July.'

'That's like two weeks away.' Jet frowned.

'Yeah, they like to give plenty of notice.'

'No kidding.' Jet smirked at his sarcasm. 'Are you going?'

'Yeah, I go to their Christmas and summer parties to keep up appearances, I won't go full time, but it shows team spirit, even from a freelancer. I'm lucky to be included, a lot of companies I work with or have worked for don't extend Christmas party invites to their contractors.'

'At least no invite at all would be the easier way to not have to make that decision in the first place,' Jet pointed out.

'You're not a fan of enforced fun?' He smiled through a yawn and got up to head to the sink, taking her plate and his cup with him.

'It's when they get crazy ideas about making you team up with someone you've never had reason to talk to in the office, just in the interest of everyone getting to know everyone else.' Jet rolled her eyes as she also got up from the table. 'It's awkward as fuck.'

'If it's dreadful, it's not far from here so we can always disappear,' he offered. 'Besides, I think there's a time limit on those type of rentals, it's not going to drag on until midnight.'

'That's a relief.'

'I think you're more suited to freelancing than you think.' He nudged her in the direction of the hall as he crossed the kitchen. 'Now get out of here before you're late. I need to go back to bed.'

TWENTY-EIGHT

'Oh, here's your bag from last night,' Mai announced, waving a shopping bag containing the clothes Jet had changed out of in the hotel room the night before. 'I don't want to take that all the way back to London with me, I need the room in the case for the things I bought today.'

'I think you're shit out of luck there, too.' Jet accepted the bag before watching Mai attempt to shove her fresh batch of shopping into the case.

'I'm glad you're OK today,' Netta said as Mai focused on making her suitcase close.

'Thanks, I'm glad he only got you guys drunk, or this flight tonight could have been hellish.'

'My head wasn't good this morning, but the pancakes helped.' Netta smiled as they both continued to watch the suitcase struggles.

'Your housemate sounds like a bit of a hero.' Mai agreed as she stood up, the case doing its best to pop a seam but holding.

'I swear it's like I wrote him,' Jet said, voicing thoughts she'd never share with anyone else. 'Who knew men like him actually existed?' Jet raised her eyebrows.

'You've been writing them for forever, one had to be out there somewhere. You had to get the idea from somewhere, right?' Mai put her hands on her hips as she surveyed her luggage.

'Wishful thinking doesn't make something real. What about unicorns?' Jet laughed. 'He has a moody loner side too.'

'Isn't that sexy in a modern-day hero?' Netta asked.

'It's borderline hiding something, but as I have my own demons, I let him maintain his however he feels necessary.' Jet ran her fingers through her hair. 'Do you need a cab? Or have you booked transport?'

'I could app it.' Mai took her phone from her pocket. 'Will my app work here?'

'I have no idea. I'm an arm in the air girl.'

'How's that working for you here?'

'About as shit as it does back in London.' Jet laughed again remembering a boozy winter's night when she'd tried to get them a cab across the city for festive frolics and failed miserably.

'I might just about squeeze all of you and your shopping into the Jeep.'

'Daryl? What are you doing here?' Jet looked him up and down as he appeared at the edge of the group bright-eyed and clean-shaven in jeans and a navy t-shirt.

'You messaged me to tell me you were dropping these

guys back to the hotel, so I thought I'd offer a lift home. I can detour to the airport, saves you embarrassing yourself with cab flagging,' he said with a boyish grin, his freshly washed blond hair falling around his eyes in the breeze which had Mai practically swooning.

'Hi, I'm Mai, Jet's editor.' She swiped her hair from her face before sticking her hand out for him to shake.

Amusement sparkled in his eyes as he took her hand then turned to Netta.

'So that makes you Netta.'

'Y-yes. Hi.' Netta also shook his hand. 'You don't have to take us to the airport.'

'But that would be lovely, thank you!' Mai cut her off and started walking towards the only Jeep parked in front of the hotel entrance.

As Netta shyly followed, Jet moved closer to Daryl. 'How long were you standing there?'

'Long enough,' he muttered in her ear, clearly amused.

'You really don't have to do this.' Jet shook her head as her cheeks flamed.

'Too late, I've offered now.' He grinned and started following the girls to help with their luggage. 'You coming?' He glanced back at her with an expression she couldn't fathom.

'Sure. Always up for a road trip.' She smiled as she watched him help Mai and Netta into the Jeep with all their luggage.

'Thank you for looking after my writer last night, Daryl,' Mai said as soon as they were all in the vehicle and Daryl was easing into traffic.

'Glad I could be there. Assholes like him give the rest of us a bad name.'

'So true,' Netta sighed. 'Are you single?'

Smirking, Daryl shot a sideways glance at Jet who grimaced apologetically as she slid down in her seat.

'I am,' he said simply and reached out to turn the radio on.

'Why?' Netta asked, the surprise barely hidden in her tone.

'Life's just busy, I guess,' he answered politely.

'Have you ever thought about acting?' Mai asked curiously.

'What?' Daryl laughed. 'No.'

'Just checking.' She poked her tongue out at Jet who shot her a black look.

'Why do you ask?' He slid another glance Jet's way.

'Mai is already looking to cast my book if it's made into a movie,' Jet said, blushing furiously.

'I look like someone you've written?' He laughed.

More than you know, Jet thought.

'Jet has a thing for writing blonds,' Mai teased.

'That is not true.' Jet shook her head a little too violently. 'The men in my books aren't all blond.'

'My favourite is,' Mai sighed.

'And mine,' Netta agreed.

'So, if you could cast any actor as your favourite, who would you pick?' Daryl asked, humouring them.

'Chris Hemsworth,' Mai said quickly.

Staring out of the window, Jet pretended she hadn't

heard or wasn't required for this part of the conversation.

'If we had to pick from the Avengers, I'd go Chris Evans myself . . .' Netta said dreamily. 'If not, Alexander Skarsgård. He's great at playing a vampire already.'

'So, the character is a vampire?' Daryl asked slowly.

'You're enjoying this too much,' Jet muttered with a smirk, meeting the look he gave her.

'Jet's main hottie isn't, no, he's a . . . a something else,' Netta said, looking for the right word and forgetting it.

'Actually, if the first book was to be made into a film, the main lead is a werewolf,' Jet pointed out quickly. 'The one you're thinking of doesn't get a lead support role until later.'

'But he IS in the first book.' Mai rolled her eyes innocently skywards.

'Then the casting director better pick carefully,' Jet said bluntly. 'If it gets that far.'

'Let's hope so,' Mai sighed.

'I'm so sorry about that,' Jet said as she got back in the car having hugged Mai and Netta goodbye at the drop-off point.

'So, is that what the meeting was about?' Daryl asked, his eyes alight as he grinned at her.

'What? Film rights?' Jet frowned, confused, then realised she'd never bothered to tell anyone. 'Yeah.'

'That's great news,' he said, his face beaming as he negotiated his way back out of the airport. 'Why didn't you say?'

'Because if I'd got all excited over it, it wouldn't have happened. Still might not.'

'You're a little too expectant of disappointment, you know that, right?'

'Yeah,' Jet sighed. 'Better to be pleasantly surprised once in a while than constantly let down though, right?'

'Is that another one of the reasons you don't date?'

'One of them. I thought we agreed not to talk about that?'

'That kind of went out the window when I had to rescue you from Roger, and after a man you weren't even on a date with tried to take advantage of you.' Daryl's face dropped. 'And you admitted as such in your drunk state.'

Swallowing hard, Jet stole a glance at him as he drove. His jaw was clenched hard enough that she saw a muscle in his neck twitch.

'Do you think he only spiked me because I wasn't taking the flirting bait he'd been throwing my way all night?' Jet asked, her voice dangerously low.

'I think a man like that doesn't need an excuse.' Daryl glanced at her. 'But the aggression he had towards you. Wow.'

'Being wary of him was what got us out of there quickly.'

'You can be savvy for your safety without winding up the dangerous types.'

'So, it's partly my fault? Is that what you're saying?!' Jet heard her voice rise and felt her adrenaline soar as she wrestled with wanting to scream or for the whole conversation to just stop.

'No, Jesus, that is not what I'm saying,' Daryl hissed out before taking a breath.

They drove in silence for a few minutes, Jet biting her lip to prevent from blurting out anything she might regret.

'Whatever this shield of armour you think you're carrying, it makes you look like you're not attracted to anyone. Hell, the way you shut down over Roger even came across as though you hate men. Some will find it a challenge. I guess I want to know why you're like that,' he said quietly. 'You told me about a few bad dates, sure, but there's more, isn't there?'

'Fear,' Jet replied simply. 'I avoid getting too close to men so that I can't be hurt, mentally or physically.'

'Like last night?'

'No,' Jet snipped. 'Like being strung along for a bet, like being dumped for the hotter model a year later, like having his mates tell you they can't understand what he's doing with someone like you, and not meaning it as a compliment . . . and if that can all happen to the same person, if you're always either an easy or convenient lay or the swamp monster . . .' Realising she was still raising her voice, Jet deflated to almost a whisper, 'you begin to wonder what else you might be put through.'

'Like an aggressive asshole getting physical with you on the front stoop.'

'Yeah, exactly,' Jet sighed. 'I'm luckier than some, last night could have been so much worse. And being strung along for a bet is far more damaging than certain romcoms make it out to be.'

'You keep saying that. Forget other people, you can't feel guilty for the cards you're dealt. Anyway, attempting to scare the bastards off is only going to scare the nice guys off too.'

'Don't start,' Jet groaned. 'And if by nice guys you mean the ones with their own problems who think you can solve their singledom by emotionally blackmailing you with their troubles, been there too. It's easier to just keep busy.'

'Right,' Daryl said quietly.

'I don't like that tone,' Jet said, turning slightly in her seat to lean against the door. 'What is your story?'

'I don't want to . . .'

'Talk about it? Bit late for that, you opened this can of worms, now spill mister.' Jet reached out and prodded his elbow. 'Trust me, you aren't the kind of "nice guy" I'm thinking of.'

'You're sure about that?'

'Well, for a start you didn't try to tell me how lonely you were just to get me to move in with you, so I think whatever story you're keeping to yourself is very different.'

'Alright,' Daryl said as he pulled off the freeway and Jet realised for the first time that they weren't heading back to Manhattan.

Watching with interest has he navigated the Jeep down a small residential area until he entered a lane leading to the edge of a lake, Jet realised how safe she felt with him. The further they drove, the further apart the houses were. Daryl only stopped the car when they reached the water's edge.

Without a word he got out of the car and walked off towards the water.

Taking a deep breath, Jet got out and followed him to a small jetty where he sat down, his feet hanging over the edge.

'I found this place when I first started exploring the state, I was looking for quiet places to clear my mind that I could get to quickly,' he said, staring out across the water, ripples glittering in the setting sun as Jet sat down next to him.

'You didn't grow up in New York City? When did you move here?'

'Truth is, I don't know.' He looked at her briefly, then back at the horizon.

'What do you mean?'

'I don't talk about my past, because I don't have much of a past to tell,' he admitted. 'At least, not one I can remember.'

'Oh. . . What happened?' Jet watched him wrestle with the truth.

'I woke up in a Manhattan hospital in two-thousand and two, with amnesia.' He continued to stare straight ahead. 'There was no ID on me. I'd been rushed in after being hit by a car, but I don't even remember that. I had a broken wrist but no obvious bump to the head. The driver said I just came out of nowhere.'

'Wow, that must have been terrifying. Did anything ever come back to you?'

'Not really. Just my name, I was able to tell them that.'

'They tried to trace you though, right?'

'Oh sure, the authorities ran searches, they tried to track me on CCTV to see whether I'd been mugged or where I might have come from, a workplace, nearby store, restaurant or anything.'

'Nothing?'

'Nothing. It was like I'd genuinely come out of nowhere.' His eyes widened as he relived the memories he had of the days, weeks and months that had followed.

'What happened then?'

'I had to start from the ground up. The doctors estimated I was about twenty-two and gave me a new birthday, the day I was found. After six months in rehab I still had nothing, so they gave me a new ID and social security number and sent me out into the world.' His lips twisted into a weird smile.

'Crazy,' Jet muttered, her own mind racing. 'This certainly isn't like anything I've heard before.' She offered him a smile.

'Anyway, I met another patient in the rehab facility, a lady who was going through physio for a new hip. Feisty woman, she knew her family and the doctors wanted her to move to a special care residency after rehab even though she had lived independently for years. We became good friends and she asked me to move into her house to look after it. She gave me permission to renovate as I saw fit, in exchange for dirt cheap rent. Just enough to keep her in gin and reading material.'

'Are you still in that house?'

'I am.'

'So, the house isn't yours?'

'Oh, it is. I managed to create a couple of lucrative websites when I realised I had a flare for coding, then some apps when they came along.'

'Whatever happened to her?'

'She passed away a few years later. She hadn't been allowed back to the house but I had been able to keep in contact with her, even visited her for a gin every Friday afternoon.' He smiled at the memory. 'After she died, the lawyers acting on behalf of the estate informed me I could stay until it went up for sale. By the time it did I made sure I was able to buy it.'

'You've done a beautiful job on that house . . .' Jet trailed off. 'What was the lady's name?'

'Rose. Why?'

'Oh my god,' Jet breathed. 'I think I'm sleeping in my old room.'

'What?'

'Rose was my gran's name, she had a house on the Upper West Side like yours, I always used to convince myself she was on Eighty-Fifth Street . . . and I always used to get it wrong.'

'You're sure?' It was Daryl's turn to look like he'd seen a ghost.

'Almost certain.' She nodded.

'Figures,' he muttered.

They sat in silence for a moment, letting the information digest as they listened to the sounds of the water lapping around the lake, disturbed only by the local wildlife.

'Is all that why you keep to yourself so much?' Jet asked eventually.

'I do genuinely like the little bubble I've created for myself. I didn't want anyone to judge me or my work differently, so I just don't talk about what I don't know. It's hard to share stories of frat parties you don't think you went to, or high school antics and past girlfriends you might not have had.'

Jet puffed out a breath through her pursed lips. 'Twenty years of hiding from a past you don't know?'

'Must sound stupid when you consider that you spend your life hiding from a past you do know?' He shot her a look but carried on regardless. 'I thought about making stuff up, just for something to talk about.' His eyes widened as he pursed his lips playfully.

'Why didn't you?'

'Lies get hard to track the more you tell. Besides, I have dreams.' His face pinched together.

'What kind of dreams?'

'Lucid, emotional dreams, often crazy stuff, but at first I kept seeing a tall woman with hair the colour of chocolate and eyes of topaz. I began to feel like I might have married her.' He shook his head before running his fingers through his hair, failing to notice when Jet had gasped in surprise.

'I wasn't found with a wedding ring, but I kept dreaming of her, I saw her so often and so vividly that I couldn't be with another woman without feeling like I was being unfaithful. I sought out new company, I tried taking it slow with dating, but the feeling that she was missing from my life was crushing, so I stopped seeking that kind of companionship.'

'That must be dreadfully lonely.'

'As I'm sure you know, you get used to it. Being alone became easier than breaking other people's hearts when I couldn't handle my own emotions.'

'Phew, yeah.' Biting her lip, Jet turned away from him for a moment. 'Did you ever get names with the faces?'

'Not really, it was always garbled, certainly nothing of use I could search for. I managed to briefly convince myself I had a brother too.' He sighed. 'When those faces eventually faded, I began seeing another.'

Frozen to the spot, Jet stared at him until he looked up at her, uncertainty in his eyes.

'Who else did you see?'

'Doesn't matter. Isn't this all crazy enough for you?'

'Getting there.' Jet widened her eyes playfully to cover her own thoughts. 'I have a feeling it could get crazier. How did you fall into the various jobs?'

'There was an old PC in the basement when I moved in. I got bored very quickly and decided to see what I could teach myself. Turns out, not a lot. Rebuilding and recoding that thing took me no time at all.'

'Like riding a bike?' Jet smiled.

'Yeah, sort of.' A smile tugged at his lips. 'The writing also came out of boredom given that my first job was pretty bog-standard IT support.'

'Ouch.' Jet winced playfully.

'I had to start somewhere,' he said with a laugh. 'It was also a colleague from that job who took me to a ball game he was writing up and introduced me to Larry. The rest is history. What I have of one.'

Opening her mouth to say something else, Jet stopped herself and closed it again.

'No, no one has ever come looking for me. There are no missing posters on lampposts in some small town featuring my mugshot.' He shot her a look.

'Who knows?'

'No one. Thankfully it's more than most people need to know. Work asks if I'm going to see parents over Christmas, I just say no. Siblings, no. Where I grew up? I'll say Manhattan but I'll change the subject if people start asking about school or stuff like that.'

'Like I did. None of their, or my, bloody business anyway.' Jet sniffed. 'Seems we've both convinced ourselves we're undateable,' she said gently.

'Can you imagine me explaining any of this to someone like Shelley? High maintenance on every level, that one.'

'That's for damned sure.' Jet laughed. 'I think I should be honoured that you told me.'

'You're different.' He offered her a twisted smile but wouldn't meet her eye. 'Come on, let's head home before it gets dark. You must be exhausted.'

'Now that you mention it . . .' Jet yawned, triggered by the very thought.

'Stop it.' Daryl yawned straight back. 'I've managed a few extra hours and I haven't walked the length of

Broadway today.'

'Not quite the length, but when you add in the extra steps to scour each shop thoroughly . . . maybe more than that,' Jet said thoughtfully, suddenly feeling very heavy. 'It's nice out here. I haven't forgotten those road trips you promised.'

'I never promised anything.' He gasped in mock horror as they got up. 'I merely wanted to gauge your interest.'

'One last question.'

'Shoot.'

'Is your favourite sport basketball?'

'Yeah, why?' He paused to look across the front of the Jeep at her as he opened the driver's door.

'Huh.' Jet stared through the Jeep thoughtfully. 'Thought so.'

TWENTY-NINE

Jet was sitting in one of the two armchairs in Daryl's library conservatory, cradling a cup of tea and enjoying the summer air with the door open when her phone disturbed the silence. Which was a pity, she considered, given that the small extension was quickly becoming her favourite part of his renovation. Books packed every shelf of the sturdy wooden units and the units themselves covered almost every wall of the open-plan floorspace.

Dinner guests could even reach around and pluck one from the antique cabinets surrounding the dining table.

A book with your wine, sir?

Breathing out through her nose in annoyance, Jet put the cup down on the occasional table she'd dragged next to the chair and reached for her phone.

'Mum?' she asked, yawning.

'Don't tell me I woke you, it's practically lunchtime over there,' her mum crowed down the phone.

'Either you have a very strange idea of lunchtime, or

you can't count,' Jet grumbled, peering at the clock on the opposite wall.

Despite writing until she'd practically passed out, sleep, when it came, hadn't lasted long. Jet had been up and in the conservatory since daybreak. She had planned on going back to bed when she was ready, but between tea and the discovery of several new books she already wanted to read, it was now 10a.m. if the clock was correct.

'Hush. Now then, a little birdy tells me you might be heading home for a visit soon?'

'Mai won't even be back at her flat yet, or if she is, she'll be sleeping off the jet lag, how the hell could you think that?'

'Oh, I know all about the little jaunt to the Big Apple your editor made. I ran into her assistant Friday night at an awards ceremony,' her mother said slyly. 'Maybe now you'll attract the attention of a bigger house. One of the big five perhaps?'

'Nothing has been agreed and I said I'd come over only IF I can get the time off and only IF I have contracts to sign,' Jet drawled, knowing her mother wouldn't pick up on any tone she served her.

'Do you want me to see if I can pull a few strings, darling? Rights deals like these rarely go unnoticed in our circles. Someone's bound to know someone, and once they find out you have impeccable literary connections, they're bound to write you that six-figure cheque.'

'I don't think literary connections matter much to

movie studios, especially not when it comes to dark fantasy films.' Jet closed her eyes and pinched the bridge of her nose. 'Don't you dare do anything to frighten them off.'

'As if.' Her mother sniffed.

'Anyway, how are you Mum?'

'Oh, the usual, your father's down the allotment and I'm baking scones to take to my weekly book club.' Jet could almost see her wave her off even though she was on the phone. 'Found yourself a nice American to settle down with yet? No, I don't suppose you have, what am I saying?'

'If I am coming home, by the way, it will be around my birthday,' Jet said even though she knew she didn't need to change the subject.

'Good, good, I'll make sure the sheets are changed on your bed. It's getting musty in there, perhaps I should rent out your room to one of those bed and breakfast websites while you're gone,' her mother said with a little laugh.

Grinding her teeth, Jet found herself wondering whether a short-term rental of her own might not be a bad idea, somewhere nearer the city centre than her parents' house in Muswell Hill. It wouldn't hurt if it was only for a week.

'I'll let you know for certain when I have flights booked.' Jet smiled, deciding that popping back to the Big Smoke for a week would be nice if she could swing it.

A beeping in the background broke into their

conversation.

'Sorry darling, got to go, that's the oven. Can't go offering my literary ladies burnt scones.'

'The very thought! OK, speak soon . . .'

Jet barely had the chance to finish her sentence before hearing her mother sing "Ta ta!" obliviously before the line cut off.

With a sigh, Jet laid her head back and let the morning summer air envelop her as comfortingly as the knowledge she was in her gran's house had. It had felt like home for some time already, knowing one of the reasons why helped to settle her soul.

Looking around at her surroundings and the sun beams sweeping across the garden, Jet lifted her phone from where she'd let it settle in her lap and scrolled through the numbers to redial.

An hour later, showered, dressed and a lemon muffin grabbed out of the fridge, Jet was headed into Central Park to meet up with Rachel and the girls.

There had been no sign of Daryl in the house, both his room doors were closed, he was either sleeping off a late-nighter himself or out for a run somewhere.

Breaking bits off the muffin as she sauntered through the Sunday sunshine, she tossed the odd crumb to the pigeons on her way to the café where she was meeting Rachel.

When she'd called, they had all been at different stages of their Sunday mornings, from Rachel, who was up and in athletic wear to Veronica, who was barely awake and in nightwear. However, they had all been arguing about the lack of food in the apartment.

Jet's suggestion of meeting for brunch had been met with enthusiasm and they'd agreed to meet at a café in the park to start the day with at least a coffee.

Given the eatery had yet to be decided, and that Jet's stomach had turned as soon as she'd thought of food, the muffin was helping to prepare her digestive system for whatever it was she decided to throw at it.

They were all still heatedly debating the matter when Jet slid up behind the group to join the line.

'Still haven't decided, huh?' She raised an eyebrow over her sunglasses.

'See how hangry I'm getting? Even Jet's noticed,' Veronica pointed out, even as she reached out for a hug.

'What on earth happened to your forehead?!' Rachel screeched suddenly, peering over her sunglasses at Jet after their hug hello.

Reaching up to touch it without thinking, Jet winced when the bruise came alive at her fingertips.

'Some jerk shoved me against a door,' Jet said with a shrug.

'Please tell me it wasn't your housemate?!' Rachel asked, horrified. 'Come and stay with us!'

'No, he was great! He actually gave the guy a broken nose for being an asshat.' Jet waved it off. 'It's fine.'

'It is not fine!' Veronica tugged at her shoulder to get a closer look.

'It is, really, the guy got a busted nose and possibly stitches in the back of his hand for the trouble.' Jet shrugged, glossing over the truth.

'You really do have some serious man trouble.' Veronica gave her another hug in support.

'Maybe switch to girls?' Tracy winked at her.

'Oh please, girls can be just as violent if they're so inclined.' Veronica gave her sister a pointed look. 'I've seen you two fight and I've seen the way at least one of your exes behaved.'

'I nearly ran over the last guy who pissed me off,' Jet admitted.

'Fuck, really?' Rachel laughed, breaking the tension.

'Well, he stepped right in front of my car . . .' Jet said with feigned innocence. 'Too many witnesses though.'

'How's that swing of yours?' Rachel grinned. 'Ever needed to punch a guy?'

'Not yet, is this about the company outing?' Jet laughed.

'Yeah… hey, how do you know?'

'I ran into Daryl. He pre-warned me,' Jet answered quickly.

'Ran into?' Veronica raised a suspicious eyebrow. 'Rach, isn't that the hot blond from your office?'

'He's the freelancer that never looks anyone sideways, until we employed Jet, practically dropped his beer first time he saw her.' Rachel looked Jet up and down as she licked her lips playfully. 'Had a drink thrown in his face recently when he turned down Jet's desk buddy.'

'Wow!' Veronica laughed as Sasha and Tracy reached the front of the queue and began ordering.

'Yeah, Jet you missed that night!'

'I had Roger to deal with that night, I think. Though I have been given several different versions since.' Jet nodded. 'Shelley told me, very angrily, herself. The tech boys told it like it was an epic saga, Daryl barely waved it off as they spoke.'

'No one knows anything about him, right?' Veronica asked.

'Not a jot. It's weird.' Rachel shook her head. 'Just keeps it all work and business. Does he even talk to you, Jet?'

'Only if it's work related.' Jet answered. 'And enough of this "even me", I don't know what that first night issue was. He hasn't so much as dropped a dirty joke, let alone actually ever flirted.'

'How can someone so pretty be so off limits?' Veronica pouted. 'Even for a test drive.'

'Turned you down flat too, then?' Jet teased.

'She didn't ask him outright, they've only met a couple of times when Ronnie has been in the area on a Friday night and met me in the bar.'

'I threw everything I had into flirting with him, though,' Veronica sighed. 'I got the impression that I just pissed him off.'

'Probably gay,' Sasha cooed as she began handing coffees around the group.

'I think Leroy would have taken a pop already if that was the case.' Rachel shot Jet a look as she accepted a coffee with a grateful sigh.

'Given how late he stays at the office sometimes, he's probably a workaholic, freelancers have to keep multiple clients happy,' Jet suggested.

'Anyway, you got me totally off topic.' Rachel waved her braceleted wrist in the air as she moved out of the way of the queue with her coffee. 'I've been helping with the arrangements at Virgo for the summer party, and I've told them over and over that people will want a night out afterwards, a few of the staff have asked if there'll be an afterparty, so I'm trying to organise one.'

'Where have you been looking?' Jet asked curiously.

'There are a couple of venues near the park so that people wouldn't have to go far from one event to the other,' Rachel said.

'What about those who want to change?'

'Good point, I'll look for places with facilities.' She narrowed her eyes as she dug into her pocket and entered some notes on her phone with one manicured hand. 'You're Upper West anyway, aren't you?'

'Yeah, it's no big deal for me to go home and change.'

'Or me, which is another reason to keep it near the park.' Rachel grinned as she popped the phone back into her pocket. 'Do you need to go dress shopping?'

'That's what I spent most of Friday afternoon doing in the end, I'm sure I'm covered.'

'Rach, you don't need an excuse to go shopping, I will even volunteer myself as sacrifice this afternoon, but can we pleeease get food first,' Veronica begged as they began wandering through the park with their coffees.

'Alright, alright. Besides, I can't shop just yet, I don't know for sure which venue we'll get.' Rachel stuck her tongue between her teeth.

THIRTY

'Jet! So glad you could join us.' Leon peered over his glasses at her as she entered the meeting room.

Stopping in her tracks, thrown off guard and wondering what she'd done, Jet glanced around the room at the rest of the team, including Daryl, before continuing to the nearest seat and practically falling into it in haste.

'Am I late?'

'Only by one full day, why weren't you at yesterday's meeting?'

Narrowing her eyes, Jet fought not to glare at Leon. He'd chosen to call her out in front of everyone. Smooth.

'I don't believe I was made aware of the meeting yesterday.' Jet shook her head in confusion.

'I pencilled in a new set of weekly Monday evening meetings last Friday,' Juliette, her project manager, muttered.

'I'm sorry, I must have missed the email,' Jet

apologised directly to Juliette, even though she knew Juliette had sent no such email while she had been out of the office. 'Could you please send it again and I'll make sure I put it in my diary.'

With no way of knowing she was in the wrong, Jet had merrily skipped out at 4:30p.m. to see a game Larry had needed to cover after a last-minute drop out. It was so short notice that Jet hadn't even mentioned it to Daryl, who looked just as confused.

'Make sure it doesn't happen again. I'd like to remind you that you're still on probation.' Leon sniffed dismissively.

Making eye contact with Daryl, whose eyes also darkened at the tone of her manager, she reminded herself not to roll her eyes in public and opened her laptop ready to take any notes required.

As the meeting dragged on, Jet wondered why on earth any of them were there in the first place. She could tell that Daryl had switched off and stopped taking notes while Juliette and Leon thrashed out how much work the team could unrealistically produce in the short time frame the client was demanding.

Sandy from graphics looked just as disheartened as the evening ticked away, they had all put forward their case for workload versus reality, but the conversation had continued as though they weren't even in the room.

When her phone buzzed unexpectedly in her pocket, Jet sat bolt upright in surprise, catching the attention of everyone except Leon. Juliette barely gave her a passing glance, Daryl shot her an inquisitive look.

Having already been reprimanded once, Jet didn't dare pluck her phone from her pocket until it was safe to do so, even though she'd set it to vibrate only so that she didn't miss anything important from Mai.

Peering out of the meeting room at the international clocks on the wall, Jet quickly decided it couldn't be Mai, midnight in London was hardly the time to be making rights deals.

'Right, so it's agreed then. We'll deliver next Friday close of play, that will allow us all to celebrate another course delivery at the summer party. Work hard everyone.' Leon beamed, seemingly blissfully unaware of the sharp objects Sandy was envisioning burying in his head.

Before anyone could counter-argue, he rose from his seat and departed the meeting and then the building in one direct line having stashed his laptop in his rucksack as he'd been speaking.

'Rights news?' Daryl asked as he packed up his own bag once it was just the two of them left in the room.

'I hope so.' Jet tugged the phone from her pocket.

'Can you believe the nerve of that asshole?' Daryl asked as he watched her check her messages. 'He has no right to speak to an employee like that in front of anyone else.'

'Well, maybe I'll decide not to be an employee for much longer.' Jet beamed as she turned the phone to show him. 'The deal is progressing towards contracts.'

'That's amazing news.' He compulsively picked her up in a bear hug. 'Congratulations.'

Squealing in surprise, Jet composed herself as he put her back down.

'I can't believe it,' Jet breathed. 'Thank you.'

'Do you think you'll get to write the screenplay?' Daryl asked as she scooped up her bag and they walked to her desk to put her laptop back on its docking station ready for the morning.

'It was something we discussed in last week's meeting, so maybe.' Jet smiled. 'I would like to have a hand in it. I don't know if I could write the whole thing.'

'If you take that on, definitely tell Leon where he can poke his job.' Daryl shook his head in the direction of Leon's empty office. 'How did you miss that meeting?'

'Larry collared me last minute to fill in, and Juliette never sent me that fucking invite, I've checked my mail. Didn't you get it either?'

'I did, but I was juggling three clients at once yesterday which was why I worked from the home office.'

'Yeah, I know you wouldn't have come downtown for it, but you looked just as lost as I did for a moment.'

'Only because I didn't know you'd missed it. When you got home late, I assumed you'd been here,' Daryl admitted.

'Nope, I was blissfully unaware I was heading towards a public flogging.' Jet scowled. 'Are you heading home now?'

'Pretty much. Unless you want to get a next-steps celebratory drink?'

'On a school night?' Jet gasped in mock-surprise.

'I'm working from home again tomorrow.' He

grinned.

'Oh, it's alright for some!'

'You can work from home too, you know.'

'Leon has made it clear that he prefers I don't whilst on probation.' Jet grimaced. 'Probably something to do with not running off with company property and secrets.'

'Total crap, of course.'

'Of course.'

'He just thinks you'll work harder and faster under his watchful glare.'

'I really hope you're joking.'

'I really wish I was.'

'Gah, yeah, let's get a drink.' Jet sighed. 'Where?'

'Let's just start heading up town and see where we end up,' Daryl said as they began heading for the elevator.

'Night guys!' Juliette called from across the office with a wave.

'Fuck,' Jet muttered as Daryl raised a hand to wave back.

'She's never that cheery.'

'And we're never so chatty in front of anyone. Think we've let the cat out the bag?'

'There's no cat or bag. So what if she makes some gossip out of it?' Daryl looked down at her.

'You have a reputation to uphold, remember?'

'Maybe it's time to build a new one.' He gave a shrug as the elevator doors pinged open.

'I will not pretend to be your girlfriend just to stop the rumour mill, if that's where that crazed grin is going with this. I thought you were better than that.'

'I am. I'm just making light of an awkward situation.' He ran his fingers through his hair.

'You feel better now that I know, don't you?' Jet slid him a sideways glance.

'I can't let a past I don't know define my whole life, can I?' He shrugged.

'I wish I didn't remember some of mine, so no, you shouldn't,' Jet agreed.

'You know what, I've got some special-occasion whiskey at home and some lonely bottles of wine. Let's head home and crack open one of those,' Daryl said brightly.

'I haven't had contracts or even a potential cash sum yet, let's not go rushing into popping corks too early.' Jet laughed.

'Alright then, but if that deal comes in, we're celebrating.'

When Jet looked up questioningly, he was gazing at her in what she could only guess was admiration.

'However and wherever you want to celebrate, we'll do it,' he affirmed.

'You're the only one who knows about the deal on this side of the pond too, you know. I haven't told Rachel and the girls because I won't risk the news getting out here before anything is settled.'

'Let's hope Juliette's hearing isn't all that good, then.' Daryl raised his eyebrows at her.

'Oh fuck, yeah!' Jet covered her mouth with her hands. 'You think she did?'

'You'll soon find out.' He winced. 'You might want to tell Rachel yourself in the morning in case it breaks.'

'Then someone else will definitely know.'

'Then she won't get offended when she finds out from someone else,' he countered.

'Good point.' Jet slid him another sly look. 'So, what are we doing? Drinking at home or drinking en route?'

'Let's see how far we get,' Daryl suggested, heading for the subway as they stepped out onto the street.

Three hours later, drunk on beer and chicken wings from the sports bar they'd stumbled into, Jet and Daryl fell in the front door of the house.

Laughing at how Daryl almost tripped over the last step, Jet retrieved a parcel from the mailbox.

'This is for you.' She chucked it lightly into the air and was impressed when he caught it.

'Ooh, I know what this is.' He tore into it as she kicked her sneakers off and closed the front door behind them.

A book tumbled out of his hands as the packaging split, hitting the floor between them.

Staring down at it, Jet blinked furiously.

'I ordered a copy of your book!' Daryl announced proudly as he reached down to pick it up.

'Fuck,' Jet blurted before she could stop herself.

'What?' His face fell, but there was a twinkle in his eye. 'Will I see into the depths of your soul through your words?'

'I mean, you didn't have to do that! I could have loaned you a copy!'

And deliberately forgotten to ever deliver it, she thought to herself.

'I've seen your non-fiction, I just want to see what makes your fiction brain tick.' He reached out and swept a stray curl from her forehead. 'I wanna know what I'll be watching in a couple of years' time. Don't panic, I promise not to think any less of you if the werewolf has his wicked way with the witch.'

Swallowing hard, Jet knew she'd be eating those words later.

'Damnit, you guessed it.' She offered an unconvincing look of shock as they began heading for the stairs.

'Might even read some now before bed,' he slurred.

'It's late, you're pissed, get some sleep. In fact…' Jet reached out and grabbed the back pocket of his jeans as he tried to head up the stairs. 'Get back down here and drink a pint or two of water.'

'Ah.' He span on his heel and agreeably followed her to the kitchen. 'I will most certainly thank you for that in the morning,' he said in a dreadful British accent.

'Yeah, ya will.' Jet smirked.

Taking the book off him and putting it down on the kitchen table, she quickly replaced it with a glass of water.

Necking the whole contents while she watched, he triumphantly handed the glass back.

Topping it up and handing it back, Jet swayed on the spot herself as she put her hands on her hips.

'Now then, off to bed with you!' she instructed and watched him bow his head, take another mouthful of water and turn to begin slowly navigating his way back to the stairs.

Drinking her own glass of water as she watched, she turned to refill it just as she heard him behind her again.

'Forgot my book,' he breathed over her shoulder, sharing a cloud of beer fumes with her.

As she followed him slowly and cautiously up the stairs with her bag in one hand and water in the other, she found herself staring at the book he held, wishing he would drop it so that she could hide it while he was steaming.

With no such luck, she watched him grin stupidly at her, wave the book and disappear into his room.

Biting her lip and hoping he'd soon pass out, Jet carried on to her room, suddenly more concerned at the tilt of the stairs and the spinning of her bed.

'Drunk on a school night.' She giggled to herself as she sat on the end of her bed and reached to take her socks off. It was only when the water sloshed over her foot that she realised she didn't have a free hand.

Dropping her bag and downing the rest of her glass of water, she got up again to put the glass on her desk before falling backwards onto the bed.

After peeling her clothes off methodically, all the while telling herself she wasn't too drunk and that work the next day would be fine, it hardly surprised her when she woke at 3a.m., in her underwear, in a sitting position on the floor.

THIRTY-ONE

'You went for a drink with Daryl after work?!' Rachel hissed in her ear, having dived around the desk when Jet entered the reception, groggy, dehydrated and carrying an extra-large coffee the next morning.

'Juliette's in then?' Jet glanced across the foyer.

'She asked me this morning whether you two are seeing each other because she heard him talking to you last night,' Rachel whispered, glancing around the reception to see who else had come out of the elevator with Jet.

'What do you think?' Jet raised an eyebrow and handed Rachel the extra coffee she'd bought for her.

'Oh, you star, thank you!' Rachel sniffed the caffeine fumes gratefully. 'Jet, I've heard your dating history, I told her not to be ridiculous. But are you?' Her eyes widened.

'Can you keep a secret? Well, two really?' Jet asked with a smile.

'I can try,' she replied honestly.

'I'm Daryl's housemate.'

'Ha, that figures. That actually makes a lot of things make a lot of sense.'

'There's something else.'

'What else? You are sleeping with him?'

'No. The reason I took last Friday off.'

'He was here then…' Rachel wrinkled her nose thoughtfully. 'Go on.'

'I write books, novels, I was at a meeting with my publishers on Friday. One of them might, just might, get made into a film.'

'Oh my god, that's so exciting!' Rachel grasped Jet's hands and danced on the spot to prevent herself from jumping up and down in excitement. 'But…oh…' She calmed quickly. 'Leon…'

'Yeah, exactly. I've already upset him once this week, I don't want to get on his bad side permanently. This deal is only a maybe.'

'Can I read your books?'

'They're available from all good bookstores, so yes, if you really want to,' Jet teased.

'Wait till I tell the girls. One of us might even have read something by you already! Or are they in your name?'

'They're not in my name. I'll give you the details later.' Jet smiled.

'Then you're not screwing the freelancer?' Rachel's face fell, disappointed.

'No, I'm not screwing the freelancer.' Jet laughed. 'I'm just renting a room in the same house.'

'I can't believe you kept that quiet!' Rachel gave her a playful slap on the wrist.

'It's not like they're New York Times Bestsellers or anything. And as for Daryl, I'm not sure whether that's for his or my safety.'

'He's made it very clear to Shelley he's off limits.'

'Yes, and we know how she took that.' Jet's eyes widened.

'Good point, hell hath no fury and all.' Rachel looked thoughtful.

'Yeah, it's just not worth it when I'm really only renting a room, I swear.'

'It's alright, I believe you, you have the worst luck with men.' Rachel nudged her with her shoulder before scurrying back behind her desk.

'You don't have to remind me,' Jet sang as she headed for the main office floor.

Wanting to hug the life out of the coffee in the hopes it would make her feel better, Jet took the lid off so that it would reach a gulpable temperature faster, popped her earbuds into her ears and set to work on the scripts she needed to finish before the end of the day.

Once the coffee was finished and she'd had a message from Daryl asking what the fuck she had been thinking letting him get that drunk the night before, Jet started to feel even more ropey.

Having skipped breakfast to prevent from feeling sick on the subway, her stomach was just about ready to eat her from the inside out.

Realising she'd reached the point where not eating

could be just as disastrous as seeking food, she decided to pop out for sustenance. Slipping her wallet into her pocket and leaving her earbuds in, she got up and headed for reception. As she reached for the double doors, planning to ask Rachel if she wanted anything, Leon stepped in front of her.

He was talking to her, having missed the earbuds lurking beneath her hair. Tugging one free, she asked him to repeat himself.

'I said where are you going at eleven in the morning?'

Her stomach churned, knowing he'd been watching her made her just as angry as being called out for doing something everyone else did all the time (within reason) and she blushed in embarrassment.

Jet took a deep breath as she tried to prevent her lips saying "I quit".

'I plan on working through lunch to get those scripts finished today so I'm just popping out to grab some food, I'll be twenty minutes tops.' Jet held her hands up to show she didn't have her bag or anything on her.

Working overtime to keep him sweet wasn't wise either, but her hangover wasn't in the mood to be stood around arguing the toss.

'If you're any more than that, make it up at the end of the day,' he sneered and stepped out of her way.

'Fucking wow,' Jet mouthed at Rachel as she finally entered reception.

'Leon off on one again?'

'Dude needs to lighten the fuck up,' Jet grouched. 'I need food asap, can I get you anything?'

'Not for me thanks, I food prepped.' Rachel waved a salad tub that was no bigger than an average-sized orange.

'I'm too hungover for salad. I'll be back,' Jet said, pulling her sunglasses off the top of her head and considering putting them on in the elevator.

When she spotted that Leroy wasn't at his post, Jet put the sunglasses on as she crossed the lobby.

'Where are you going?'

'What is it with that question this morning? What are you doing here? I thought you were working from home?' Jet scowled as Daryl dragged himself up the steps in front of her. 'Wow, you look worse than I do.'

'Thanks for that,' he said with a glare at her. 'I've been called in, seems Leon's slave driving is going to go on until this course is also delivered.'

'At least it's not as broken as the last one.' Jet grinned. 'I haven't eaten, and I might be sick if I don't, so I'm going searching for food, but I've had to promise to work through lunch just to be allowed to do so.'

'He stopped you on the way out?'

'Yes, he did.'

'Great. Well, if he's in that kind of mood, I'll come with you, I'm not working hungover without snacks.' Daryl turned back the opposite way and started heading down the steps. 'Where were you heading?'

'I don't really know, I usually just use Starbucks as it's the closest.' Jet looked up and down the street as she followed him back down the steps.

'There's a little deli one block over. They sell bagels,

baguettes, pizza slices . . .'

'Cake? I might need cake if I'm here until it's done tonight.'

'Yes, they have cake and confectionery.'

'Time, indeed, to stock up then.'

'That's my plan,' Daryl agreed.

'We definitely drank too much last night.' Jet laughed through her pain. 'What the hell possessed us?'

'We got carried away with the game they were showing, then you started daydreaming about how you could buy your own townhouse and get me to decorate it if your film is a huge success.' Daryl frowned.

'Ah, yes. I can't even remember how many rounds we ordered. You started drawing on napkins.'

'I started trying to show you all the things I'd do to another house if I could buy a fixer upper and what I'd do differently next time.'

'You threatened to put in a pool.'

'That was an awesome idea.'

'Do any of the other townhouses in the neighbourhood have pools?'

'They might. Certainly not in the tiny backyard, but maybe in the basement,' Daryl reasoned.

'You can't draw for shit.' Jet smirked.

'How dare you! We were both pretty wasted by that point.' He waved her off. 'In here.'

'Oh my god, I'm going to do some serious calorie damage today,' Jet said as he steered her into the store and she stopped and stared at the array of baked goods in the cabinet.

'You weren't kidding,' Daryl said as they left the deli five minutes later with a bag full of food each.

'I don't kid about snacks,' Jet declared. 'Oh, and we were spotted last night. Juliette had already asked Rachel about there being an "Us" before I got in this morning. But she didn't know about the book.'

'What did Rachel say?'

'She told her I have shit luck with men and must have been mistaken.'

'She's not wrong,' Daryl teased.

'Gee, thanks.'

'Hey, it's none of my business unless they need a good punch on the nose.' Daryl glanced down at her.

'Once again, let's leave it at that,' Jet said, staring down at the sidewalk.

'I'm going to go and get a coffee so that we're not seen walking back in together. I won't ask you if you want anything,' he said pointedly.

'Fair. See you in there.' Jet nodded as he crossed the street.

She watched him go, wondering whether he'd tried to read any of her novel before passing out. With a shrug to herself, she guessed perhaps not and headed back to her desk where she managed to keep her head down for the rest of the day, her bag of goodies keeping her company right up until 6p.m. when she put the scripts in a zip file and sent them to the booked proofreader.

Leaning back in her chair with a stretch and checking the time, she glanced down towards the back of the office where the developers all sat clustered together.

Whatever they were working on, they were all heads together thrashing it out.

Deciding not to disturb Daryl and ask him if he was working late — it was obvious he would be — she packed up and headed home to catch up on some sleep.

Tugging her phone from her pocket to check for messages, she found just the one, from Rachel, informing her the girls wanted to turn their movie nights into a book club.

With a smile, Jet replied, asking her what they wanted to read first, though she had a feeling she already knew the answer.

THIRTY-TWO

'I cannot believe you get to see that guy whenever you get home.' Veronica swooned. 'Have you seen him topless yet? Or even better, in nothing but a towel?'

'His bathroom is en suite, so no, sadly not, but even I have to admit, that's got to be a wonderful sight,' Jet said wistfully, wishing she'd had a better view from the garden that night. As her memory tried to fill in the blanks, she picked up her glass of wine and took another sip.

'I'll bet,' Veronica agreed as Sasha came in the front door and threw her keys on the kitchen island. 'Heya,' she called to her sister, 'where's Tracy?'

'That asshole has made her work late tonight,' Sasha bit out as she leant on the island and poured herself a glass of wine, slugging back half the glass in her first mouthful. 'She said she'll get here as soon as she can.'

'Maybe we should take the party to her, give her boss a piece of our minds!' Rachel declared.

'How much has she had?' Sasha looked to Rachel then

Veronica.

'Maybe she has a point,' Jet agreed. 'She needs out of there.'

'I don't think us getting her fired is quite what she's hoping for.' Sasha fixed Jet with a hard stare. 'Jobs like hers don't exactly grow on trees in this city.'

'I get that it's competitive as shit,' Jet agreed. 'But if her boss is threatening her, telling her she won't get another job as good as that one if she leaves, then she needs to do something, for her own stress levels if nothing else.'

'Did you ever start that podcast the two of you have been talking about for ages?' Rachel asked Sasha.

'Of course they haven't.' Veronica eyeballed her sister.

'You have an idea for a podcast?' Jet sat bolt upright. 'Why the hell not? Give it a shot.'

'We looked into the equipment and everything, but we can't afford anything like the setup they have down there at the radio station,' Sasha admitted. 'Tracy is a damned good sound editor, so she's picky about getting good equipment.'

'What about turning our book club into a podcast?' Rachel suddenly squealed.

'Yeah, we could even run extra publicity for Jet's book when it's made into a film,' Veronica suggested.

'Let's not get carried away. Sasha already said they have an idea,' Jet soothed. Sasha raised her glass in thanks.

'But if we started tinkering about with a smallish fun

podcast about the books we're reading, that could just be something to practise on, get a feel for the market and how it works?' Veronica offered Sasha. 'Plus, if it was something we all did for fun to start with, then we could all chip in for some half-decent equipment?'

'That's a great idea!' Rachel shuffled to the edge of her seat.

'I'd be up for that,' Jet agreed. 'In case you hadn't heard, I got a sweet deal on my rent.'

'And you might be writing a movie script before the summer is done.' Sasha lifted her glass again, this time in salute. 'We can float it with Tracy later and see what she thinks. She might hate the idea.'

'Ah well, if she does, can't say we didn't try.' Veronica nodded.

'Anyway, you have to read the book first.' Jet chuckled. 'When are we going to do the first one?'

'My copy was delivered to work today.' Sasha gestured towards her handbag on the floor by the front door.

'I found one too, it should be here by the weekend. Give us a week to read? Next Saturday?'

'No can do, we have a company event.' Rachel waved her wine glass in Jet's direction.

'The week after that, then? We can't all be speed readers. Tracy is going to be sharing my copy,' Sasha admitted. 'Sorry, I probably shouldn't admit that to the author.' She glanced at Jet, who waved it off.

'You've bought three copies between you as it is! If I had author copies lying around, I'd have handed them over. Sadly, they're all in London.'

'You could read to each other,' Rachel said soppily.

'We might,' Sasha agreed, 'Though that depends on the quality of the writing. Is there a reason there's no audiobook?'

'Not really, my publisher is quite small and when I started writing the rights for audio just weren't picked up, so the whole series would now have to be recorded as a back-catalogue, I guess.'

'If you get a movie deal, it might be time to get that sorted,' Sasha pointed out. 'Even self-published authors get themselves on streaming sites these days.'

'Would you read it yourself?'

'How cringeworthy would that be!' Jet shuddered. 'Where is that pizza we ordered? Shall we save Tracy's?'

'Tracy says not to wait for her, she'll pick something up on her way home.' Sasha consulted her phone. 'She can't stand cold pizza.'

'She's moved in then?'

'Pretty much.' Sasha grinned coyly.

'She had been here most of the last three months, it made sense.' Veronica smiled at her sister. 'We all agreed, and it helps with the bills.'

'It also helps them save for their own place.' Rachel pouted sadly. 'They've been talking furniture budgets already.'

'It was going to happen one day Rach, we'll just have to marry each other and downsize.' Veronica sniggered.

'Or get another roommate?' Jet frowned.

'You're not looking anymore, though.' Rachel's pout intensified.

'We're not going anywhere yet!' Sasha threw the nearest dishrag at Rachel.

'See that you don't!' Rachel got up to refill her wine glass. 'We should start making a list of all the books we want to read, so that we can pull the next one out of a hat or something each time we finish one.'

'Don't try to organise us on a Friday night.' Jet wagged a finger at her.

'It was only a suggestion. Maybe it's this dress though, I should go and change.'

Without a second thought, Rachel left her glass on the island and shut herself in her room to get changed. They were all still in their work clothes having sunk one quick drink at the bar with the usual suspects. Veronica had met them there before heading to the apartment via a grocery store for snacks.

'She makes a very good point.' Veronica smoothed down her white dress shirt. 'Fuck it, I'm not likely to spill red wine down it or anything.'

'You're drinking white wine,' Sasha snarked.

'Exactly.' Veronica winked at her.

'And to think, you got the brains,' Sasha countered.

'We can't all be creatives, who'd handle the money?' Veronica smirked.

'I handle other people's creations, not my own,' Sasha bit out, even though she looked to Jet as she said it.

'Yet.' Veronica smiled. 'Slip one of your designs onto the pile one day. See if they notice.'

'You think your company wouldn't notice if you suddenly added a phoney accountancy certification to your wall?'

'To go with all the others? They might not actually.'
Veronica considered the thought as Sasha headed for
the door to let the delivery in.

'Who the hell ordered a pizza-sized cookie?' Sasha
asked as she started opening pizza boxes.

'I did!' Jet exclaimed, jumping up from the couch.

'Why?' Sasha turned the box to show her sister, then
Rachel as she emerged from her room in a shorts and t-
shirt set.

Instantly jealous, Jet reminded herself to pack spare
clothes next time they had a girls' night straight from
work, jeans were not summer in New York attire.

'Because they're pretty good,' Jet said guiltily. 'The
first one I had was free though, not sure how I swung
that.'

'Daryl paid?' Rachel waggled her eyebrows.

'No one paid, it randomly came with our order the
first night I moved in.' Jet's lips twisted into a smile. 'I
made him eat half.'

'You guys better be willing to split half between you,
I call dibs on . . . this half.' Veronica drew a line above
the cookie with her finger sectioning off the half nearest
her.

'Fight you for it,' Rachel said delightedly.

'See, I knew it was a good idea.' Jet smirked.

'Saturday night book club rule number one,' Rachel
declared. 'Must always be accompanied by pizza
cookie.'

'That's one rule I can live with.' Veronica grinned.

THIRTY-THREE

The door to Daryl's bedroom flew open as Jet headed down to breakfast Saturday morning. Stopping, in case he ran into her, she narrowly avoided catching a holdall to the ankles.

'What are you up to this weekend?' he asked, appearing in the doorway.

'Nothing but writing. Where are you off to?'

'Haven't decided yet. Fancy that road trip?'

'Um . . .'

'How much writing have you got to do?'

'Couple of chapters before Sunday night.' Jet looked down at the bag.

'I have an article to write but I don't want to do it at that desk for a change.' He tossed his head in the direction of his study causing his hair to flick away from his face as he folded his arms. 'How was girls' night?'

'Interesting, we might be starting a podcast.'

'Don't you have enough work to do?' He shook his head, baffled.

'Probably,' she laughed half-heartedly as she ran her fingers through her hair. 'Take it you didn't stay at the bar too late last night?'

'No one did, we lasted one more drink, even Leroy gave up and headed home. It was a bit flat. So, you coming?'

'When are you leaving?'

'As soon as you're ready, or in ten minutes.'

'I get longer than ten minutes if I say yes, right?'

'Sure, I can stretch to eleven.'

'You don't even know where you're going yet.' Jet frowned at him.

'No, but ideally I don't want to drive more than four hours in any direction.' He moved away from the door for a moment, only to toss another t-shirt on the bag when he returned. 'Are you hungover for the second time in a week?'

'Not really, but I am awake earlier than expected and would appreciate breakfast before hitting the road at least, do I have time for that?'

'Toast and coffee?'

'That'll do.'

'Go back upstairs and shove a few things and your laptop into a bag and I'll have breakfast waiting for you when you get downstairs,' he offered.

'Alright. Thanks.' Jet smiled. 'Give me twenty minutes.'

'Twenty!'

'I can be showered in ten, but no less, twenty is about as good as you're going to get.'

'OK, twenty it is,' he agreed with a shake of his head.

Running back upstairs, Jet grabbed her rucksack from the floor and threw it onto the bed. Unplugging her laptop, she tossed that and the power cable onto the bed too and stuck her head into the closet to grab a couple of outfits and sling them on the pile.

Shimmying out of her shorts and t-shirt, she chucked those on the bag too, knowing she was prone to forgetting nightwear when in a rush.

'Eighteen minutes,' Daryl said, impressed, checking his watch as she dropped her bag in the hall next to his and entered the kitchen.

'Have you decided where we're going yet?'

'I think I've got it all worked out.'

'And?'

'It's a surprise.'

'You don't really have a plan, do you?'

'Plans are for wimps. We'll use the Force.' He grinned and slid a plate of toast and a mug of coffee her way. 'Let's hit the road.'

Five minutes later they were throwing their bags into the back of the Jeep. Four hours later, Daryl woke Jet from a two-hour nap she hadn't intended to take.

'Long week?' he asked quietly as he shook her shoulder gently and she checked for embarrassing levels of drool on her other shoulder.

'Sorry, I guess so. Some company I was.'

'Ah, it's fine, I usually drive these distances by myself, you were great up until we stopped for that comfort break.'

'Shouldn't have drunk so much coffee either.' Jet scrubbed her hands over her face to wake herself up. 'Where are we?'

Peering out of the window she saw that he'd pulled up out front of a large white Georgian hotel. The street they were on was lined with what Jet recognised to be ever more brightly coloured Federal and Georgian homes of all shapes and sizes, nestled between fluffy green trees.

'Massachusetts?' she asked hopefully as he climbed out.

'Is it that obvious?'

'I'm just wishful thinking.' Jet felt her face split into an uncontrollable grin. 'Salem?'

'Salem.' Daryl nodded and laughed gently when she covered her mouth with her hands and did a full 360 in the parking lot. 'Where else should you take a supernatural writer on her first road trip?'

'Oh my goddess,' Jet muttered to herself with a smile.

'I called ahead, this is the only one with a vacancy tonight.'

'*A* vacancy?' Jet asked, dragging her attention away from her surroundings.

'I asked for two rooms.' He frowned. 'Let's go in and find out.'

Retrieving her bag from the back seat, Jet followed him up the steps to the front door.

'I'm sorry but it really is only the one room. At such short notice, you're lucky we had that,' the receptionist explained moments later. 'It's twin queens, when you said you were friends, we didn't realise . . .'

'What do you want to do?' Daryl glanced down at Jet.

'We've come this far. It would be a bigger waste to head home again. I'm happy to take it if you are? I trust you.' Jet smirked.

'Ladies choice,' Daryl agreed, turning back to the receptionist. 'We'll take it.'

'Have you ever been to Salem before?'

'I haven't, there's so much I'm going to want to see.' Jet looked to Daryl as he also shook his head.

'Well then, you won't exactly be spending much time in the room anyway.' The receptionist smiled sweetly. 'Let me know if there's anything else you need, breakfast is served eight till ten.'

'Thank you.' Jet returned her smile before they headed for their room.

'Are you sure you're OK with this?' Daryl looked concerned as they wandered up the stairs.

'We shared a bed last Friday night, how hard can this be?' Jet widened her eyes playfully.

'Yeah, well, you could have spewed all over me had I dared so much as roll you over that night.' He nudged her with his elbow.

'Are you alright with this?' Jet asked seriously.

'It's an adventure, and I don't think either of us sleep naked,' he said pointedly.

'No, generally not,' Jet said, amused, as they reached the first floor.

'Only one desk,' Daryl observed as they entered their room.

'I can write on the bed.' Jet waved him towards it, causing him to take the bed nearest the window where the desk was situated.

'This would make an awesome writers' retreat.' Daryl peered out of the window as he set his bag down. 'It's not much of a view as such, but that helps, just the trees blowing in the background, a few people going about their business.'

'You sure you don't plan on writing a novel?' Jet glanced up as she put her bag on the end of her bed.

'Not had the inclination yet,' he said as he continued to peer out of the window.

'Right, do you want to head straight back out or get an hour's writing in first?' Jet asked, patting her pockets and then her head to check she was ready to go; phone, wallet, sunglasses.

'After the drive, a walk would be nice, scope out somewhere for dinner, make a list of things you'll want to do next time and see how we go.' Daryl turned from the window, pocketing the key card.

'Next time?'

'Well, this is only a flying visit, I presume there's going to be a bunch of things you'd like to do that we might not have time for?' Daryl checked his own pockets, a questioning look on his face.

'Good point. I bet this place looks amazing in October.'

'I've driven through this area around Halloween, they take it pretty seriously.'

'I should bloody well think so,' Jet replied, raising her

eyebrows. 'I'll be covering the front stoop in pumpkins. Just to warn you.'

'Who says I don't?'

'Do you?'

'Only once,' he admitted, 'Forgot to remove them though. The neighbours didn't appreciate rotten pumpkins being kicked down the street when some drunk kids spotted them.'

'Whoops.' Jet grimaced. 'Maybe we won't get too many then.'

Stepping out of the B&B and checking their bearings, phones in hand, they headed for the Salem Witch Museum as a place to start.

As Jet made a list of things to pre-book the next time she could get to Salem, Daryl watched how she lit up in her element, finding her enthusiasm so addictive that he forgot to keep an eye out for places to eat.

Eventually they wandered beyond the city centre and found a steakhouse near the water's edge. Sitting at an outside table in the late afternoon sun, they enjoyed a drink in silence while contemplating the menu.

Glancing over the menu at her companion, Jet found him watching her.

'Have you decided what you're having?' he asked quickly but maintained his gaze.

'Just about,' she replied, slowly feeling her cheeks warm when her brain tried to turn the look in his eyes into something more. 'You?'

'Yeah, it was an easy decision really.'

'What can I get you two?' The waitress appeared out

of nowhere at that moment to take their orders.

When she'd gone, complete with additional drink requests, they both focused on finishing their existing beverages.

'Thank you,' Jet said, staring down at her glass awkwardly. 'For bringing me here mostly, but also for looking out for me recently. I know you didn't have to.'

'It's been my pleasure.' He met her eyes when she looked up. 'I mean that.'

'Surely not all of it.' Jet chuckled.

'Well, most of it. Grazing my knuckles on some other dude's nose was a low point, sure.' He smirked even as Jet grimaced. 'But last weekend also made me realise something.'

'Like what?'

'Like how good it feels not to bottle my shit up around you. I haven't been this . . . I don't know . . . content, maybe, since your grandmother was alive. Even though those were hellishly confusing times, she had a no bullshit way of talking me through it.'

'Did she know you had dreams?'

'Yes.' His brow creased slightly as he drew on the memories. 'She always had this knowing look in her eyes when I spoke of them and told me not to worry about it, that it would all make sense one day.'

'Hmm, I wonder.' Jet raised her eyebrows before taking the last mouthful of her drink when she spied the waitress heading their way with the next round.

Three hours later, fully loaded on burgers and a couple of beers, they found themselves sat in their hotel room as the sun set outside, heads down, keyboards clicking away.

Daryl had opened the window as he'd sat at the desk, a box of milk duds at his elbow.

As the summer air dragged the smell of freshly cut grass and the sounds of the pool filter running in the courtyard below into the room with it, Jet looked up and watched him work for a couple of minutes.

Every time he paused to catch his train of thought, he'd reach for a dud that had rolled from the box.

Smiling to herself, Jet reached for another square of chocolate from the broken-up bar on her bedside table.

He stopped again, long enough for Jet to notice, she glanced up to find him looking over his shoulder.

'What can I chuck you?' Jet asked, nudging the bag of snacks they'd bought on the walk back with her toe.

'I'm alright for a moment.' He looked thoughtful. 'Just wondered how you were getting on with being on the bed.'

'I'm fine, me and this laptop have written in stranger places than on a hotel bed, trust me,' she said with a smile.

'Is the next novel in the same series as your first book?'

'They're all the same series essentially.'

'So you can't tell me what you're writing, as that would be a massive spoiler.'

'Good point. How is the reading going?'

'I read the prologue, after we went drinking, so I don't remember any of it,' he admitted. 'I'll get back to it, I promise.'

'No rush.' Jet smiled, still hoping he'd forget to bother.

'Maybe we should declare Sunday evenings library evenings,' Daryl suggested.

'If we're in.'

'If we're in,' he agreed and turned back to his own laptop.

Writing until her eyes could no longer focus, Jet eventually put the TV on to give herself a five-minute concentration break, which turned into an hour's nap. Daryl had turned to his headphones to concentrate on the last of his article before she'd needed to put the TV on but when she woke up, her laptop had been moved to the bedside table, the television turned off and Daryl had gone to bed.

Getting up off the bed as quietly as possible, Jet retrieved her nightwear from her bag. Keeping an eye on Daryl to make sure she didn't wake him, she tiptoed to the bathroom with her washbag and got herself ready for bed.

Finding Daryl in exactly the same position when she left the bathroom, she classed him as being out for the count and, retrieving her laptop, saved copies of her work, sent Mai her completed chapters and shut it down.

Snuggling down into the marshmallow mattress and pillows, Jet reached out for the light, noticing as she did that Daryl had switched the aircon on when he'd shut the window.

Tucking the duvet around her shoulders in case the room chilled down too much, she turned over and let herself relax back into sleep.

THIRTY-FOUR

Waking suddenly, her heart hammering in her throat, Jet was briefly unsure where she was.

Reaching for the light, she stopped herself when she remembered she wasn't alone in the room. Only to realise that the other person in the room was the reason she was awake as Daryl let out another shout.

Turning her lamp back on and jumping out of bed, Jet sat next to him, hoping the light and the movement would be enough to bring him out of it.

When he thrashed out and turned towards her, Jet caught his wrist gently before his fist could land on her knee. Stiffening at first, he soon relaxed.

'Daryl?' she whispered, unsure whether he was genuinely asleep or in between outbursts.

Putting his arm back down, she nudged him on the shoulder.

'Daryl?' she repeated a bit louder.

'Hmm, what?' he asked groggily, his eyes barely open.

'You're having a nightmare,' Jet explained. 'Are you

alright?'

Opening his eyes fully, he saw her sat next to him and almost rolled out of bed in the opposite direction.

'It's only me, sorry.' She stood up in order to back away. 'Are you alright?'

Looking spooked, his eyes darted around the room before sitting himself up and rubbing at his face. Instinctively, Jet handed him the glass of water on his bedside table.

'Shit, did I wake you?' he asked quietly after draining the glass.

'A little, but it's fine.' Hands on her hips, Jet watched him closely. 'Take a moment.'

'I'll be alright.' He shook his head. 'Sorry, you can go back to bed.'

'You have night terrors?' Jet asked.

'Sort of.' He ruffled his hair as she took the glass back off him and waved it at the bathroom, when he nodded, she went and refilled it. 'Thanks.'

'It wasn't one of *those* dreams, was it? You said you don't really get those anymore.'

'I don't, but this is something else. I get about one a month. Sometimes there are faces, sometimes it's a lucid bunch of random events in which lives are at risk. The lives of people I keep seeing but don't know.' Putting the glass back down, he patted the bed as he sat back against the pillows.

Sitting next to him, Jet stretched her legs out and shuffled close enough that he tipped his head against her shoulder.

'What did you see?' Jet asked quietly.

'It doesn't matter.'

'Might help to talk about it.'

'I can't talk about them with you.'

'Why not? You told my gran, I might be able to impart some wisdom.'

'I can't tell you, because yours is one of the faces I see.'

'Even just now?' Jet looked down at the top of his head.

'No, not in the terrors, thankfully. Sorry if that's really weird.'

'I had my suspicions if I'm honest.' Jet pressed her bottom lip thoughtfully with her free hand. 'How long for?'

'You've always been in them. From the moment I moved into that house.' He sat himself back up and glanced at her. 'That's why I was so off with you to begin with. It really was like seeing a ghost.'

'You're telling me,' Jet said sarcastically without thinking.

'Have we met before?' He turned to her fully, his eyes pleading for information.

'Not in person, I mean, not physically, no,' Jet said slowly, her heart aching at the look on his face.

'You think I might have seen a photo of you in the house?' He looked down at the sheets in thought. 'No, Rose had all her personal possessions put into storage long before I moved in.'

'I promise we haven't met before. I was eighteen and

still in school in the UK that year.'

'I thought . . . to begin with, that you were from my past, coming to check up on me. Then as I got to know you, I realised that wasn't . . . couldn't be the case, you had no idea. Especially when you listed off your exes in a milkshake haze.'

'I'm not sure what to make of that.' Jet scowled.

'I may have thought I was married to the brunette, but I convinced myself I loved you.'

'O-oh,' Jet stuttered.

'Yeah. Always dangerous to love someone before you've met them,' he said as he looked away.

As her heart split in two, Jet waited for him to say something, anything, else. When he didn't, she decided to hammer the nail into the crazy coffin.

'You'll think I'm bonkers, but you also seemed familiar to me that day. The why is even weirder.' Jet bit her lip when he looked at her again.

'The book? The character Mai and Netta were talking about?'

'No, a different one. One who didn't make it into the final edit.'

'And when did you make the final edit?'

'Two thousand and two.'

'That can't be a coincidence.' He met her eye. Jet held it, purely so he could see for himself that it was the truth.

'Too crazy to be true though, right?' She pursed her lips in her best attempt at a smile.

'Right,' he muttered and settled back against the

pillows again.

'Shall I put the TV on for a bit? Random shows or films usually help my mind reset after a nightmare.'

'Yeah sure, if you can reach the remote, if not don't worry about it.'

'It's here, on your nightstand.' Jet reached out without having to move too far and, picking it up, handed it to him. 'You can drive.'

When Jet next awoke, she found herself on Daryl's bed, the TV still on, offering them Sunday morning talk shows and news.

Just as she realised they were spooned together, Daryl's arm around her waist, the alarm on her phone started blaring.

Before she could decide what to do, he released her and rolled onto his back.

'Is that your alarm?' he grumbled through a yawn.

Deciding it was best she pretended she'd been asleep too, Jet gingerly sat up herself. 'Shit, yeah that's mine.'

'Why did you set an alarm?' he asked, sitting back against the pillows as she crossed to her own bed and, sitting on the cold sheets, grabbed her phone and shut it up.

'Because we have to check out half an hour after they stop serving breakfast, so whether you want a shower, or food, or to be out of here on time, we needed to at least be aware of the time.' Jet smirked at him after rubbing sleep from her eyes and ruffling her hair.

'Fair point,' he muttered as he turned his bleary eyes to the TV. 'Do you want first dibs on the shower?'

'Do you want an extra ten-minute snooze?' Jet asked, glancing at the TV herself, wondering what he suddenly found so interesting on the news.

'Yeah, I'm not ready to move just yet.' He closed his eyes with a grateful smile.

'OK then, me first,' she said gently, careful not to sound upset, and headed for the bathroom, grabbing her rucksack and taking it with her.

Locking the bathroom door behind her, she let out a deep sigh. It had been a long time since she'd woken in the arms of a man. Hell, it had been a long time since anyone had pulled her close for the sake of just holding her close. Damn that alarm.

Running her fingers across her waist as she undressed, she found herself wondering what his strong arms would have felt like against bare skin.

Swallowing hard and chastising herself, a ball of embarrassment settled in the pit of her stomach as she recalled how quickly he'd turned over when the alarm went off, and how he'd avoided looking at her afterwards.

Toying with her hair in the mirror as she tried to decide whether the slept-on curls would survive the day or not, her eyes kept drifting to the rest of her body. She'd never be an athlete, could never match his dedication to the gym, but she didn't care, having come to love her softer bits in her thirties.

With another sigh, she stepped into the shower and lost herself in the warmth of the water and the rich floral scents of the complimentary shampoos, gels and soaps.

Emerging from a cloud of steam with a T-shirt on and a towel around her waist and hair a little while later, Jet found Daryl wandering around the room in his boxers. He was tidying up and making sure his bag was repacked, a pair of jeans and T-shirt on the chair next to the bathroom ready to go.

Almost dropping the towel she was holding around her waist, Jet stopped and stared. Until he turned and caught her.

'Hey, my turn?' He smiled as he looked her up and down. 'Or do you need to go back in?'

'It's too much like a sauna in there to get my jeans on.' Jet felt herself blush as she tried to keep her eyes level with at least his chest. 'I'm done.'

'Great.' He walked towards her.

Stepping out of the way to put her bag back on the bed, Jet nodded as he moved around her.

The air was thick with silence, but the expected click of the bathroom door closing didn't come. Instead, he slipped up behind her and lay his chin on top of her head, wrapping his arms around her shoulders.

'I'm sorry I woke you last night. I didn't mean to freak you out,' he said quietly.

'It's OK, anything I can do to help.' Closing her eyes, Jet reached up to pat the back of his hand.

'Won't be long, I can't wait to find out what's for breakfast,' he said brightly as he released her and shut himself in the bathroom before she could turn her head.

Jet was barely fully dressed or packed when Daryl re-emerged from the bathroom.

'You weren't kidding about breakfast, were you?' She laughed to see how damp his T-shirt looked.

'You were right about the sauna,' he retorted as he pulled at his T-shirt. 'It was a nightmare getting my jeans on.'

'You should have waited until you were out here.'

'Haven't I flashed you enough this morning?'

'Not enough to be illegal,' Jet teased with a shrug. 'You could have asked me to turn around.'

'Well, I do need you to turn around,' he laughed, 'in the direction of the breakfast room.'

'We still have snacks for the road.'

'Snacks are not breakfast.' He made a twirling motion with his finger to indicate that she needed to about-face and head downstairs.

'Alright, alright,' Jet huffed playfully and, reaching for the door, led the way down to the dining room.

'We are coming here again,' Daryl declared when he saw the array of breakfast options both on the buffet and on the menu.

'Are we now?' Jet raised an eyebrow, though her lips twitched in a smile.

'Perhaps we should book a whole weekend in October, if they have one.' He glanced over his shoulder in the direction of the reception desk.

'Wouldn't hurt to ask.' Jet followed his gaze.

'I'm going to go ask.'

'Now?'

'I can't possibly order off this menu without knowing

whether I'll get a second shot at this.' He tossed it onto the table and got up.

Laughing to herself, Jet watched him go with a shake of her head.

He was back barely two minutes later.

'They only had one room available for the first weekend in October.'

'Same room?'

'Yup.'

'So, you booked it?'

'Yup.'

'Fine by me.' Jet smiled as a waiter headed over to take their order.

THIRTY-FIVE

'What the hell is this?' Jet looked puzzled as she approached her desk on Wednesday morning. Daryl had followed her in and paused behind her.

Touching, then lifting the blank envelope from her desk, Jet put her steaming coffee cup down and looked at Daryl who then glanced around the office. Hardly anyone else was in quite so early but it was clear that whatever it was, only Jet had received one.

A concerned scowl settled on his brow as he watched her shrug her bag off her shoulder and start opening the letter.

'Oh, for fuck's sake,' she whispered, glancing up and around the office to see if anyone was watching or listening.

'What is it?'

'We missed another meeting when we went to that theatre review last night.' She looked in the direction of Leon's office. He was in it, but turned away from the room gesturing wildly as though he was in a call.

'How?' Daryl sounded baffled.

'I have no idea, but I've had my first written warning.' Jet handed him the formal letter in her hand.

'You should have had a meeting with HR before something like this was issued, surely?' He looked disgusted as he skim-read the document.

'I would have thought so too,' Jet muttered, downhearted. 'I've never been in trouble during probation, though. Saying that, I would have expected to be fired on the spot.'

'They can't discipline you for not attending meetings that are called last minute out of hours, they've never done that to me before. I have no idea why they're so keen to please this client so badly.'

'Well, they might need the money, and if they need the money, it won't be about the client, they will want rid of me.' Jet sighed, exasperated.

'Jet, Daryl, can you come to my office, please.'

Looking up, they found Leon leaning out of his office door. The odd employee who had made it into the office early looked from Leon to the pair in the Learning Design corner with confusion.

Grabbing her bag and coffee, Jet followed Daryl as he put himself defensively between her and her boss. His eyes had darkened as they'd been summoned. He stalked across the office ahead of her.

'If this is about the meeting last night, neither of us had any idea you'd even called it,' Daryl cut in as soon as as Jet closed the door behind her.

'You are both aware that this client needs us to be on

our toes out of hours. The meeting was called at five-fifteen, you both left at five last night, that's half an hour ahead of our standard working office hours. The fact that you left together goes against our intra-office dating policy in the first place.'

'We're…' Jet started but Daryl was ahead of her.

'I am not a permanent employee, and therefore I fall outside of your office rules…'

'That is the only reason you haven't received a warning yourself,' Leon said as he pointed a finger at Daryl. 'We've never had reason to question your work ethic over the years but since Jet started working here, your loyalty has been questionable.'

'I have no need to be loyal. I work for a variety of clients at any given time, I cannot afford to be loyal to any single one over another. As a freelancer, if you don't like my work, you don't book me.' Daryl put his bag down and folded his arms.

They hadn't been invited to sit and expected Leon to say his piece and let them go.

'That can be arranged.'

'By all means. Clear it with Tom. Say the word and I'll stop turning up.' Daryl maintained eye contact with Leon in a manner that made the manager shift awkwardly in his seat.

Breaking eye contact, though Daryl's gaze was fixed, Leon turned on Jet.

'As a staff member on probation, you should be keeping your nose extra clean, Jet,' Leon began, though his eyes darted to Daryl. 'You will only receive one written warning, the next time you let me down, you will be handing in your pass and clearing your desk. Do I make myself clear?'

'Crystal,' Jet answered bluntly and caught Daryl smirk slightly.

'Is that all you have to say for yourself?'

'I know I didn't miss the meeting deliberately. You seem to think I did, the letter is on my record now,' Jet replied evenly.

'I don't think you're taking this too seriously at all.' Leon narrowed his eyes. 'I'm revoking your space at the summer party on Saturday.'

Feeling her face heat through a blend of anger and embarrassment, Jet opened her mouth to say something she'd regret but Daryl beat her to it once again.

'Fine. We'll stay clear.'

'I haven't revoked your invite.' Leon looked up at Daryl.

'We both made the mistake. We'll both take the punishment.' Daryl's eyes blazed. 'Now, if you'll excuse us, we're here early because we have a deadline to hit.'

Taking the hint, Jet turned and led them back out of the office before Leon could say anything else.

'That was out of order,' Daryl said quietly as he paused in an empty part of the floor and lowered his head towards her. 'Promise me you'll tell him where to stick his job as soon as you land the contract with your publisher.'

'Thank you for backing me up.' Jet smiled up at him. 'The way I'm feeling right now, he'll be lucky to see me

Monday. Once this course is delivered, why wait?'

'Sounds like a plan to me,' he said with a nod.

'What about you?' Jet's smile turned worried. 'What if they stop booking you?'

'They won't, they've threatened it so many times before to try and get me to go permanent. But I don't need them, I have a good rotation of other clients. If they let me go, I won't have the time to come back. And if they fire you for something they've done, they might not see me again anyway.' He narrowed his eyes and glanced over the top of Jet's head to where Leon was still watching them.

'It might be best if I just go.' Jet looked around the office, her mind racing over her options.

'You don't need this place to write,' he reminded her. 'Now, let's get this latest course cleared and out of the way. Late night meetings should be a thing of the past after the delivery on Friday.'

'Yes. Let's,' Jet agreed as they parted ways and headed for their desks.

'What was that about?' Shelley asked as Jet rounded her desk. Shelley was in the process of hanging her cardigan on the back of her chair and slipping her handbag into the lockable bottom drawer of her desk.

'Last minute meeting last night. I didn't get the memo before I left and neither did Daryl.' Jet huffed out a sigh as she sat down. 'We both missed it.'

'You both missed it?'

Catching the suspicion in her voice, Jet chose her words carefully as she turned her computer on and stowed her bag.

'Yeah, but of course the only one in trouble is me,' Jet bitched. 'Leon even accused us of dating as that's against office policy.'

'Not with a freelancer,' Shelley pointed out. 'I checked, of course.'

'Of course.' Jet smiled knowingly.

'What did Daryl say?' Shelley glanced at Jet through her lashes.

'He wasn't impressed, even though it wasn't his neck on the line,' Jet replied simply as her instant messages began flashing the second she was logged in.

Rachel: "Leon's just told me you and Daryl aren't permitted at the party on Saturday! What happened?"

Jet: "We missed a meeting by leaving at 5 last night, it's punishment."

Rachel: "That's insane!"

Jet: "He now also thinks we're dating, because we left at the same time."

Rachel: "You know the rumour mill has been turning for a while on that one."

Jet: "Great."

Rachel: "I laugh it off, so most people drop it quite

quickly."

Jet: "I'm not sure that's much better."

Rachel: "I've booked a venue for an afterparty, Leon never stays at those long, we can sneak you both in when he's gone."

Jet: "Thanks, I'll see how it turns out."

With a sigh and a large mouthful of coffee, Jet popped her earbuds in and selected a playlist she'd made especially for days when she was pissed off but needed to focus. One that was mostly full of heavy metal.

She'd barely found her rhythm when there was a tap on her shoulder.

Almost lurching out of her seat, though bouncing high enough to have headbutted Gabrielle from HR if she'd been standing any closer, Jet bit back the profanity she had almost blurted.

'Sorry, Jet,' Gabrielle said with an apologetic smile, 'but you clearly haven't seen your emails and I just need to you confirm your address for me, please.'

Having turned to look at her when she'd started speaking, Jet's eyes dropped to the piece of paper Gabrielle was holding out to her.

'Why?' Jet asked suspiciously as she took the piece of paper and lowered it to her lap in case there was anything her nosey, eagle-eyed desk mate might not want to see on it.

'We spotted a duplication on our system and just wanted to make sure we have everyone's records correct for payroll this week.' Gabrielle smiled. 'If it's all OK, you just need to sign it.'

Glancing down at the form, Jet realised it was a change of address form that they had quickly scribbled the address down on. Her eyes narrowed, if they'd found the duplication on the system, she knew damn well where the duplication was.

Someone was investigating them.

Scowling, she signed the document quickly and handed it back.

'I rent a room at that address,' Jet said pointedly, 'in case you need a reference or proof of residency from my landlord or anything?'

'What would you need that for?' Shelley peered over the desk.

Shooting Shelley a look that suggested she had a secret to share, Gabrielle then smiled sweetly at Jet, folding the paper in two.

'Thank you, we can make sure you're paid on time.'

And with that, she was gone.

The day was going to the dogs.

Reaching for her phone to restart the music, Jet almost swore again as it started ringing.

Picking it up and glancing at the London clock on the wall, Jet made a dash for the kitchen.

'Hi Mai, tell me you have good news,' Jet said quietly even though she found the kitchen empty.

'I have awesome news,' Mai squawked on the other

end of the phone. 'They're liking our contractual terms so far and we seem to have received an email with a large number on it.'

'How large?' Jet crossed her fingers but as she turned around, she saw Leon creeping out of his office, his eyes locked on her.

'Well, I can't promise you that you could retire on it, but you could certainly take a year off to write me many, many, many sequels.' Mai hesitated before giving Jet the actual figure down the phone.

'Oh my fucking god,' Jet whispered in response, barely able to move to even reply.

'I take it you're as pleased to hear the news as we were?'

'Probably more so . . .' Jet watched Leon getting closer, his face darkening as he approached her. 'There is something I am now going to have to do however, can I call you back?'

'When?'

'Oh, not long.'

'You'd better,' Mai warned before hanging up.

'Give me your phone,' Leon held his hand out.

'Now why would I want to do that?' Jet asked loudly, making him blink in surprise but darken an extra shade.

'You have a deadline to hit and you're taking personal calls.'

'What is it about me that bothers you, Leon?' Jet arched one eyebrow as she paused for a response.

He didn't seem to have one.

'You know what? I don't care. Whatever you have

against me, you can keep it to your fucking self. I'm out of here.'

'You can't leave with a deadline to hit!'

'You were about to have to fire me anyway because there was no way I'd give up my phone just to soothe your ego.' Jet leaned towards him. 'I quit.'

'What the hell?' Brad rounded the corner, entering the kitchen as Jet spoke, with the rest of the tech team, including Daryl.

'What's happened?' Daryl asked her directly.

'I took a call from my publisher, Leon tried to confiscate my phone, so I'm saving him the trouble of firing me.' Jet grinned in a manner that made Tom and Brad take an exaggerated step back.

'About time someone answered you back,' Tina deadpanned when Leon opened his mouth to fight his corner.

'I knew something was going on!' Shelley yelled appearing out of nowhere to join the party, pointing at Jet, then Daryl in turn. 'They live together!'

THIRTY-SIX

'Well, that was fun,' Leroy panted half an hour later as he took a seat on the front steps of the building beside Jet. 'I've never actually had to go all security on anyone's ass before.'

'I'm so very glad you did.' Jet laughed to try and cover the shaking in her fingers as the last of the adrenaline ebbed away. 'Do you think she'll be waiting for me round the corner?'

'I'll get you a cab before we risk that, honey,' Leroy promised.

'Oh good, you're still here,' Rachel said as she approached from behind and, tugging her short skirt down, also lowered herself onto the steps. 'Are you alright?'

'I'm fantastic. Really. Has it calmed down a bit in there?' Jet asked, looking up and offering Rachel a smile.

'What the hell actually happened?' Leroy asked.

'The office discovered just how much of a male

chauvinist my manager is at almost exactly the same time Shelley found out I'm living with Daryl.' Jet widened her eyes in an exaggerated fashion. 'Shelley let rip just seconds after I told my manager I quit.'

Dumbstruck, it took Leroy a moment for his mouth to catch up with his brain.

'I'm not sure which part of that I'm going to need you to explain first,' he said finally.

'I've been renting that room Daryl didn't-then-did have available since I moved out of the hotel. When I couldn't find anywhere suitable, he changed his mind.'

'Have you seen him naked?!' Leroy squeaked, his voice high pitched enough for both girls to wince.

'No, she hasn't,' Daryl said as he appeared through the main entrance.

'Is everything alright?' Jet looked up.

'Shelley will be allowed back on the premises once she's calmed down,' Daryl said as he crouched with them.

'It's amazing what jealousy can do to people,' Leroy said.

Nodding, Daryl changed his mind and took a seat. Jet watched him closely, he wouldn't meet her eye, but she could tell he was uncomfortable at being in the middle of the explosive episode.

'Luckily she only raised her voice in the kitchen, had any of the client calls been disturbed, I doubt she'd have gotten off so lightly,' Rachel agreed.

'She feels lied to. It looks like we've been keeping secrets from everyone for as long as I've been here. But that's not the case.' Jet ran her fingers through her hair, noting how the shaking had almost stopped. 'Still, no excuse to name-call on a personal level in a workplace.'

'Especially when nobody had done anything wrong.' Daryl narrowed his eyes as he finally looked at Jet. 'You haven't broken any rules, you're not even guilty of the negligence Leon accused you of this morning.'

'It's not against the rules to date a freelancer,' Leroy and Rachel said at the same time.

'So everyone keeps telling us, but we wouldn't be breaking that even if it was a rule,' Jet said in frustration, meeting Daryl's eyes again. 'What's happening with you?'

'I told you, they need me. Nothing was said to me, I'm expected to go straight back to my desk and carry on working as though nothing happened,' Daryl said, his voice momentarily thick with aggression. 'I tried telling Leon the situation from my side, he just waved it off and walked away.'

'I don't think anyone believes you.' Leroy shot Daryl a look but smiled sadly at Jet. 'I can't believe I'm not going to see you every day.'

'You will still see me though, I'm not going anywhere.' Jet chuckled, reaching out for a hug and laughing when he pulled her in for a proper squeeze. 'We can totally hang out.'

'And there's nothing to stop her meeting us for lunch or drinks,' Rachel reassured him. 'She's not exactly going back to London.'

'Oh, that's a point,' Jet said, relieved. 'I don't have to

ask permission to go back for a holiday next month now.'

'You are going back?!' Leroy looked horrified.

'For. A. Holiday,' Jet repeated. 'I'll only be gone a week. I'll have some papers to sign at the publishers.'

'You work for a tech company . . .'

'*Worked* for a tech company.'

'Whatever. Surely you can sign that stuff from anywhere?'

'Oh yeah, of course, but they like any excuse for a boozy working lunch at my publishers and asked me if I'd be up for flying back. It's probably about time I check in on my parents. I'll probably be gone over my birthday though, so we'll make sure we celebrate big time when I get back.'

'Well, now everyone knows where you live, I guess we could throw you a little party at the house when you get back.' Daryl beamed suddenly making Rachel and Leroy stare at him. 'You guys could help me organise it.'

'Sure,' Rachel said slowly as they looked from Daryl to each other open mouthed.

'When is your birthday?' Daryl asked.

'First week in August. When is yours?'

'Last week in July.' He smiled.

'Summer party central up in here!' Leroy grinned. 'Right, sorry my love, I'm going to have to get back to my post. Will you be alright?'

'I'll be fine.' Jet nodded as they all clambered to their feet. 'You two had probably better go back in too,' she said to Rachel and Daryl.

'Sadly, you're right,' Rachel agreed and reached out for a hug. 'Call me if you need a girls' night to get over this.'

'Always.' Jet grinned. 'Do they sell ice cream by the litre?'

'By the gallon. I'll keep an eye on her,' Daryl reassured.

'I bet you will,' Leroy teased and scurried inside with Rachel, the pair of them looking back as they reached the door.

Laughing gently, Jet shook her head and reached down for her rucksack, full of the meagre items she'd needed to rescue from her desk.

'I'll see you later then I guess.'

'Are you sure you're alright?' Daryl asked quietly.

'Mai was calling to give me a rather large slice of happy pie. I'm more than alright. I'm free.'

'You'd best find us a place to celebrate then,' he said thoughtfully, remembering his promise.

'I'll work on it,' she agreed before turning to head down the steps and hail a cab.

Daryl, watching her go, only went back inside once the cab she snagged was out of sight.

THIRTY-SEVEN

Flopping down on the couch, Jet kicked her heels off and stretched out her toes as she closed her eyes and lay her head back with a groan.

Wiggling her toes, she listened to Daryl kicking his shoes off in the hallway, hanging his jacket up and pausing before he headed for the kitchen.

Without opening her eyes, she raised her eyebrows as she heard him fire up the coffee machine. The electric hum drifted down the hall ahead of the smell of freshly ground coffee beans. She wasn't sure what time it was, but it had been 2:05a.m. when they'd fallen into a cab and she'd last checked her phone.

London would be awake shortly, but she wasn't about to check for messages before going to bed. As far as any of them were aware, she was long-since in bed and out cold, though Mai might also have been boozing it up in celebration.

Her eyes snapped open as her whole body flinched awake at the sound of a mug being placed on the table in front of her.

'It's ok, it's not coffee,' Daryl murmured as he slid onto the opposite end of the couch.

Reluctantly, she willed her body to lean forward and inspect the offering.

Hot chocolate with marshmallows.

'You star,' she sighed, scooping it up and snuggling back into the corner of the couch, her bare feet tucked under her.

'Hot choc before bed, one of your pre-hangover things?' Jet peered at him over her cup.

'Not tonight. Mine's coffee.' He too closed his eyes for a moment and considered laying his head back.

'Dear god, why?'

'I have an article to read over and send before I hit the hay. I wrote it last night to keep tonight free but wanted to let it brew before I sent it.' He took a large mouthful of hot coffee. 'It won't take me long, it's not on a deadline as such.'

'Pfft,' Jet blew out between pursed lips. 'Do it tomorrow when you're sober, it feels too much like homework on a Saturday night.'

'Ah, but I get paid for this.'

'Fair.' Jet shrugged and nibbled on the edge of a marshmallow over the rim of the mug.

They sat in companionable silence as they sipped their drinks.

'Are you doing much with your Sunday?' Daryl broke the silence after draining the last mouthful.

'Beyond waking up whenever I want, I hadn't really

thought about it,' Jet said and, unfolding herself off the couch, took his cup off him and headed to the kitchen to rinse and leave them on the draining board.

'Brunch if we're hungover? Or a run if we're not?' he asked, appearing in the kitchen doorway as she turned.

'Why not both? Blow the cobwebs out with a run, reward with a dirty brunch?'

'A dirty brunch?' he chuckled, folding his arms across his chest.

'I've seen what you can put away on a normal Sunday and when hungover in the week. What constitutes weekend hangover food in your physique's lifestyle?' Jet raised an eyebrow playfully. 'Cos this physique is used to fried eggs and bacon and now it's in this country that comes with pancakes and maple syrup rather than fried toast and black pudding.'

Having risen an eyebrow of his own at her reference to his body, Daryl took a moment to blatantly review her appearance in her littlest black dress. And not for the first time that evening.

'Your body seems incredibly happy as it is,' he said, his eyes locking on hers.

Blinking at him, Jet's words failed her.

'I eat pancakes for a hangover too,' he said quickly. 'Life would be boring without pancakes. Though a side of waffles may further help vanquish a hangover.'

'Sounds like a plan then,' Jet said, cheerier out loud than she had intended as she crossed the kitchen. 'We'll almost certainly need the run though if we don't sleep all day. I think it might be way past our bedtime as it is.'

Leaning against the kitchen door, Daryl failed to take the hint and remained rooted to the spot. Jet took a step towards him, hoping he'd turn and head to bed. When he didn't move, she flipped the kitchen light out and slipped past him to retrieve her handbag.

'Don't stay up too late.' She paused at the bottom of the stairs to study him. He turned slowly, making eye contact but clearly thinking of something else.

'You really do look amazing in that dress,' he said. 'You know that, right?'

'What do you mean?' She frowned, reaching out for the banister to ground herself.

'Just then, in the kitchen . . . you don't like compliments. You bat them away the same way you bat men away.'

Biting her tongue, Jet willed herself silent, she had never taken compliments well and opening her mouth would only have been self-derogatory.

Daryl moved across the hall to stand in front of her in the time it took her to quiet her inner voice.

'You are beautiful.'

'I am?' Jet said vacantly as his cologne hit her. Whatever he wore, it had filled her senses in the cab on the way out, but since it had dulled and mixed with his own natural scent and the general comforting aroma of a boozy evening.

True to his word, he'd let her pick a restaurant, then they'd stumbled on a jazz club and carried on drinking until they felt brave enough to dance. That was until they realised what they were doing and awkwardly agreed it might be home time.

'I don't think I've ever met anyone like you,' he said, his voice quieting still. 'I think you're amazing.'

'The feeling is mutual,' Jet muttered, her head swimming as he took a step closer and she momentarily lost the ability to speak.

'Is it?' he murmured. 'It's impossible to tell with you.'

'What?' Jet breathed as her brain refused to process his words.

'It's impossible to know whether you feel anything for me at all,' he whispered, a desperate edge to his voice.

'Why make a fool of myself when you love a version of me I don't live up to,' Jet said sadly, wanting to reach out and run her hands up the front of his shirt.

'You're right, you're not the vision I thought I'd had a relationship with,' he admitted. 'You're so much more than that.'

'I'm not a disappointment?' Jet looked up, her eyes glittering with tears.

'No,' he said gently, though his eyes narrowed suspiciously. 'So you do feel what I'm feeling?'

He moved closer still, pausing uncertainly, leaving less than an inch between them. Jet closed her eyes and breathed into his shirt as he lowered his head enough that he could smell the coconut treatment balm she used in her hair to keep her rich mahogany curls in check.

'Yes. A million times, yes.'

Her breath caught when his fingers trickled up her arms, resting momentarily on her shoulders as her hands instinctively found his hips, sliding upwards until they came to rest on the warm curve of his muscular waist.

His left hand slid into her hair, causing her to tilt her face upwards and their eyes to meet.

Without giving her time to think, he closed the gap and kissed her softly but not without an undertone of raw tension.

Parting her lips to catch her breath, she felt her body pressing against his on autopilot as he deepened the kiss hungrily.

'I don't think I will finish that article tonight,' he whispered, breathless as he rested his forehead against hers, eyes still closed.

'I think that's for the best,' Jet agreed, tipping her head up until she could nudge his jawline with her nose and kiss his throat.

As he let out a sigh, Jet disentangled herself from his arms and taking his hand, began heading upstairs. When they reached his room, she paused, turning to see if he'd kiss her again or bid her goodnight.

His hands drifted to her hips as he walked towards her, backing her up against his bedroom door where his lips found her neck and collarbone.

'This isn't working,' he muttered between kisses.

'What isn't?' Jet asked, her senses too flooded with desire to think straight. 'Oh!'

With his hands still on her hips, he shimmied her skirt up slightly and lifted her to a more accessible height.

With the dress raised, Jet was able to wrap her legs around his waist and surrender her throat and chest to his mouth.

'Lean against me, I need to get the door open,' he breathed, quickly sliding an arm beneath her as his other hand reached for the door.

Arms clinging around his neck and giggling as he carried her to the bed, Jet half expected him to throw her down and for what was to follow to be the frantic scratching of an itch. Instead, he lay her down gently and sliding onto the bed beside her, spent the rest of the night making love to her.

The sun had risen by the time they finally fell asleep, naked and in a heap of sheets in the middle of his king-size bed and when Jet awoke, it wasn't to an empty bed.

He was right there, next to her, and when he saw her blink her eyes awake, he pulled her gently to him with a kiss and they dozed some more tangled together.

THIRTY-EIGHT

Waking again late in the morning, Jet found herself alone in the middle of Daryl's bed.

Pulling the sheets around her, she sat up, realising that neither of them had bothered to close the heavy curtains at the windows and that it was the first time she'd been in his bedroom.

On hearing the coffee machine, Jet smiled to herself and reclined against the pillows to take in her surroundings.

Dark hardwood on the floors and a deep teal on the walls, with bronze floor lamps and two bedside tables pretty much the only other items of furniture in the room. He'd managed to make the large room feel like a warming cocoon. Even the white bedsheets couldn't spoil how enveloped in luxury she felt.

'Hey. You're awake.' Daryl beamed as he nudged the door open with his hip because he was carrying two steaming mugs.

'Hey. You made coffee.' Jet grinned back.

'Lattes, I think.' He peered into the two mugs as he handed her one and sank back onto the bed to sit beside her.

'Looks good to me.' Jet also peered into her mug as if she was marking him on a test. 'Thanks. What time is it?'

'Just after eleven,' he said before blowing on his coffee and trying to take a sip.

'There goes the run.' Jet watched him struggle with the temperature and lowered her mug into her lap, which caused the sheet to slip from her chest. 'Fuck.'

'I think I know what they look like by now.' Daryl chuckled as she tried to recover herself.

'I'm not worried about you. I'm worried about the neighbours.' Jet blushed.

'Why? They *wish* they had such a good view.' He grinned but having seen her discomfort, reached over and kissed her on the shoulder. 'Shall I close the curtains?'

'They're under control for now. You close those curtains, and it might take more than coffee to wake me up.' Jet stifled a yawn. 'It's too nice a day to waste sleeping.'

'If we stay in this bed all day, would we really sleep?' Daryl slid her a sideways glance.

'I can't believe you've gone from active flirt avoidance to shall we stay in bed all day, overnight.' Jet shook her head with a smile as she attempted to sip her coffee.

'I can tone it down if I'm moving too fast?' He grinned as though he didn't mean it.

'Oh no, no, it just gives me equal excuse to go from can't flirt to filthy minded overnight.' She raised an eyebrow as she glanced at his boxer shorts over the top of her mug.

'How can this feel so right?'

Putting his coffee down on the bedside table, he reached out, hooking one arm under Jet's knees and another around her shoulders to bring her closer, laying her legs over his and reclining back into the pillows with her nestled into the crook of his arm before retrieving his coffee.

Smiling up at him as something within her settled contentedly, Jet wrinkled her nose before turning her head to kiss his chest.

'Maybe I really did write you.'

'Maybe you did.'

'That doesn't weird you out?' Jet looked up.

'It would answer many strange occurrences over the years.'

'Such as?'

'I don't seem to be able to leave the country.'

'You don't have a passport?'

'Oh, I do. Just every time I've booked to go anywhere, or a client has tried to send me somewhere, it's always gone wrong in the strangest darn way.' His lips twisted into a smile. 'I couldn't even get to Canada in the Jeep. In fact, the endeavour almost cost me the vehicle.'

'Huh. Yeah, that is strange.' Jet frowned.

'Just as strange as dreaming about the same woman for two decades before she walks into your life,' he snarked with amusement.

'I guess I'll need to change my answer next time Leroy asks me whether I've seen you naked,' she said playfully.

'Given that conversation the other day, I don't think I hid my feelings as well as I thought. Well, from everyone except you, that is.'

'It certainly seems that way.' Jet widened her eyes. 'I'm so very glad they were right.'

'Me too,' Daryl said as he ran his free hand up and down her arm. 'What shall we do today? As much as staying right here is incredibly tempting, we promised each other breakfast.'

'Is there anything in the city you haven't done?' Jet asked thoughtfully.

'I've been amusing myself for twenty years in this city, I've had a lot of time on my hands.'

'That'll be a no then.'

'Well, I'm sure there has to be something I haven't done, but to all the obvious things . . . probably.' He looked to the ceiling for inspiration. 'Why? Is there something you wanted to do?'

'As the newbie, a lot of the things we've done have been about me. I think it's time you chose.'

'OK, I have got something, we can get breakfast on the way.' Daryl smiled. 'One last question before we have to untangle.'

'Yeah?'

'Your bath or my shower?'

'Your shower now, my bath later?' Jet smirked.

'Though I will need to go upstairs for clean clothes.'

'Your little black dress will not, sadly, be suitable for today's activities,' Daryl agreed as he peered over the edge of the bed to where it lay on the floor.

'Noted.'

Once coffees were drunk, and sheets or underwear had been discarded, Jet let Daryl show her into his en suite wet room where they washed each other with his shower products.

As she left the room to head upstairs, she dropped her towel onto his bed, hearing him sigh in tortured exasperation as she opened the door.

For being a tease, he sprayed her retreating backside with his cologne as she went.

Two hours later, after promised pancakes and waffles, Jet found herself walking her food hangover off on Brighton Beach.

'Don't tell me you've never ventured out here before?' Jet asked, glancing up at Daryl through her sunglasses. He had barely let go of her hand since they'd left the diner.

'Oh I have, of course I have,' he said as he peered over his own sunnies. 'But there's one thing I'd never do on my own, despite having wanted to.'

'We are not having sex on the beach,' Jet warned him playfully.

'Didn't think that would be an option, to be honest.' He raised his eyebrows. 'Nope, not that. I've never ridden the Cyclone.'

'Oh, we are so doing that.' Jet grinned and started

walking a bit faster in the direction of the wooden rollercoaster in question. 'How's your stomach?'

'I think it will handle a rickety old rollercoaster,' he said thoughtfully. 'Yours?'

'I've been on bigger and badder than Cyclone.'

'With a hangover?'

'With a hangover,' Jet confirmed. 'Let's do this.'

THIRTY-NINE

'How does it feel not having a job?' Rachel asked gently down the phone.

'I'm loving it.' Jet grinned down the phone as she settled herself at the kitchen table with a cup of tea. 'I've been able to talk to my editor while she's actually in the office and I've been writing at sociable hours now I have the house to myself whenever Daryl is at a client office.'

'He was still at Virgo when I left tonight.'

'He went in late. Start late, end late, I guess. How are things there?'

'As if nothing ever happened essentially, except that Shelley and Daryl are no longer to be placed on the same courses wherever possible.'

'Did they ask for that?'

'No, the project managers agreed it with Tom and Leon.'

'Sounds like that's for the best. Daryl was ready to quit too but we talked it over and it would be counterproductive for him to cancel his current contract. He can decide next time they renew, if they do.' Jet bit her lip and wondered whether Rachel would pick up on how casually she'd used the term "we" as she spoke.

Jet knew Daryl's late start was her fault too, after riding the rollercoaster and the Ferris wheel at Coney Island, they'd walked along the beach some more until the summer sun got the better of them and they returned home. Daryl had reminded her about Library Sundays, and they'd taken an armchair each in the conservatory with the doors open onto the sunset. That was until Jet, having grown bored of the book she'd chosen, realised Daryl was reading her novel.

Having taken it off him, tossing it over her shoulder, she'd silenced his protests by sitting on his lap and taking her t-shirt off.

The quickie that followed had been full of laughter on the library floor.

They'd finally fallen into her bed after a long luxurious soak together in her bathtub and slept straight through to 10a.m.

Biting her lip, Jet realised she'd missed the last thing Rachel had said.

'Sorry, what?'

'I asked if you're still coming over Saturday night for girls' night. The book club.'

'Oh, yes, of course. I also have some ideas for the podcast if they're still up for that?'

'Yeah, I think so, what ideas?'

'Remember our first lunch in the park when you said you and the girls could fill a book with dating horror stories…'

'Oh my god, that would be so cringeworthy.'

'But hilarious?'

'Yeah definitely.' Rachel laughed to herself, mentally reliving some memories of her own. 'We'd change the names though, right?'

'Obviously!' Jet exclaimed, instantly wondering how hard anyone had ever been sued for shopping their exes to the world in the name of entertainment.

'So, what did you do with your weekend in the end?'

'We celebrated the progression of the movie deal with my publisher.'

'There you go with the whole "we" thing again,' Rachel said suspiciously. 'Don't think I haven't noticed.'

'*We* should have been out with you guys anyway, so rather than sitting in our rooms playing with our computers, we went out instead,' Jet answered smoothly, wincing inwardly every time she used the word again.

'I wish you guys would just get it on already.' Rachel sighed. 'Everyone is waiting to see whether it will happen, especially now you've left. They all come to me for the gossip.'

'Rather than spying on us over their partitions,' Jet drawled.

'Exactly,' Rachel said delightedly. 'We only have Daryl to watch now and, pretty as he is, he gives fuck all away.

You were the only one he ever really spoke to, he was always different when you were here.'

'Because we're housemates.'

'Even before you were housemates.'

'Anyway, do you want me to bring anything with me Saturday?'

'Can you get hold of a microphone by then? Tracy gave me a shopping list, I'll message you as it has specific instructions regarding the spec, etcetera.'

'I should be able to manage that, sure,' Jet replied, picking up her tea and taking a testing sip as she glanced around the kitchen, her gaze settling on the fridge.

'Great, I'll check that off the list.'

'Did anyone disgrace themselves horribly at the party?' Jet asked.

'Brad caught a ball with his head and made us think he had concussion for a bit, but he got pretty wasted at the afterparty and turned up to work this morning. So, he's fine. That was about as dramatic as it got. Everything else paled in comparison to the fireworks from Wednesday,' Rachel said, sounding bummed about the lack of gossip.

With little else to scandalise over, Rachel soon signed off, leaving Jet to get up and investigate the contents of the fridge.

As she contemplated cooking something to have ready for when Daryl got home, she found herself returning to her chair, chastising herself for being dreadfully presumptuous and a little clichéd.

Instead, she wandered back to her desk with her tea

in hand, but not before popping her head into the library, wanting to pick up his copy of her book and see how far he'd read.

It wasn't there.

She did a full lap of the room, hoping it had been kicked under one of the chairs during their floorwork, but no such luck.

Wandering slowly back up the carpeted stairs to her room, feeling the way the piling got thicker under her socked feet as she climbed to the top floor where it was less-trodden, Jet settled in for an extra couple of hours writing.

Popping her earbuds in, she soon found herself lost in a playlist she'd built especially for building the right atmosphere for the novel in progress.

So lost that she jumped in her seat when Daryl nudged the door open sometime after dark.

'Sorry, I didn't mean to startle you.'

'I'm not used to you letting me know when you're home.' Jet smiled through a teary yawn, swiping at her eyes in time for him to crouch next to her to kiss her hello. 'Hey,' she said quietly.

'Hey, yourself.' He smiled. 'I didn't mean to be home this late.'

'You don't need to explain yourself to me.' Jet shook her head with a chuckle.

'Well, it's just, once everyone went home and while I was waiting for an upload to take, I got reading.'

'You took the book to work with you?'

'I often do, when they leave me to my own devices in

the evenings and something requires a lengthy up or download, it gives me something to do. I can read on the train as well,' he said quietly as he reached up to wipe a yawn tear from her cheek. 'You look as tired as I feel,'

'Straight to bed, then?' Jet smiled gently. 'Actual bed, it's been a long couple of days.'

Instinctively, she reached out and ran her fingers through his hair.

'Your place or mine?'

'Haha. What time do you need to be up tomorrow?'

'I'm working from home tomorrow, so it doesn't really matter. As I dropped my bag at my bedroom door and have to go back down anyway, shall we stretch your legs a floor?'

'Sure.' Jet stifled another yawn. 'You go ahead, I'll be down in a minute.'

'Alright.' He nodded and, as he stood up, kissed her on the forehead.

Listening to his footsteps retreat down the stairs, Jet saved down her work and switched the computer off. Changing into the camisole set discarded on the end of her bed, she looked around the lamplit room, wondering whether she'd sleep in it much in the future.

When she nudged open the door to his room, Daryl was already in bed, the open book in his hand.

'Are you genuinely enjoying that or just trying to get through it as quickly as possible?' Jet looked to the book in his hand as she climbed into the bed next to him.

'I'm getting to know another part of you, and me in a

way. I'm not going to pretend that I read supernatural romance on the regular, but I can see how this could be turned into a movie.' He turned it over in his hand, letting Jet see that he was almost halfway through.

'And has the werewolf had his wicked way with the witch yet?'

'You know that's not how it goes down, but yes, he has.' Daryl shot her a look. 'And that's my would-have-been-wife I believe you're talking about.'

Biting her lip to cover what she was sure would have been a cheesy but contented smile, Jet picked up the book she'd brought with her and wriggled down into the pillows, settling her head against his shoulder to read until she passed out.

FORTY

Waking when Daryl's alarm went off, Jet rolled over into the empty space in the bed next to her. Peering through the gloom caused by the velvet curtains, she realised the bed was hot and damp with sweat.

'Daryl?'

Sitting up, she found him sat on the edge of the bed, his head in his hands, breathing heavy.

'I'm fine, go back to sleep,' he said quickly.

'Another nightmare?' Jet asked as she got to her knees to move closer.

'Yeah, but I'm OK, honestly. Go back to sleep.' He glanced over his shoulder at her when she reached him.

Laying her hands on his clammy shoulders, Jet kissed his cheek softly. 'My offer to talk it out still stands. When, if ever, you're ready.'

'I know,' he breathed, attempting a smile as he got up and locked himself in the bathroom.

Concerned, she listened as he turned the shower on.

Determined to stay awake despite the temptation caused by the blackout curtains to do as he suggested, she waited for him to reappear.

The longer he spent in the bathroom, the more awake she felt until she decided she'd better get up and get on with her day.

The water was still running as she drew the curtains and made the bed, leaving his side of the covers pulled back to air. When the shower stopped, she sat on the bottom corner of his side of the bed to see if he'd go straight to his desk. She waited ten minutes, people-watching the early morning routines of some of their neighbours in their kitchens and breakfast rooms as she listened to the birds chirping in the garden.

When she heard the tell-tale bleep of a computer booting up, she got up and let herself out of the room, walking quietly up to her own room so as not to disturb him further.

It was already a balmy morning and the idea of leaving one hot mess of a bed just to climb into a cooler one was incredibly tempting, but making the mistake of checking her phone, she found the choice taken away from her.

Mai: Call me when you get up, we'll go over travel arrangements, book you some flights and get dates and meetings in the diary.

'Work to do,' Jet sighed as she pressed the power button on her laptop.

Giving the device time to wake up, she opened the

bedroom window and took a deep breath. She knew early morning summer air in the city was unlikely to ever make it as a scented candle, but for Jet it was a better drug than caffeine.

Shimmying out of her camisole set as she crossed the room to the closet, she grabbed a pair of denim shorts and a black t-shirt before heading through the bathroom to open the windows in the back bedroom so that the air could flow.

Once back at the desk, the breeze from the open window at her shoulder, Jet picked up her phone and dialled the London office.

'Fuck, you're up early,' Mai said with surprise when she grabbed the phone, having recognised the number on her extension.

'It's just gone nine, not that early really.'

'Early for you, I've only just had my lunch,' Mai said as Jet heard her put the coffee cup she had been swigging from back down.

'Still running to the coffee houses for your lunch?'

'Hey, it helps the economy.'

'You think those guys would really shut up shop if you stopped buying a large americano and tuna melt every day?' Jet teased.

'You never know, maybe,' Mai sassed straight back. 'Right, so, everything is pretty much good to go, we're waiting on the contracts being signed their end, then we'll get you to sign this end.'

'Isn't that a bit backwards?' Jet frowned.

'These things go how they go. Between time zones,

offices and a wayward author . . .'

'I am not wayward.'

'Darling, you're practically halfway between the two offices involved in this deal,' Mai pointed out, though her tone was jibing. 'And you didn't write me a single thing this weekend.'

'We were both out celebrating, I doubt you were in a fit state to read anything I sent anyway.'

'That's beside the point.'

'We couldn't speak on the phone yesterday because you were hungover, you even sent me an email warning me not to call.' Jet rolled her eyes fondly.

'Yeah, hangovers after thirty are no laughing matter.'

'They most certainly are not,' Jet agreed, reaching out to pick up her pen and start doodling on the nearest notepad.

'Right, so, let's get you here asap. There are some great deals on flights on the last Sunday in July.'

'Because it's a Sunday,' Jet pointed out. 'I can't do that date.'

'Why not? You're not working.'

'It's Daryl's birthday.' Jet kept the "we think" that popped into her head out of the conversation. 'Things are already arranged.'

They weren't, but Jet intended to change that.

'What does that man do for fun?' Mai asked dreamily.

'Builds software, codes programs, rides rollercoasters and takes authors out to dinner and jazz clubs to celebrate their successes,' Jet answered coyly.

'He took you out?!' Mai almost dropped the coffee

she'd retrieved for another swig. 'Like on a date?'

'Not exactly.' Jet squeezed her eyes shut as she grinned to herself. Glancing at the door to her room, pushed closed, she wondered just how much it was worth divulging.

'Does he shag as beautifully as he looks?'

'Mai!'

'I'll take that as a yes.' Mai laughed. 'I could tell you'd been up to something as soon as I answered the phone.'

'There was no *shagging* as such,' Jet said quietly, suddenly scared he would somehow be standing right outside the door and hear her. 'It was so much more than that.'

'Wow,' Mai said slowly, blinking stupidly as she glanced at the row of books on her shelf, a handful of them with Jet's pseudonym displayed on the spine. 'I've never heard you sound genuinely happy that a sexual encounter occurred. Spill.'

Keeping her voice quiet as she quickly told Mai as much as she was willing to, Jet kept a constant ear on the house beyond her door. His office space was directly below hers.

'You lucky fucking thing,' Mai sighed dreamily when Jet got to the part of having slept in his room the night before.

'Shh, don't jinx me.' Jet giggled.

'Hopefully there'll be more for you to tell me when you fly over,' Mai said as she realised her coffee was empty.

'Do you need anything highly American brought

over?'

'No one in this office is going to say no to some whacky snacks,' Mai replied.

'I think I can handle that. Just text me if there's anything specific you think of before I fly. I might be able to pick some things up from the airport.'

'Alright, I'll have a think.' Mai looked up and saw Netta peering over her monitor at her and waving a copy of one of Jet's books around. 'Oh, Netta wanted me to ask you to pick up some peanut butter M&Ms.' She nodded and gave her a thumbs up.

'That's an easy one.' Jet smiled as she noted it down. 'So, let's go for the following Thursday, I can be there for the weekend and mid-week might also be cheaper for flights?'

'They're all red-eyes anyway, you know that, right?'

'I hadn't forgotten,' Jet deadpanned. 'I'll just have to see if I can get myself an upgrade when I get to the airport. Travelling by my lonesome might mean I can fill a random spare if they have one.'

'You're not bringing lover boy with you, then?'

Jet opened and closed her mouth a couple of times before her thoughts caught up with her tongue.

'I hadn't thought about it to be honest. A lot has happened this weekend. However, can you imagine introducing him to my parents?!'

'Hmm, good point, you sound like you would actually like to keep this one a while.'

'Yeah, that'd be nice,' Jet said sarcastically.

'Right, so if you're not going to be distracted, I can

happily find ways to fill your calendar.'

It didn't take Mai long to carry out her threat. Between meetings, drinks, a theatre reservation and a quick book signing, Jet just about managed to block out some time to see family, realising she'd have little time to miss Daryl in the week she'd be back in the UK. Finding herself wondering how that might feel as she finally signed off, she listened again to the house and realised he hadn't left his office all morning either.

Stretching out her back, she got up, put her phone on charge and walked slowly down the hall and down the stairs to the kitchen. She shivered as her bare feet met the tiled floor of the kitchen.

Turning the coffee machine on to warm up, she wandered to the fridge and, opening the door, leant against it as she surveyed the contents.

Having been so concerned with her own thoughts of brunch and whether Daryl had eaten, she didn't see or hear him enter the kitchen. The first she knew he'd followed her was when he slid an arm around her waist and kissed the back of her head.

'Sorry about this morning,' he said quietly. 'That one caught me totally off guard.'

'Are they getting worse again?' Jet asked softly as she laced her fingers through his.

'I hope not.' He sighed. 'I can't let them destroy the potential for a future with you.'

Squeezing her tighter as he spoke, Jet felt butterflies dance beneath his hand on her stomach. Men didn't use the word future around her, unless it was incredibly short term, like how they'd get home in the morning.

'You want me in your future?' Jet whispered.

'I don't care if that's fast or presumptuous, I just know that this feels right here and now. That I need you in my arms.' He lay his other hand over hers on the door and shut it as he pulled her backwards away from the fridge.

'Coffee?' she asked, her voice husky as his hands reached for her hips.

'In a minute.' He paused and Jet wondered why he hadn't turned her around.

'Kitchen table?' she breathed when his hands began to drift.

'Kitchen table,' he agreed as he reached for the button of her shorts.

FORTY-ONE

'Are you good to start this tonight?' Tracy peered over a bottle of beer at Jet as she leant on the island to pour herself a glass of wine.

'Of course! What do you mean?

'You look exhausted,' Sasha commented.

'You look like you've been getting some at last.' Veronica laughed. 'That's a happy exhausted.'

'You'd be happy too if your novel was getting made into a movie,' Rachel teased.

'Shh! Save it for the podcast!' Sasha shrieked.

'Nah, it's definitely more than that.' Veronica was looking at her intensely when Jet shifted her attention and blushed furiously.

'No. Fucking. Way,' Rachel said slowly. 'I knew it!'

'Knew what?' Tracy frowned.

'Daryl,' Rachel said simply, though not without a smug look of her own. 'Damn, Leroy is going to love this. We almost placed a bet on it.'

'Well, someone had to, eventually.' Veronica sighed

with mock jealousy, then muttered, 'I'm going to want all the details later.'

'You can't even attempt to deny it.' Rachel gave a shocked laugh.

'Nope, there's no point in that.' Jet smirked coyly, knowing that if they were going to have a combined birthday gathering at the house, it would be more than obvious by then. 'But that's not the reason I'm tired. Sorry, I've tried naps and caffeine today to catch up, clearly I haven't done as good a job as I thought.'

'Writing all day, fucking all night?' Veronica asked dreamily.

'Not quite,' Jet muttered. 'With the heatwave this week, we've not been sleeping very well at all.'

'Oh, it's a "we" already?' Tracy looked up from where she was untangling wires and setting up the two mics they had bought between them.

'We live together, it already seems weird to sleep in separate rooms.' Jet shrugged as her lips quirked into a twisted smile.

'How long has this been going on?'

'Only a week.'

'For real?' Rachel shot her some narrow side-eye.

'Genuinely.' Jet nodded, her eyes wide.

A rollercoaster of a week, Jet thought to herself. After their antics in the kitchen, Daryl had chosen to work from home the rest of the week and around work, they'd barely kept their hands off each other. She'd even jumped him in the basement after a workout, having found it hard to concentrate on her run on the treadmill while he took out a sleepless night on the punchbag, with no shirt on.

It was the nightmares disturbing their sleep, which had grown more frequent and more intense as the week had gone on. Jet was getting used to listening for the signs of distress in her sleep so that she could wake him out of it.

He wouldn't talk to her about them, and on two occasions had even asked her to leave him alone until he'd calmed down. They'd seen the sun come up that morning, laying together in silence, Daryl's head on her stomach as she'd run her fingers through his hair, hoping he'd drift back off.

When neither of them had, they'd ordered breakfast to be delivered at the earliest opportunity and eaten it in the garden.

They'd agreed that they wouldn't let his past trauma get the better of them, but Jet was getting increasingly concerned. It was even harder not knowing what his dreams were about. Given the way he looked at her sometimes as he came out of sleep, she suspected that she had started to feature in some of the nightmares.

'OK ladies, we are good to go,' Tracy announced. 'The sooner we make a success of this, the sooner I can tell my boss to stick his Hot Asian Babes magazine up his ass.'

'Sorry, what?!' Jet and Veronica exclaimed at the same time.

'I found a copy on his desk.' Tracy's face contorted in disgust.

'Wow, that guy sounds like more and more of a catch every time you mention him,' Jet growled and handed Tracy a fresh beer as they gathered around the setup on the coffee table.

'If he'd been the one to have hired me, I'd have a different kind of ethics case on my hands,' Tracy said sourly, 'Thankfully, he wasn't.'

'Well, even if this podcast never makes us millions, at least it might get your talent noticed at last.' Sasha leant over and kissed her on the nose as she sat down.

'How are we for soundproofing?' Jet looked up at the high ceiling.

'That's what the blankets are for.' Tracy pointed to where everyone had thrown their bed covers onto one of the couches as Rachel started carrying the stools from the island over. 'I'm hoping that if we can create a mini fort around us, the bedsheets will absorb a lot of the echo and background noise. As these windows are too big for curtains, we'll have to rethink our location if this doesn't work.'

'Break into one of the spare booths at the station?' Sasha suggested.

'There are a couple of people who might let me get away with that, but we'd have to time it right,' Tracy mused. 'What can they do, fire me?'

'Well, yes,' Rachel drawled.

'I'm getting more inclined to say it's worth a shot.' Tracy grinned. 'Did everyone do their homework? Jet, did you re-read it?'

'No… but then, surely my opinion would be biased.

You could always do a small interview with me?' Jet suggested.

'Ooh, I like it.' Veronica pointed at her.

'I might need one more of these before you do, though.' Jet finished her glass of wine and reached for the bottle sitting at her foot. 'Given that you all now know my work.'

'So, Jet, when did you first realise you were sexually attracted to werewolves?' Rachel asked, peering at Jet as though she was a serious journalist.

'What?!' Jet almost choked on her drink. 'You aren't really going to ask things like that, are you?'

'Maybe.' Sasha grinned. 'Your reaction might have made some entertaining listening.'

'Not if she shrieks like that again, it won't,' Tracy said with a wince. 'I've got to fix the sound levels if you do.'

'Noted,' Jet agreed.

With the equipment set up and the alcohol flowing, Tracy set the mics to record and they were off. It was awkward at first but soon they were all discussing her book and some of their past favourites it had reminded them of as though the microphones weren't even there.

When the fifty-five-minute timer Tracy had set herself went off, she rounded the group up, introduced the next book they would be reading and announced the end of the show.

'Oh my god, I feel like that went really well,' Rachel said as she shook her hair away from her face and off the wine glass it kept getting stuck to.

'Shall we listen to it back?' Tracy asked.

'No! No, I don't think I'm ready for that yet.' Veronica hiccupped. 'You can premier it for us when you've cleaned it up a little.'

'I'll share it between us when it's ready.' Tracy nodded. 'But I think we have enough usable material, swearing included,' she said with a look at their resident Brit.

'Hey, my book, I'm allowed,' Jet pointed out. 'If they can't handle my swearing on the podcast, they'll hate the book itself.'

'Where did you get the idea to set Dracula as the next book?' Rachel frowned.

'We've read a modern day take on vampires, why not compare it to one of the earliest examples next?' Tracy suggested. 'Reading Jet's book made me realise I've never read it.'

'I think that's a great idea, because interestingly, neither have I,' Jet admitted.

'OK, Dracula it is then.' Veronica toasted the last of her wine into the air before draining the glass.

'Well, it's picked now, you don't have a choice, not if we're going to publish this podcast,' Tracy reminded them.

'I can't wait to hear what you do to it.' Jet smiled. 'For now though, I think I'd best head home and collapse into bed.'

'It's early yet, you could sleep on the couch!' Rachel pouted.

'It's almost midnight,' Jet said, glancing at her watch.

'Ron's half asleep too, we won't last much longer anyway,' Sasha said with a shake of her head.

'I'm fine.' Veronica stopped herself mid-yawn.

'Why don't we catch up midweek when I've had a chance to play with this?' Tracy looked up from the laptop.

'I'm covering another comedy gig Tuesday,' Jet suggested. 'We could discuss it after over cocktails?'

'Too soon, give me a chance!' Tracy shook her head. 'Thursday evening? Here?'

With glances all around, there were shrugs and nods to confirm.

'That settles that, then. Night all.' Jet also yawned as she stood up and headed for the island in the kitchen to put her glass in the sink.

Less than twenty minutes later, she was tiptoeing up the stairs to her own room in the darkness. Both of Daryl's doors were closed and there was no light from beneath. Not wanting to disturb him if he was finally sound asleep, she crept up to her own room and stripped down to underwear before falling on her bed.

Listening to the sounds of the city, very much awake as always but even more so because it was only midnight on a Saturday night, Jet barely startled when her bedroom door opened.

Daryl's footfall was careful, and he slid into the bed behind her gently, only reaching for her when she moved.

'Sorry, I thought you were asleep,' he whispered.

'I'm only just in, I didn't come to your room in case you were getting a good night's sleep.'

'No chance,' he muttered into her hair as he shuffled

in behind her. 'I just woke up.'

'Another one?'

'Not this time,' he said in a way that told her he was smiling.

'Well, that's something,' she mumbled as she reached for his hand and he kissed her on the shoulder.

Waking to a chill at her back and the morning sun streaming through the curtains, Jet sleepily reached for the covers. Glancing over her shoulder to see whether Daryl was still there, she found him sat up in the bed reading.

'I'm wondering whether you should stop reading that,' Jet admitted when he looked up.

'I'm almost at the end,' he said as she sat up to snuggle into him.

'It's just . . . the nightmares have been almost nightly this week, and it's either something I've triggered in your psyche, or it's the book.'

'It's really not that scary.' He said with a teasing chuckle.

'I don't mean that.' Jet bit her lip cautiously before continuing. 'It's just, well, what if reading about that universe is triggering half-formed memories?'

The book dropped an inch in his grip as he considered her words. Turning the book over in his hands, he studied the cover before putting it down.

'Are there memories you don't want me to see?'

'No. Not at all. I'd be happy to tell you more about my early writing. But the version you're holding in your hands is mostly derived from the darker side.'

'I'm guessing from the side of you that already felt like happily ever after was for other people?' He shot her a look before picking up the book and tossing it onto the nightstand.

'That's another one of the reasons I switched the characters.' Jet reached out to take hold of his hand and gave it a gentle squeeze.

Blowing out a sigh, he ran his fingers through his hair with his free hand, before reaching over to scoop her up onto his lap.

'I'll stop reading it and we'll see what happens,' he promised before kissing her good morning.

'Worth a shot.' Jet shrugged playfully. 'Speaking of which. Mai actually suggested you come to London with me.'

'I'd love to.' He nudged her nose with his. 'But you know it might not work.'

'I'm going to be stupidly busy, but I'd love to be able to show you London.'

'I would probably have to work from the hotel anyway, but if anyone can get me there, it's going to be you, right?' he asked, his voice husky as he ran his hands up her thighs.

'Oh, I'll get you there.' Jet smirked, raising an eyebrow as she tilted her hips and he gripped her by the waist. Leaning forward, she whispered in his ear, 'This Sunday we can stay in bed as long as you like.'

FORTY-TWO

Coffee in one hand, laptop balanced in the crook of her other arm, Jet wandered into the lounge and sank into the couch. Reaching out to exchange her caffeine for the remote control briefly, she put the TV on and selected a movie she'd seen countless times before for some background noise.

Putting her feet up on the coffee table, Jet watched the first twenty minutes while she finished her beverage.

She knew she was putting off the task at hand.

Finally conceding and discarding the empty mug, she returned to the document open on her computer, the cursor blinking insistently at her.

Having spent all of Monday thinking up ways to get Daryl to London, Jet had eventually simply tried to book him a ticket on her flight.

The merry dance she'd performed with the British Airways website and various other independent booking sites had driven her to wanting to throw the laptop out of the window.

Ticket availability was different on every site she tried, her card was refused when she could get a seat, or the seat would disappear in the time it took her to confirm her selection. Eventually conceding that he was right, there was something going on, she began brainstorming other solutions.

The cursor continued to mock her hesitancy.

Finding herself distracted by the movie again after watching a further half hour of it, Jet snapped the laptop shut and ran up to her room to ransack her bags for one of her notebooks.

Eventually settling on one she could rip the pages out of if she needed to hide the evidence, Jet returned to the lounge.

Setting the laptop aside so that she could see the brief outline she'd typed out the day before, she pulled the coffee table nearer to the couch in order to lean on it and scribble down the short story idea she'd had before her nerve completely went.

The credits were rolling on a second movie by the time she leant back into the couch, feeling her back scream in protest after being hunched over for the best part of two hours.

Staring down at the neat pile of pages she'd already torn from the pad, Jet chewed on her thumbnail.

'I've done it now,' she said to herself and, with a glance at the TV, checked the time on the clock sitting on the mantlepiece.

She was meeting Leroy for dinner and taking him with

her to the comedy gig. Before returning to her room to change, she snatched up the laptop and tried one more time to book Daryl a flight.

On her way out of the house, she tiptoed into his office, knowing he'd be at Virgo until late, and used his machine to print off the booking confirmation and boarding pass. Leaving it on the keyboard for him to see when he got home, she smiled to herself as she shut the door behind her.

'Hey baby, sorry I'm late,' Leroy breathed as he collapsed into the booth next to Jet and leant over for cheek kisses before righting himself and taking the seat opposite.

'No worries, gorgeous.' Jet smiled. 'I got you a beer.'

'Superstar!' Leroy beamed after necking half the bottle. 'Will we make the gig?'

'It's only a block over, we'll be fine,' Jet reassured him.

'Excellent, I'm famished. So, who's tickling our fancy tonight?'

'We have three comedians, one's a singer, all local.' Jet followed his gaze around the cheerful chain restaurant they'd agreed on. 'How are things with you?'

'Pretty good actually.' He grinned. 'I'm seeing someone.'

'Is this the someone you had that date with?'

'It is.'

'The one with the blue lipstick and mermaid hair?'

'The very same.' He waggled his eyebrows. 'Turns out

Star performs with a troupe of merfolk. They do events, shows, kids parties . . . where a pool is available of course. The tails they have are amazing, I borrowed one when we went swimming on our third date and now I *really* want one of my own.'

'That's fantastic! You should have brought Star with you.' Jet nudged him with her elbow.

'I wanted to catch up with you! But I won't say no to a double date sometime soon.' Leroy winked at her. 'I knew I wouldn't see Daryl here tonight, he was still in the office.'

'He started late, he'll be finishing late.' Jet nodded.

'Girl, you have seen sights I could only dream of.'

'I should imagine that whatever you dream of is pretty close to the truth.' Jet smirked.

'You'll have to let us know if he shares anything about his cryptic past.' Leroy shot Jet some side-eye as he peered down at the menu.

'What do you mean?' Jet asked innocently.

'No one knows anything about him, you know he doesn't really talk much anyway, but we've never so much as even discovered what college he went to. He can't be stalked on social media because he doesn't use it,' Leroy complained. 'Virgo employed him based on his LinkedIn profile and that's not exactly the place to find a juicy back story.'

'He's just private, that's all.' Jet shrugged with a smile.

'Now he's got you at it.' Leroy shot her a look that told her he was unconvinced. 'You can't tell me he hasn't told you anything.'

'I know enough,' Jet said, her eyes bright. 'It's not my place to gossip about my new boyfriend, though.'

'Boyfriend, huh!? So, it's not all about the sex?' He grinned.

'Nope,' Jet admitted, blushing.

'Oh, it's so good to see you so happy,' Leroy gushed, reaching out to grasp her hands. 'I think your luck has finally changed.'

'Let's hope both our dating fortunes stay this way.' Jet raised her glass.

'Amen to that.' He clinked his glass against hers.

Allowing herself to be carried away with Leroy's office gossip and then on a wave of laughter at the gig, Jet had completely forgotten about the ticket she'd booked until she was jumping out of a cab outside the house sometime around eleven.

Fuzzy on a few too many beers, she scowled to find the house in darkness and glanced up and down the street to see if Daryl happened to be arriving home and was walking up the street, before letting herself in.

Kicking her shoes off, she tugged her phone free of her pocket to see whether he'd tried to contact her at all.

There were no messages.

Heading straight for his room, she crept inside in case he was asleep.

He wasn't there.

Slipping through the bathroom to the office, she felt her stomach sink to find he wasn't at his desk either. The flight documents were still sitting on the keyboard where she'd left them.

Jet considered calling him, or at least sending a message of her own, but she didn't want to come across as needy, so she left her phone in her handbag to stop herself.

Yawning as she wondered what could have kept him in the office so late, she returned to the bedroom and, stripping down to her underwear, climbed into the bed to wait for him to come home.

FORTY-THREE

Sitting bolt upright in an empty bed, Jet felt her heart race. She hadn't meant to fall asleep and wondered how heavily she must have slept not to have felt him get in or out of bed.

Leaning over to grab her phone and check the time, Jet rubbed at her eyes.

She'd also slept later than normal. It was past nine. If he'd needed to be in an office, he would have left over an hour before.

'Daryl?' Jet's voice shook as she called out, knowing she wouldn't get an answer.

Not wanting to move, her bladder eventually forced her to get out of bed. Inspecting the bathroom for signs of a morning shower or any part of Daryl's routine and finding none, she progressed to the office.

The tickets were where she'd left them, so he hadn't been in there even if he had been home.

Biting her lip against a wave of nausea, Jet returned to the bedroom and picked up her phone.

She considered calling Rachel to see if he was there, but knowing that would sound odd and that he wasn't necessarily at Virgo even if he was with a client, she decided against it.

Instead, she fired off a message to his number apologising for being out for the count and playfully blaming Leroy so as not to sound like a total stalker.

With a deep breath to steady her nerves, Jet headed to her own room to shower and get dressed.

Daring to look at her phone only once she was downstairs in the kitchen, Jet was disappointed but distracted by a message from Tracy with a link to the first cut of the podcast for her to listen to.

Pacing around the kitchen as the kettle boiled, Jet smiled to herself as she listened to the first couple of minutes of the track.

Considering their make-shift setup, Tracy had worked wonders with the sound quality and with the whole group's blessing, it would be launching over the weekend. Jet made a mental note to pick up a copy of Dracula for her flight to and from London.

The podcast was interrupted by a message alert.

Almost dropping the mug she was planning to make a cup of tea in, Jet grabbed for the phone and felt her world tilt.

'No,' she breathed. 'That can't be right.'

On the screen, accompanied by a red exclamation mark, was an alert informing her that her message to Daryl was undeliverable. Number unknown.

'No, no, no, no, no,' she said as she ran from the

kitchen, phone in hand, all the way to her bedroom. 'You can't do this to me now. Please, no.'

Shoving the phone in her pocket, she ransacked the desk in a blind panic for the short story she'd written the day before.

Finding it, she collected all the pages and hurried downstairs to the garden, stopping along the way to retrieve a box of matches.

Tossing the pages into the firepit in the middle of the garden, Jet threw a lit match onto the pages.

Fighting back the tears, she stared into the flames. Wrapping her arms around her waist, Jet fidgeted on the spot until the fire had gone out and there was nothing more than ash left in the pit.

Trembling as she reached into her pocket, she sent the message again, hoping it was just a glitch and that she was overreacting.

To distract herself from her own thoughts, Jet headed to the park to walk laps around the reservoir and listen to the podcast.

She listened to it twice over before pausing to sit on a bench and people watch. Anything to take her mind off her thoughts about where Daryl might have gone.

Taking deep breaths through a wave of anxiety, she reminded herself that it was irrational to think some of the things she was thinking. Then reminded herself that it was equally as irrational to believe he'd materialised from the pages of a book.

Before she could think herself into full hysterics, she returned to the house and spent the rest of the day trying to write. When that failed, she called Rachel once she knew the office would be closed.

'Hey! Have you been listening to the podcast?' Rachel answered on the first ring. 'I listened to it on my commute this morning. It's so cringe!'

'It's great! But yeah, listening to yourself back is super awkward. I think Tracy has edited it just right.' Jet smiled down the phone. 'Are you headed home?'

'No,' Rachel said coyly. 'I have a date.'

'Ooh, with who?' Jet asked, excited for her.

'Someone who came in for a client meeting asked to take me out to dinner. He's pretty hot, so I thought why not.' Rachel grinned to herself. 'Speaking of hot, what have you done with our freelancer?'

'What do you mean?' Jet asked around a very dry mouth.

'He was supposed to be here for a meeting today and didn't show. Leon is seriously pissed.'

'He's not here with me,' Jet said, feeling light-headed. 'Maybe something urgent came up and he got caught up with another client?'

'Well, if you don't know, that's anybody's guess.' Rachel sighed in a manner that suggested Leon had been on Rachel's case about it, maybe even tried to get her to call Jet and chase him up. 'Anyway, I'd better run, I've got twenty minutes to freshen up. He's even meeting me here!'

'OK, yes go, have fun!' Jet said as lightly as she could before hanging up.

Putting the phone down and standing from her desk,

she paced the floor and shook the tension from her arms.

He wasn't where he was meant to be, he hadn't been home. Far short of calling all the hospitals in Manhattan, to see if. . .

No, Jet shook her arms harder, she couldn't think like that.

Her second message hadn't been rejected like the first.

FORTY-FOUR

Shoving her rucksack further up her shoulder, Jet entered the regular Friday night haunt. Instantly spotting Leroy and Tom, she smiled to see friendly faces.

She knew she looked like hell, having hardly slept for two nights.

When Daryl hadn't come home a second night, she'd spent all of Thursday contacting hospitals, police stations and even mortuaries with an increasing degree of trepidation.

After a third night, her nerves were shot and the ache in her chest was unbearable.

One of the stations she'd called had taken a description and added him to their missing persons list. They tried to reassure her that given his history, he would be in the system and therefore easily identifiable should he turn up.

It hadn't helped.

Having spent Thursday night mostly sat upright in her

own bed staring out of the window, Jet had decided to get an earlier flight back to the UK.

'Hey, honey.' Leroy leant over to give her air kisses as Jet threw her bag into their booth. 'Are you alone tonight?'

'Yeah, just me. I thought I'd swing by before grabbing a cab to the airport. I'm flying back to London tonight.'

'You weren't supposed to go until next week!' Leroy gasped. 'Is Daryl alright with that? Where the devil is he anyway? I hear Leon's been having an aneurism over his tardy ass this week.'

'He's caught up with another client,' Jet lied.

She'd gone over a multitude of tales to tell and that seemed like the simplest option. Telling everyone he had vanished into thin air wasn't something she wanted to deal with until she got back.

Especially not if it was her fault.

'He's skating on very thin ice with Leon, but you need to tell him to call me. Even if he's caught up with another client, he could at least answer my calls.' Tom shot Jet a look over his beer before taking a large mouthful. 'Are you alright?'

'Me? I'm fine,' Jet squeaked unconvincingly, toying with her own bottle of beer.

'Nervous flyer?' Leroy patted her hand.

'Something like that,' Jet agreed, grateful for his intervention. 'I had hoped Daryl would fly with me, but never mind.'

'He does need to learn how to take a holiday once in a while,' Tom grouched. 'Just not right now.'

'I've got a lot to do while I'm back, he was hoping to work from the hotel,' Jet informed him. 'At least this way I don't have to risk introducing him to my parents yet. Where is everyone tonight?'

'Brad and Tina are working on something Daryl should have completed this week, I had to promise overtime and a crate of beer sent to the office.' Tom's look blackened further making Jet regret asking.

'Rachel has another date.' Leroy waggled his eyebrows.

'Good for her!' Jet smiled and took another swig of her drink.

'Right, missy, don't you have a plane to catch?' Leroy asked pointedly, putting his own glass back down and shooting a look at the bar where Shelley was waiting for a drink.

'I most definitely do,' Jet agreed with a playful grimace before hurriedly finishing her beer. 'I don't have any luggage to check in, but I do have some duty-free shopping to do.'

'A bottle of vodka for the flight?' Tom smirked.

'Sweets for the publishing house, the weirder the better.' Jet grinned. 'I had a request for peanut butter M&Ms but I got those already in case the airport didn't have any.'

'What do a bunch of Brits high on American sugar look like?' Leroy asked, batting his eyelashes playfully.

'I'm about to find out.' Jet laughed, sliding out of the booth. 'I'll see you guys when I get back.'

'Gonna miss you, girl.' Leroy pouted as he leant over

for a tight squeeze of a hug.

'You too, babe.' Jet kissed him on the cheek. 'I'll be back in a couple of weeks.'

'Promise?'

'I have to come back, we're going on a double date, remember?'

'Star is totally up for that, by the way,' Leroy admitted shyly.

'Then we'll get that booked soonest.'

'Safe flight!' Leroy called after her as she turned to blow him a kiss on her way out of the bar.

Slinking out the door unseen, Jet hailed a cab and headed for JFK.

Gazing out of the window as they left Manhattan, Jet found herself wondering how she could return to a version of NYC without Daryl in it.

FORTY-FIVE

When the plane landed at Heathrow and all her fellow passengers stood up, eager to collect their luggage, Jet remained in her seat, staring out at the early morning sunshine. July in England was behaving for once, it seemed.

Unable to sleep or read, Jet had tried listening to the Dracula audiobook on the journey. It had been pointless.

As the plane emptied, she shifted her heavy limbs just enough to reach down and retrieve her bag from underneath the seat in front of her.

Moving her flight had come with a major downside.

Her accommodation in the city couldn't be extended, she needed to stay with her parents for a few days.

She hadn't bothered to tell them she'd be turning up early, they would have insisted on picking her up from the airport. Jet needed to smell the London Underground in the morning, experience the summer heat created by thousands of tourists jostling together, and walk the familiar streets between Highgate Station and her parents' house.

By the time she approached the door to her childhood home, Jet had been travelling for eighteen hours, including the leisurely brunch she'd treated herself to between tube changes.

And the call she'd made to Mai to let her know she was in the city.

And the drink she'd subsequently snuck in with her editor.

Ringing the doorbell as a pre-warning, Jet let herself in anyway.

'Mum? Dad? I'm home,' Jet called out cheerily.

'Jet?' Her mum appeared from the kitchen as Jet ventured up the tiled entrance hall of the large Victorian her parents owned. 'What are you doing here?'

'Nice to see you too, Mum.' Jet kissed her on the cheek as she attempted a hug, but her mother was wearing a food-smeared apron and did her best to keep her distance.

'I'm covered in cake batter, darling. You should have let me know you were coming,' her mother scoffed and, turning on her heel, headed back into the kitchen.

'It was a last-minute thing, really.' Jet sighed, keeping her bag on her shoulder as she leant on the kitchen doorframe. 'Sorry, am I interrupting something?'

'Well, yes, we have Geraldine and Samuel over for dinner tonight, I'm in the throes of cooking a three-course meal.'

'Can I help at all?'

'Yes, keep out of the way.' Her mum waved her off. 'It will be boring for you, anyway. We can catch up tomorrow, can't we?'

'Sure, Mum,' Jet said quietly, 'Is Dad in?'

'He's in his study.'

'Great,' Jet muttered, slinking back down the hall to the stairs and making her way to the spare bedroom her dad had turned into his own personal man cave.

'Hello, Father,' Jet chirped, pushing the door open and finding him sat at his mixing desk with headphones on.

Looking up, startled, her dad's face split into a grin as he got up to give his daughter a hug.

'Hello, Daughter. How's my city?'

'She's as magical as ever.' Jet smiled.

'And the house?'

'Granny's house?' Jet frowned, realising she hadn't told them. 'I've been living there.'

Her dad frowned, confused.

'Well, where else would you live? She left it to you.'

'Oh,' Jet managed as the floor wobbled beneath her. 'Yeah . . .'

'What state was it in after being empty all these years?'

'Don't worry, it looks great,' Jet said, forcing a smile through the white noise in her head.

'If your mother's schedule ever clears, we'll come over and see it for ourselves. I'm guessing she's told you we're entertaining tonight?'

'I've been warned to make myself scarce, yes. Pub roast tomorrow?'

'You bet.' He beamed before sitting back at his desk and retrieving his headphones.

Taking that as her cue to escape, Jet crossed the hall to her bedroom and, closing the door behind her, clamped her hands over her mouth and nose to take deep breaths as she sank to her knees next to her bed.

When the tears began to flow, she sank to the carpet to curl into a ball against the aching chasm in her chest.

Crying herself into exhaustion, Jet rolled onto her back and stared at the ceiling until it started to get dark.

She'd heard Geraldine and her husband arrive, could hear their distant muffled chatter through the floor.

When her dehydrated, jetlagged body had nothing left to give, she sat herself up and reached under her bed for her box of pyjamas.

Laying her hand instead on a box of old writing, Jet dragged it out and peered inside.

Everything else she'd ever written about Daryl was in that box.

Unable to bring herself to read any of it, she collected everything she could find and tossed it into the fireplace in her bedroom and set it alight before she could give herself time to think.

FORTY-SIX

Staring down at the bag holding her lunch, Jet decided miserably that she didn't really want it.

Sighing into the bag of food and putting her sunglasses back on, she reminded herself that she'd always expected to grow old crazy and alone as a pang of heartache swirled in her gut.

After spending a tense week living under her mother's roof, Jet had been pleased to finally get into the apartment she'd booked for herself.

Thankfully, Mai had kept her busy signing books and bookplates and dreaming up social media campaigns and competitions for her to run. She also suspected something was up, but hadn't mentioned it.

Eternally grateful for her editor and friend's knowing discretion when it was really needed, Jet had thrown herself headfirst and with gusto into anything Mai and her publicity team could cook up. They'd even found her a desk in their Camden office.

The flight she had booked Daryl on had landed just a

few hours earlier. Jet had been tempted to skulk off to the airport and watch the arrivals just in case, but she'd known it was pointless.

She hadn't even been able to bring herself to send him a birthday message, in case it bounced.

Glancing around Leicester Square for wherever Mai had gone to get her lunch from, Jet found the fountain bubbling away quietly and smiled sadly to herself.

It was just about ready to give some of the kids running around a good soaking. A group of small children from three different families had banded together to become best friends for the day and dare each other to run in and out of the jets in the paving surrounding the main fountain.

The August sun was in good form for it. As if on order, a heatwave had hit on the first of the month.

Most of the kids were already drenched, some of the parents had made them take their shoes off. Jet wondered with a smile how far they each had to go to get home, Londoners or not, from Leicester Square there was almost always going to be transport requirements.

Perhaps they'd take them down to Trafalgar Square after, where there were less trees to shade them, so they could dry off in the sunshine. Provided none of them tried to swim in the fountains down there.

Plucking a sandwich from the bag, and watching a daring pigeon take up residence at her feet in hope of a few crumbs, Jet opened the packaging and began deliberately dropping bits of crust to the ground.

Checking her phone as she spotted Mai heading across the park, dodging the soggy children as she went, Jet realised she hadn't heard from anyone in New York for a couple of days.

Tracy had let her know that they were getting listeners for the podcast already and Leroy had asked her to bring him back a Union Jack T-shirt.

'I saw that look.' Mai was already standing over her. 'Is everything OK?'

'I hope so, I'm hoping it's just a spike in anxiety. We've got a lot going on here. The world is about to see inside my brain in glorious technicolour.' Jet laughed to cover herself.

'Darling, we've always been able to see inside your brain, and it's glorious without the need for technicolour,' she said with a giggle as she sat down next to her and planted a KFC bag between them.

'Aww man, why didn't I think of that.' Jet compared Mai's lunch with her own.

'I'm grease-loading before Friday night drinks. What's your excuse?' Mai asked before plucking a bunch of fries from the bag and popping them in her mouth.

'I was saving the grease-loading for after the Friday night drinks.' Jet laughed.

'You've got a brownie in there, haven't you?' Mai narrowed her eyes at Jet's swag.

'Of course, and a cookie.'

'For me?'

'Obviously.' Jet shot her a look and let the pigeon have the rest of her crusts.

'I'm so glad you decided to head over early, it's taken so much pressure off this week.'

'You're telling me. Who was I kidding to think I could spend a week *relaxing* at my parents' house?' Jet lifted the second half of her sandwich out of the bag and started picking at that too.

'It's all done bar the shouting . . . or in this case, maybe the casting,' Mai said excitedly. 'Just the screenplay to write.'

'Around the edits to the last delivery.'

'While that first draft is being read through and marked up, you'll have a couple of weeks to make a start. Then the next steps bounce back and forth, blah, blah, you'll have plenty of time.'

'You usually prefer me to start the next one asap.'

'I think the fans will understand a slightly bigger gap between releases next year, especially when they find out there's a film in the works.' Mai grinned.

'The fans,' Jet repeated with a chuckle.

'Yes, you have fans, get over it. You've seen how we've started to stir up attention on social media already, now that there's word of a movie deal, sales are starting to creep up.' Mai met her eyes. 'For the whole back catalogue. People are getting curious. Anyway, sales have never been as low as your modesty would have people believe. You need to start getting used to the idea that people like your stuff, and that one day you might have to talk about it on TV.'

'No one is going to want to talk to an unknown author on a talk show. The actors get called in for that, not the writers,' Jet pointed out.

'Meh, we'll see.'

Smiling fondly, Jet abandoned the last quarter of her sandwich to the pigeon, who had been joined by his mates while they'd been talking.

'Shoot,' Mai squeaked, checking her watch. 'I'd better take the rest of this back to the office, I have a call in thirty minutes, it will take that long to get back. Are you coming?'

'Not today, I'm going to soak up the sun now you've had your way with me this morning. I'm all meetinged out.'

'But you're coming for drinks later?'

'I'm only staying a couple of tube stops away from here, I'll be around, let me know where you end up.' Jet watched her get up and roll the top of the KFC bag down so that she could carry it back to the office. If it was an online meeting, Jet knew she'd turn her camera off and finish her lunch when she didn't need to speak. 'Don't forget your cookie.' Jet waved her lunch bag at her after retrieving the brownie.

'Oh no, mustn't forget that!' Mai took the bag with a grateful smile. 'See you around four!'

Waving her off, Jet stole a glance at her watch. It was getting on for 2p.m. There was little point leaving the park. She had her book, the fountain and a spot on the bench already, two hours was nothing.

Reaching back into her bag to put the brownie away for later, Jet retrieved her water and copy of Dracula. Sitting with the book on her lap, she watched the children getting braver with the fountain. The next cycle hadn't started yet.

People watching for a few minutes while she waited for the fun to start, Jet caught movement out of the corner of her eye as a figure approached the bench to sit next to her.

They didn't sit, but they were clearly considering it as they stood over her.

Willing herself to look up, her breath caught.

Daryl was looking down at her, an unreadable look on his face.

'Hi, Jet,' he breathed, in a manner Jet could have sworn was relief.

Without a word, she leapt up off the bench and threw herself into his arms.

'Hey, hey, hey, what's wrong?' he soothed, scooping her up off her feet as she clung to his neck.

'I thought I'd lost you.' Jet bit back a sob of relief.

'You thought you'd lost me? I'm the one who woke up in an empty house last weekend. All you left behind was the tickets, what the hell happened?'

'I thought you'd gone,' Jet whispered as he set her back on the ground. 'You hadn't been home since Tuesday.'

'Oh my god, I'm sorry,' he said, exhaling heavily as he gripped her tighter. 'That's never happened before, explains the lost days though, I thought my memory was on the blink again.'

'I think it was my fault.' Jet sniffed as a tear rolled down her nose. 'I tried to fix your travel issue . . .'

'Well, I think you did that.'

'I burned it all, I won't do it again,' she babbled. 'I'm so sorry.'

'OK, it's OK,' he hushed, his grip easing so that they could sit down. 'So, you didn't freak out and leave me?'

'No! Oh my god, is that why you didn't call?'

'Sort of,' he chuckled awkwardly. 'I refused to believe it was over when I found the tickets. Then I convinced myself it would be best to surprise you . . . I've been here a few days,' he admitted.

'You didn't take last night's flight?' Jet blinked at him.

'I couldn't wait to see you again without knowing what had happened. I went straight to the airport to see if I could jump an earlier flight. They put me on standby so I didn't think I'd make it, but after camping out at JFK overnight . . . well, here I am. I've been hanging out here every day since.'

'Why here?'

'At the Shakespeare Fountain?' He shot her a look. 'You told me it's your favourite place. Especially in summer.'

'Of course I did,' Jet barely whispered as she looked across the park.

The fountains were back in full swing.

Glancing over with a laugh as he stayed close, Daryl watched the kids run between the jets.

'I can see why,' he said, laughing after one of the boys got a full stream up the nose.

'I can't believe you're really here.' Jet smiled finally as she reached for his hands.

'Neither can I.' With a shake of his head, he met her eyes before reaching out to wipe the tears gently from her face, her grip slipping to his wrists, unwilling to let him go.

'Wherever you came from, wherever you went,' Jet whimpered, 'I can't imagine my life without you in it.'

'I'm not going anywhere.' He smiled softly. 'Not on purpose, anyway.'

'I'm finding it very hard to believe any of this is real.'

'Maybe it's not. But fuck it, let's run with it,' Daryl muttered as he reached out to pull her closer and, threading his fingers through her hair as he leant in, kissed her softly.

ACKNOWLEDGEMENTS

Thank you to all the friends and family who have listened to me harp on about books and writing over the years, some of you have the patience of a saint. Especially my sister, Chloe, who saw several versions of the front cover while I learned how to master Book Brush. Thanks also to my proofreader, Jenny, hopefully we've managed to meet for ice cream or cake by now. To those in the know, you finally know where he went.

Printed in Great Britain
by Amazon

36165710R00223